Rebel Bear

Aloha Shifters: Pearls of Desire
Book 2

by Anna Lowe

Twin Moon Press

Editing by Lisa A. Hollett

Covert art by Kim Killion

Contents

Contents   i

Other books in this series   iii

Free Books   v

Chapter One   1

Chapter Two   11

Chapter Three   21

Chapter Four   29

Chapter Five   39

Chapter Six   53

Chapter Seven   63

Chapter Eight   71

Chapter Nine   81

Chapter Ten   89

Chapter Eleven   99

Chapter Twelve   111

Chapter Thirteen   123

Chapter Fourteen   133

Chapter Fifteen   141

Chapter Sixteen   149

Chapter Seventeen   159

Chapter Eighteen   169

Chapter Nineteen   177

Chapter Twenty   187

Chapter Twenty-One   197

Chapter Twenty-Two   209

Chapter Twenty-Three   217

Chapter Twenty-Four   225

Chapter Twenty-Five   237

Chapter Twenty-Six   249

Chapter Twenty-Seven   259

Sneak Peek: Rebel Lion   273

Books by Anna Lowe   275

About the Author   281

Other books in this series

Aloha Shifters - Pearls of Desire

Rebel Dragon (Book 1)

Rebel Bear (Book 2)

Rebel Lion (Book 3)

Rebel Wolf (Book 4)

Rebel Alpha (Book 5)

visit www.annalowebooks.com

Free Books

Get your free e-books now!

Sign up for my newsletter at *annalowebooks.com* to get three free books!

- *Desert Wolf*: Friend or Foe (Book 1.1 in the Twin Moon Ranch series)

- *Off the Charts* (the prequel to the Serendipity Adventure series)

- *Perfection* (the prequel to the Blue Moon Saloon series)

Chapter One

Hailey smoothed her hands over the silky contours of her dress and frowned into the full-length mirror.

Her mother tapped her shoulder. "Don't make faces, honey. It will give you wrinkles."

Hailey's frown deepened as she looked down. "I thought only the bride was supposed to wear white at a wedding."

"It's cream," her mother insisted.

Hailey squinted into the mirror. Was that a trick of the bright overhead light? "It's still too close."

Her mother shrugged. "It's Isabelle's wedding, and if she wants her bridesmaids in cream, she can have them. Besides, it brings out the blue of your eyes."

Hailey turned this way and that. The dress looked good. Almost too good, what with the way her long, golden hair flowed over the silky fabric. But she was just a bridesmaid, for goodness' sake. A reluctant one, at that, because she barely knew the bride. On the other hand, Isabelle was known for having quirky tastes.

"I think she just made me a bridesmaid to be polite."

"Nonsense, honey. She likes you. Her future sister-in-law." Her mother winked.

Hailey just about stamped her foot. "Would you stop that? Just because I've seen Jonathan a few times doesn't mean I'm marrying him."

She nearly added, *In fact, it's been more about him wanting to see me.* Their brief, long-distance relationship had barely given them time to talk in person, and it seemed impolite to break up on the eve of his sister's wedding. She didn't want to jinx Isabelle.

1

Her mother made a vague, *mmm-hmm* sound and tugged the shoulder strap of Hailey's dress to one side.

Hailey tugged it right back. "Mom..."

Her mother huffed. "You know, you didn't use to fuss so much."

Hailey nearly blurted, *That was when I was a kid and I had no choice.* But that only would have gotten her mother started on her whole *How can you be so ungrateful when I've done so much for you* speech, so Hailey held her tongue and swung her jaw from side to side instead.

"Don't do that. It's not pretty."

Her mother didn't used to get on her nerves this badly. But lately...

"I'm not on the clock, Mom."

"People will still be watching you." Her mother smiled like that was a good thing.

Hailey made a face. People were always watching. Commenting. Sneaking pictures and whispering, *It's her! It's her! Hailey Crewe!* She'd had to live with that for the past three years, ever since her modeling career took off.

An accidental career she kept meaning to end, a lot like her relationship with Jonathan. She just had to find the right time to break the news. Hailey looked out the open window at surfers bobbing in the water off Waikiki, waiting for a perfect wave. They looked so relaxed, so free. So spontaneous. Everything she couldn't be.

Not in her current life, anyway. She fingered her necklace and let her gaze drift to the craggy crown of Diamond Head. Hawaii might be just the place to make that break and start something new. She closed her eyes, picturing it.

It was getting to be a little fantasy with her — making her career-ending announcement, then kicking up her heels and turning her back on it all. Make that, *running* away from it all. The intense schedule. The constant dieting. Sexist producers. How superficial it all was.

Of course, if Hailey did that, her mother would have a heart attack — or fake one. Her agent would flip, and the media would whip themselves into a frenzy if she didn't time it exactly right. Maybe when another top model hit the news with a record-breaking deal or shocking news, like a bombshell divorce or a drug arrest. Hailey didn't wish any of that on anyone but, heck. If one of those things did happen, she'd grab the chance for a quiet exit, stage right.

She must have been smiling at the notion, because her mother chuckled. "Ah, I see you're dreaming of your own wedding."

That snapped her out of the fantasy with the force of a car slamming into a brick wall. "Marriage isn't my major goal in life, Mom."

"Which I can't understand, not when you have a good man like Jonathan."

Good meant *rich*, Hailey knew. As in, billions. She hadn't even realized at first, but the more she'd gotten to know Jonathan, the more she'd realized how much money ruled his life.

"He's only a few years older than you," her mother went on, extolling his virtues. "He's in good shape, and you look great together..."

Hailey rolled her eyes. Was that important?

Her mother sighed. "Would you stop fiddling with that ugly thing?"

Hailey bristled. Her pearl was a family heirloom, but since it wasn't the round, shiny type — just an oblong, bumpy pearl — it wasn't good enough in her mother's eyes.

Her mother tugged the shoulder strap down again. "You have such nice shoulders, honey. Nothing wrong with showing a little skin."

"At a wedding?"

"Gotta make a splash." Her mother grinned.

No, she didn't. When would her mother get that? She'd had her lucky break and made it big. Modeling had lifted her and her mother out of poverty. Why did her mother always demand more?

"This a wedding, Mom. Not a publicity event."

"Everything is a publicity event." Her mother practically beamed.

"It doesn't have to be. I'd really like to go to this wedding as myself, not as someone else's vision of who I should be."

Her mother gave a theatrical sigh. "If I let you do that, you'd go in ripped jeans and a T-shirt. And your hair would look like you'd skateboarded to the event."

Hailey snorted, not because her mother was wrong, but because the astronomical insurance policy her agent had negotiated didn't allow anything fun. No skateboarding, no horseback riding. Nothing. All the simple fun she'd had as a kid was suddenly off-limits. Heck, she couldn't even go out on the beach and rent a surfboard for an hour. And anyway, she'd be mobbed if she did.

"Making it big is supposed to let you live the way you want to live," she murmured.

Her mother shook her head. "You have another ten years — at best — in this business. You have to milk that time for all it's worth."

An apt description, Hailey thought. She was the golden cow that had to be milked for every penny. How much would she need to earn to satisfy her mother?

"Now about your hair..." her mother said before Hailey could snap those words out.

She pursed her lips and counted to ten. A woman really ought to have shown her mother the limits by the time she hit twenty-eight. But the first years of Hailey's whirlwind career had been like falling into a shark tank, and her mother had had her best interests at heart. For every success, there had been another step of the ladder to climb, and Hailey had been too focused on her part of the equation to battle her mother.

But now... Hailey sighed. She was going to have two difficult conversations soon. One with Jonathan and one with her mother. She appreciated her mom — she truly did — but it was time to carve out space for her own life on her own terms.

She turned away from her mother, covering her hair. "I can do it."

"You want it to look good for the wedding, dear."

"Not my wedding."

4

"You never know," her mother said under her breath. "I mean, when the great day might come."

Hailey gave her mother a side-eyed stare and started forming a twisted chignon.

"Needs more volume," her mother said.

Things pretty much continued in that vein until they left their penthouse suite for the hotel lobby, where Jonathan waited. Or rather, where he spoke on his phone. He flicked his fingers up in a little salute then turned his back on Hailey to finish the call.

"Yes, twenty-six. And verify the ETFs." He checked his hair in a pair of slanted mirrors that threw back an infinite number of images of him. "What are the numbers from Nagoya?"

Hailey gnashed her teeth. What had she ever seen in him?

She looked toward the fountain bubbling cheerily in the lobby of the beachside hotel, but her thoughts were a thousand miles away. She'd first met Jonathan near his hobby ranch in Montana, and he'd been different then. More relaxed, more outdoorsy. Sporty, even, with hair that hadn't been blow-dried just so. Had that all been a show? Maybe she'd been desperate to see him in a better light — or desperate to get away from her mother, who guarded against men like a hawk. When Jonathan came along, however, her mother had been all fluttering eyelashes and happy coos.

Three reporters rushed across the lobby to snap pictures, making her mother wind an arm through Hailey's elbow and beam.

"Miss Crewe! Miss Crewe!"

Hailey tried not to frown. Why did reporters always talk at the same time?

"What are your thoughts on this big day? Are you excited? Nervous?"

It was only a wedding. What was the big deal?

"Back up. Back up."

Lamar, Jonathan's head of security, stalked over with his usual glare and pushed them all back, but that didn't improve things much. Lamar made Hailey cringe, even if she couldn't explain why. His low bark of a voice and permanent scowl made her imagine all kinds of evil deeds, like he'd come straight from strangling someone in the woods. Which was a terrible thing to think of someone, but somehow, that's what always came to Hailey's mind.

Jonathan, on the other hand, had a serious man-crush on his head of security. "All set to go, man?" He thumped Lamar on the arm like they were close buddies instead of boss and hired gun.

Lamar gave his usual pissed-off nod and growled. "All set to go."

Jonathan turned to Hailey, beaming as if she'd only just walked up. "Honey, you look beautiful!"

Hailey turned her cheek before Jonathan's lips could hit hers. Did the man ever notice anything other than her appearance? No *I've missed you* or *How was your morning?*

Jonathan turned to her mother. "Mrs. Crewe. You two look like sisters."

Her mother ate that up, but Hailey rolled her eyes. No, they didn't look like sisters. Her mother looked every bit a woman who'd struggled most of her life to make ends meet. A woman who'd spent years at the stove of a diner, grilling burgers and fries because that's what you did to pay the rent, especially if you were widowed young and left with a kid, a crippling mortgage, and a car that barely ran. To Hailey, the wrinkles and stooped shoulders made her mother beautiful, not the styled hair or designer clothes she'd cloaked herself in ever since Hailey's modeling money had started to roll in.

Hailey sighed at her own train of thought. God, she really was in the wrong industry, wasn't she?

"You look great, Jonathan," her mother cooed.

Jonathan flashed his country club smile, smoothed a hand over his perfectly straight tie, and winked. "It's the big day."

Hailey's mother winked back, making her pause. Those two were up to something. But what? Jonathan did look good, she had to admit. Of course, it was his sister's wedding, and his family had spared no expense. Kind of a rushed wedding, but whatever. That wasn't Hailey's business, so she'd never really asked.

"Shall we go?" she asked.

Jonathan grinned like she was one of the adorable little flower girls who skipped by and not a grown woman who could think for herself. "Soon." He gave Lamar a cryptic signal and let him bustle ahead. "Let's make sure everyone is ready to go."

Jonathan *loved* making an entrance — another thing he hadn't revealed in Montana. When Hailey had seen him in California between jobs, she was shocked at the cheap thrill he got out of limos and red-carpet events. Sometimes she wondered whether he only supported charitable projects for the publicity.

The fountain bubbled quietly, providing an oasis of calm and tranquility Hailey didn't feel in the least.

At least she'd never slept with Jonathan. Thank goodness for that. She'd kept it to dinners out and a quick kiss on the doorstep of her Brentwood condo.

Not going to invite me in? Jonathan had asked with a glint in his eye every time.

She'd blabbed about going slow and forming a meaningful relationship before taking the next step and a bunch of other nonsense that had held him at bay. So far, she'd kept it at that. And *that* was as far as it was going, because she had no intention to continue seeing Jonathan. He'd booked a suite for Hailey and her mother across the hall from his own, and *across the hall* was where she planned to keep him until she found the right time to break it off gently.

"One more thing," Jonathan said, reaching into his pocket. "I brought you a gift."

Hailey looked on, mortified, as he held out a jewelry box with a magnificent pearl necklace. There were at least twenty pearls in it, each pink, shiny, and perfectly round.

"Oh, it's lovely." Her mother pressed a hand to her own chest as if picturing them there.

"Yes, they are." Jonathan grinned.

Hailey bit her lip. "Thank you, but I couldn't possibly accept."

Jonathan frowned. "Of course you can. They're beautiful."

As if beauty was all that counted. Hailey sighed then ducked away before he could loop them around her neck.

"I don't understand why you don't want them. They're much better than yours." Jonathan's eyes narrowed.

She could have thrown out any of a dozen answers, starting with *Because they'll make you feel like you own me* and moving on to *Because my grandfather gave me my necklace and I love it.* But Jonathan wouldn't listen, and he'd never understand.

He stared at her through icy eyes until her mother intervened. "Please forgive her, Jonathan. It must be all the stress. She'll come to her senses before long."

Hailey gritted her teeth. If only her mother knew.

Jonathan pocketed the necklace, slowly composing himself, then spoke in a strangely flat tone. "Oh, I'm sure she will."

I already have, Hailey was dying to say. But that would just get Jonathan worked up and make it harder to have a calm, sensible conversation when the time came. The sooner, the better.

"Oh, this is so exciting," her mother chirped, fanning herself.

Hailey peeked outside. The Royal Hawaiian was a Waikiki landmark that opened onto a golden beach with turquoise waters, all framed by a line of bright pink sun umbrellas.

Where would you have your wedding? Jonathan's sister Isabelle had phoned to ask a few weeks ago. *Somewhere in Hawaii, right?*

Hailey had nearly said *At home in Montana*, but okay. Hawaii would be nice, too. Someplace small and off the beaten track, like one of those tiny missionary-era chapels she'd seen in the in-flight magazine.

Leave it to a member of Jonathan's family, then, to stage an event in the middle of bustling Waikiki.

Sure, she'd told Isabella. It wasn't her wedding, anyway.

Outside, a bell chimed, and the crowd bustled to the white chairs set in two long lines. Everyone hushed and craned their heads expectantly. Hailey looked around too. Isabelle must be on her way any minute now with her beau.

"Okay," Jonathan said, puffing out his cheeks. They were pinker than she'd ever seen. Jonathan was all worked up about his sister's wedding, which was cute. "They're ready for us."

See? she told herself. He did have some redeeming qualities. Not enough to want to stay with him, but enough to make her feel better about getting involved in the first place. She let Jonathan take her arm and guide her out onto the lawn.

"Nice," she murmured, tilting her chin upward as they stepped into the sun. She'd only arrived late the previous night and had been cooped up in her suite all morning.

A ripple of excitement went through the crowd, which Hailey supposed was par for the course. Isabelle would be next — that's what they were anticipating, right?

But everyone's eyes were fixed firmly on her — hundreds of pairs, though few she recognized, because they were all Jonathan's family, friends, and business partners. Her step faltered, and her stomach churned, because something felt off. Really off.

She touched her hair. Was it a mess? Or, God — she knew she shouldn't have worn that dress.

Everyone was smiling, but there was a vibe in the air that made her want to turn and run. As if everyone knew something she didn't. She reached up with one hand, touching her pearl for reassurance. Jonathan, on the other hand, was beaming like a man with four aces up his sleeve.

Hailey took three more steps, then stopped short. Isabelle, the bride, was sitting off to one side in the first row of seats, wearing a yellow dress, and her fiancée was nowhere in sight.

"Uh, Jon—" Hailey started, then stopped as Jonathan sank down to one knee and looked up.

Cameras flashed. Palm trees rustled, and her mother squeaked. The guests seemed to hold their breath, and Hailey did too. What was going on?

Jonathan cleared his throat and spoke loud enough for everyone to hear. "I know you love surprises, honey..."

She hated surprises — so much, she couldn't speak or move. She stood like a deer in headlights, knowing doom was a split second away but still not processing exactly what it was.

The crowd chuckled on cue, and Jonathan went on, his clammy hands clasping hers. "The day I met you, I knew you were the one. My one. My only. My princess."

Hailey wanted to tug him to his feet, but there were too many alarms going off in her mind for her to take action of any kind.

Jonathan held out a tiny black box and smiled at her. No, wait. He was smiling at the box in one of those *Aren't I awesome?* looks he flashed from time to time. The crowd gasped when he opened the box, revealing a massive diamond ring.

"I know we haven't known each other that long, but I don't need any more time to decide," he announced.

Jesus, Jonathan, she wanted to bark. *I sure do.* Or rather, she didn't need any time to decide because she already wanted out. Really out.

"Are you nuts?" she hissed as quietly as she could.

The women in the nearest seats giggled. *Isn't that cute?*

No, it wasn't cute. It was appalling. Why would Jonathan put her on the spot like this?

He grinned like he thought it was cute too. "You said you wanted more spontaneity in your life."

"I didn't mean this." She jerked her hand at the scene. "What were you thinking?"

Jonathan's grin stretched. Obviously, it hadn't occurred to him she might not go along with his crazy plan.

"I was thinking about forever, sweetheart. I was thinking about how much I love you."

The crowd sighed audibly, but to Hailey, the words sounded stale and rehearsed.

"Hailey Crewe," he continued. "Will you marry me?"

Chapter Two

No, Hailey wanted to scream. She didn't want to marry Jonathan. Ever.

She settled for "What — here? Now?"

Glancing around frantically, she saw many bright, hopeful faces in the crowd, but none that were her friends. Some of the guests laughed — nervously in the case of those who realized the spectacle they'd come to witness might not be going according to plan.

Jonathan plunged ahead with confidence — and a little more force. "Of course, here and now." His hand squeezed hers a little too tightly, and his eyes took on a look of warning.

She'd seen that look before, but only aimed at people negotiating business deals. No wonder Jonathan had made so much money so young. He'd taken the start-up loan his father had given him — a cool million, or so she'd heard — and turned it into a business empire that stretched from coast to coast.

An empire he wanted to pull her into as his next prize. The sinking feeling in her gut turned into an all-out plummet as she looked around. Everyone was in on this trick wedding but her.

She turned to her mother, who wore a stiff smile below viper eyes that said, *Don't blow this.*

Hailey cringed, knowing that look all too well. She'd gotten it the first time she'd bussed tables at the diner when she was twelve. *Don't blow this.* Her mother had pierced her with the very same look the time the just-passing-through-town photographer called Hailey over to his table on the fateful day that changed her life. Not to mention the time Hailey had signed her first six-figure contract, or the time she'd been interviewed for her recent modeling job with a fragrance line.

Don't blow this, her mother ordered without saying a word.

It had made sense the first couple of times. They'd desperately needed the money, and Hailey was eager to help as best she could. But now, they were long past worrying about keeping a roof over their heads.

Hailey took a try at her own eye-talk back. *It's not about survival any more, Mom. It's about my pride. My independence. My life, damn it.*

But her mother didn't so much as blink. In fact, her stare intensified.

Hailey's jaw swung open. Wait a minute. Her mother knew Jonathan had been planning this all along?

Mom, she wanted to wail. *How could you?*

A guest cleared his throat, and Jonathan frowned the way he did when a steak wasn't cooked exactly to his taste.

"I know it's a surprise, princess, but I love you," he said in a tone that was half coo, half order.

Did he love her, or did he love the idea of loving her? She studied his eyes and found more *I* than *you* in them.

"Jonathan," she whispered, trying to tug free.

His eyes hardened. When Lamar, the security man, stepped closer, Hailey paled. How far would Jonathan take this? What if she said no?

"Let me just have a word with my mother," she squeaked, buying time.

It took a forceful yank to get away from Jonathan, but Hailey turned the momentum into a quick spin toward her mother. But trying to get her mother to budge was like moving a boulder, so Hailey hurried to one side, forcing her mother to follow.

"Are you crazy?" her mother hissed as the crowd erupted into shocked chatter.

"How could you?" Hailey rubbed her eyes. "You knew what Jonathan was planning, and you didn't say a word."

"Of course I didn't. You would have said no."

Hailey stared. "And you really think I'm going to say yes now?"

"Of course you will. In front of all these people — how could you spoil everything?"

Hailey's eyes went wide. This could not be happening.

But it was, as her mother indicated by grabbing both of Hailey's shoulders.

"Think. Just think for a change."

Hailey's head snapped up. For a change?

"This is our chance. I mean, your chance." Her mother corrected herself quickly.

"Chance at...?"

"Securing a future. Making it big. Jonathan's brother is running for Senate, and you know it won't be long before Jonathan does too."

Hailey blinked. Apparently, her mother wasn't just greedy for money. She was greedy for power too.

"But I don't love him," Hailey protested.

"Love?" her mother nearly spat. "Love doesn't keep the repossession team away. Love doesn't put food on the table. Love doesn't secure a future."

Hailey felt all her energy drain away. Did that mean her mother didn't love her either?

"But you loved Dad..." she tried.

Her mother snorted. "I was young. Stupid."

A bubble formed in Hailey's throat. She could barely remember her father, but her grandfather had filled that gap as best he could. He'd read bedtime stories and told her about the grandmother who'd died before Hailey was born. He'd taken her for long walks and let her pretend the dog was obeying her commands, not his. He'd raced her across his fields and let her win every time, cheering *Run, Hailey! Run!*

Hailey bowed her head as the stark truth lit up in her mind like the old kitchen bulb that used to buzz and blink before blinding her with harsh fluorescent light. Everything she'd learned about love, she'd learned from her grandfather. Everything about survival, she'd learned from her mom.

"We can secure our own future," she said, trying to use language her mother would understand. "We don't need anyone else for that."

Her mother practically bared her teeth. "Now listen to me, and listen well."

Hailey pulled back, but her mother wouldn't let her go.

"You will turn around and say yes. . ." her mother started.

The hair on the back of Hailey's neck rose. Jonathan was coming up behind her. Soon, she'd be trapped.

Help, she wanted to scream. *Help!*

"You will do the right thing. . ." her mother went on.

Hailey twitched, dying to stand tall and release the outburst on the tip of her tongue. *No, I will not marry Jonathan just because you're crazy enough to think I should.* Then she would turn to Jonathan, give him a curt, *No means no, you got that?* and march out of there.

The problem was, she'd had an outburst along those lines at a recent photo shoot when her mother wouldn't stop harrying the photographer, caterers, and even the hairdresser.

Enough, mother! Enough! Hailey had finally roared.

Unfortunately, there'd been a reporter waiting in the wings, and she'd ended up in all the gossip rags for the next weeks, along with bold headlines like *Hailey Flips Out* and *Ungrateful B*tch.* So she forced herself to hold her tongue. Anything she said now was likely to be twisted and misinterpreted. But, Jesus. What could she do?

She looked around in desperation. The beach seemed miles away, but the lobby was right behind her, nearly deserted. The fountain gurgled quietly, and the marble floors gleamed.

"Hailey," Jonathan said in the same tight, uncompromising voice that uttered orders like *Schedule that meeting for three* or *Get me first class on the seven o'clock flight.*

Her heart thumped faster, and the sound of pounding surf filled her ears. Or was that the panicked rush in her veins?

This isn't happening, she wanted to scream.

But it was happening, and if she didn't act fast, who knew where it would end?

"You will march right back out there. . ." her mother continued.

Jonathan touched Hailey's shoulder, and she flinched.

No, wait. She did more than flinch. She spun and pushed Jonathan away — hard enough for him to stumble back, giving her just enough space to...

Half her mind was blank with fear, but the other half filled with her grandfather's voice.

Run, Hailey! Run!

Not a playful voice. A panicked one, just like that day out in the fields that started beautifully and ended in such horror. The day he died.

And just like that, she ran. The dull thump of her shoes along the flagstones turned into a sharp tap over the patterned marble floor of a long breezeway. Pink arches blurred by on one side, and yells broke out.

"Wait a minute," Jonathan snapped.

"Hailey!" her mother barked.

Hailey slowed just long enough to yank off her shoes before pushing through the front door and sprinting onto the bustling sidewalk outside.

She took off to the right and glanced back. Two reporters sprinted out in pursuit along with Lamar, who looked as murderous as ever. She gasped and ran on. God, she'd made it all worse by running. She should have just talked it through.

Jonathan, I'm not going to marry you. Mom, I'm not going to listen to you.

But bullies didn't listen to mere words, and both Jonathan and her mother were bullies in their own way.

So she ran, dodging pedestrians, losing hope with every step. Where could she go? To the police? The airport? Would she hide in an alley and hope never to be found?

A glance back showed Lamar was catching up. Jonathan had joined the posse that had taken up the chase. Her mother burst out onto the sidewalk next, screaming at the top of her lungs.

"Hailey, get back here!"

It was insane. And even more crazy was how life-and-death it all felt, like she was the rabbit and they were the wolves, out for a kill.

The wide sidewalks of Kalakaua Avenue stretched ahead with traffic too backed up for her to jump into a cab and make a quick escape.

"Best sale ever," a teenage girl announced to a friend, swinging a shopping bag that banged Hailey's arm.

Hailey darted around them and pivoted into the shopping center on her right.

"So rude," the girl muttered as Hailey raced on.

Hailey scowled. She wasn't being rude. She was running for her life.

The rough concrete under her bare feet turned to cool tile as she jumped on an escalator just ahead of three big, beefy young men and their giggling girlfriends.

"So rude," one of the girls snipped.

Hailey rolled her eyes. Would no one give her a break?

As luck would have it, that very group of teens did, because they clogged the escalator, blocking Lamar's way. Hailey clawed her way upward, making the most of her chance, and turned a tight corner to ascend to the next floor. Then she raced down a long corridor and over an open footbridge that gave her much too good a view of the hubbub below. Dozens of wedding guests were milling around outside, looking for her.

Think, Hailey. Think! she yelled at herself.

At the next escalator, she skidded to a stop, making a split-second decision. She was on the third level, overlooking a food court. A food court with lots of nooks and crannies where a woman on the run might be able to hide. She jumped onto the downward escalator and ducked out of sight. Lamar and the others were far enough back not to have seen her last moves, so she might just slip out of sight. *If* the tourist couple before her would stop taking selfies long enough for her to pass. Finally, she just pushed through.

Rude, I know, she nearly said, but she was panting too hard by then.

She jumped long before her step rolled to the bottom and made a sharp turn as the smell of Chinese cooking hit her. Then she ducked behind a potted plant and looked up. Lamar and several others sprinted along on the upper floor. They might not be tricked for long, but she'd bought herself a minute. But now what? Going down to street level would bring her right into the thick of the crowd. Where could she hide?

Her heart hammered as her eyes swept the area. Suddenly, she froze, catching a stranger at a nearby table staring at her. A big, broad-chested man who sat at one of the ridiculously small food court tables, sipping a drink through a straw. Except he'd stopped the moment their eyes met and started staring at her. *Into* her, almost.

At first, his frown made him downright terrifying. But instead of going cold with fear, Hailey found herself warming up, and for the next ten seconds, all she could do was register the color of his eyes. Hazel eyes, deep and dark as a forest. A forest with rays of sunlight streaming through it, because those eyes seemed to spark and glow the longer he looked at her.

Her leg muscles twitched with the instinct to keep running, but something told her to wait. So she did, staring into his ever-brighter eyes. Deep, soulful eyes that accomplished everything that silly fountain in the hotel lobby had failed to do. A sense of peace and serenity washed through her. Her heart rate slowed, and she rose out of her half crouch without understanding why. The man wasn't wearing a police uniform, and she didn't recognize him. But something about him called to her the way a lighthouse led a boat to a port of refuge, and she found herself taking a step closer.

"There she is!"

Her head snapped up at the sound of Jonathan's yell, and she broke into a run.

No, something deep inside her cried. *Not so soon...*

Which was crazy, because that man was a stranger, and she was in a rush. So she ran, winding past a sushi bar, an ice cream shop, and a burger place where the scent of sizzling grease made her think of the diner where she used to work. The memory made her run faster, pivoting this way and that until even she lost track of where she was. Someone was selling watches. Another person was collecting money for a charitable cause. A third manned a stall with perfume samples, surrounded by a pack of teenage girls. Hailey rushed around them and raced down a narrow corridor with a few barely visited shops, a couple of restrooms, and—

"Shit," she blurted, staring at the dead end.

She turned to retrace her steps, then backed up slowly. If she ran straight out, she might bump into Jonathan or Lamar. She backed away, then whirled and tried a side door. Locked. The next one was locked too, and the one beyond that. Finally, she ran into the second to last shop on the right — a sports store. The girl at the sales counter barely looked up as Hailey rushed in and continued through the pair of saloon doors at the entrance to the changing rooms. The narrow hallway had stalls on each side and a window at the end. A big, wide window she could easily fit through, if only it weren't too high to reach, not to mention two stories up. Mall sounds drifted up through it — footsteps, chatter, the rattle of a delivery trolley.

Hailey froze, undecided. A second later, she ducked into one of the changing stalls. The curtain screeched as she yanked it closed, and she winced.

Shit. Now she really was cornered. The area went still but for the distant sounds of shoppers, and Hailey buried her face in her hands in one of those *I wish I could teleport myself into a new life* moments she'd started experiencing lately. But this certainly took the prize.

Big mistake. A huge mistake. . .

She snorted. Running into the changing room was the least of many recent mistakes. She closed her eyes, vowing to get her life under control ASAP.

Over the next few minutes, everything remained quiet, though her heart barely slowed down. It would take a massive stroke of luck to go unnoticed by Jonathan, Lamar, and the others. Maybe she should have stayed out in public, because who knows what would happen if they found her behind closed doors? Jonathan had never been violent with her, but his piercing eyes had made her wonder how far he would go to get what he wanted. And Lamar. . . She shivered. Lamar had always scared her.

Maybe she should try the window. Maybe there was a fire alarm she could pull. Maybe she could—

The saloon doors squeaked, and she clapped a hand over her mouth to stifle a gasp. Quickly, she pulled her feet up and out of sight.

All she could see was the tiny cubicle of the stall, but she could hear the saloon doors swing on their hinges as someone came in. Slowly, the doors stilled, and nothing moved — including whoever had pushed those doors open. That person had to be standing just inside the doors, listening as closely as she was.

Obviously, it wasn't a woman coming to try something on. The steps had come in heavy clomps, indicating a person in boots.

Her mind whirled. Not Jonathan, then. He would have burst in yelling her name. Was it Lamar?

Every hair on her body stood in alarm as the steps advanced, one sure clomp after another. Left. Right. Left. Right. The boots came to a stop in front of the stall beside hers, and the curtain moved.

Her hands shook as she looked up. She would never be able to climb over the divider without being spotted. She'd be caught. Exposed. Helpless.

The steps shifted sideways, and she caught a brief glance through the gap between the curtain and the edge of the stall. A piece of gray clothing flashed past, bulging with muscle. She saw combat boots. Thick legs and huge, chiseled arms.

Her mind spun. Had Lamar been wearing short sleeves?

The steps stopped directly in front of her stall until all she could see were the worn toes of those boots. The curtain rustled, and she cringed. The room grew quieter still — a silence she was sure would be broken by a shout at any time.

I found her, whoever that was would yell out, calling the others in. Then he would thrust the curtain aside, yank her out, and—

Hailey squeezed her eyes shut, picturing the worst.

Chapter Three

It wasn't every day Tim entered the ladies' changing rooms. But the second he'd seen the woman with the piercing blue eyes, something in his soul stirred. When she'd glanced around the mall in terror, his inner grizzly had growled to life. And when she'd started running, he'd nearly run too.

Help her. Save her. Keep her safe, something deep inside him screamed.

Which was crazy, because bears didn't charge into action before thinking things through. Bears didn't so much as un-sheathe their claws without considering all options, exits, and backup plans. They were the quiet observers, the ones who said afterward, *I told you so.*

Well, okay — maybe he'd gotten into hot water a few times in spite of that. But that was in his younger, wilder days. His first two tours of duty had worn that out of him pretty quickly, and most of the messes he'd gotten into after that were a result of sticking close to his brothers, not his own hotheadedness. He was the one who tagged along to make sure things didn't get entirely out of control, and the one who saved their asses when whatever stupid idea they came up with didn't go according to plan.

So, what the hell was he doing, going all Lancelot with a woman he didn't know?

Sit, damn it, he had ordered his bear back when he'd first spotted her. *Calm down.*

There was no reason to get mixed up in someone else's business. For all he knew, the woman had been shoplifting. But his bear had roared and rampaged, tearing him apart. His human side might have learned to play by the rules, but his animal side still tended to rebel from time to time. The beast didn't rile easily, but when it did...

Get moving already, it growled.

No, he would not. He was more human than bear, and he lived in a human-dominated world. He was in a food court, for goodness' sake, not a war zone. And frankly, he didn't have to be a hero anymore. He didn't *want* to be a hero, because he'd learned the hard way that there wasn't a nice, clean line between good guys and bad guys. More like a blur, and if a man wasn't careful, he could find himself fighting for the wrong side.

He crossed his arms. The bear could rebel all it wanted. It wasn't getting its way now.

But, Jesus. The beast was hollering and kicking like never before.

She needs us, and we need her.

That was the most preposterous part. He didn't need a perfect stranger. And he wasn't about to lumber after a woman like a wild animal in heat. So he had forced himself to sit at that cramped little table in the food court and look the other way.

That lasted about three seconds, because his bear forced him to turn right back.

Watch! Help!

He gave in the teensiest, tiniest bit. Just enough to try to calm his bear down. *Okay, fine.*

But he didn't watch the woman. He watched for what she was running from.

A man yelled from the floor above and started charging down the escalator three steps at a time. A man with ruthless eyes and clenched fists who looked like he was out for blood. Tim could picture him charging through a combat zone, what with that quick, compact way he moved.

Tim sat up a little straighter. Whatever the woman had done, she didn't deserve what that man was about to dish out.

Two other men followed the first, all of them dressed to the nines, and one of them was cussing.

"Damn it, Hailey..."

Tim glanced over toward the corridor she'd disappeared down. Hailey? Was that her name?

The bear part of his mind went all dreamy, like he'd just licked an entire pot of honey or walked through a grassy meadow filled with spring flowers. The human part, meanwhile, tried to puzzle out why a woman in a nice white dress would be running barefoot through a mall.

Tim pushed his backpack aside with one foot, clearing a little aisle in case he decided to get involved, after all. A woman could run whenever and however she wanted; that was none of his business. But a woman running from two... three... four guys? He'd *make* that his business, damn it.

The first man — the dangerous one — reached the bottom of the escalator, ran a few steps, then stopped and sniffed. Really *sniffed* the way an animal would, with his nose turned up a little, his nostrils wide, his eyes half closed.

Tim froze. Like an animal — or a shifter?

He sniffed deeply, but the tangle of scents in the food court was hard to pick apart.

The man with the murderous eyes hesitated at the intersection where the woman had peeled off to the left, and Tim found himself gripping the table. But that man waved to the others rushing up behind him and took off to the right. His accomplices fanned out in different directions, with the one in the fancy gray suit taking the hallway the woman had disappeared down.

Connor, Tim barked to his brother, using the mental connection all closely bonded shifters shared.

But Connor was all the way across Honolulu and too busy to reply.

Just go already, his bear grunted.

Tim cursed and stood, finally giving in. After a quick check of the area, he followed.

"Try this one. It's a new scent from Chanel," a saleswoman said, spraying perfume across the wrists of six enthusiastic girls.

To a human, that artificial floral scent might smell subtle, but to a sensitive bear snout...

23

Tim wrinkled his nose, trying not to gag. The good news was that smell had probably masked the woman's trail from the man who'd sniffed the air.

His eyes locked on the back of the man stalking down that left branch-off. Video games beeped and pinged from an arcade, and a table of sport shoes stood in front of the next shop. There was a dollar store and a phone place before the hall ended in a set of double doors marked *Fire Exit. Alarm will sound.* Clearly, the woman hadn't gone that way. So where was she?

The man in the gray suit peered into each shop, and Tim followed. His bear claws pinched the undersides of his fingernails, itching to be released. He balled his fists, keeping the claws safely tucked away while he—

He whipped around to the left. *There,* his bear cried. *She's in there.*

He looked past the tennis rackets and discount shoes of the sport store. What made the bear so sure? He couldn't pick out her scent, and there was nothing to indicate she was there.

Believe me, she's there.

It was weird, how certain he was. The way he could always tell where his brothers were from a sixth sense that was hard to explain.

A phone rang, and Tim watched as the guy in the gray suit stopped to pat his pockets.

"Damn it," the guy muttered, pulling out a phone. "Hello? Yes. I mean, no. No sign of her yet. What?"

Tim pretended to look at baseball caps while he listened in.

"No. She couldn't have come through here. Call me back," Gray Suit barked into his phone. Then he walked back toward the food court, shooting Tim an annoyed look like it was all his fault the woman had run.

You're the one she was running from, asshole, Tim wanted to say.

But even if he had said something, he doubted the man would listen. He knew that type. The *you're not important enough to exist in my world; therefore, I will ignore you* kind.

A man of wealth and privilege, judging by the way he barked orders — not to mention the tailored clothes, the smooth shave, and the perfectly manicured nails.

Yeah, Tim noticed the nails. His bear got its cheap thrills by comparing weeny human nails to his own blade-like claws. What could he say? Every shifter species had its own little quirks.

"I'm on the second level," the man in the gray suit said, walking back to the food court.

Tim dropped the baseball hat and walked into the sports store, sniffing hard. The woman's scent was easier to track back there. It led him to a narrow hallway with a pair of saloon doors, and beyond them, a row of changing rooms with privacy curtains. He checked the store again, but the two employees took no notice of him, too busy showing each other pictures on their phones. Then he stepped through the saloon doors and stopped, wondering what the hell to do. The woman was in the last booth on the right, if his nose was right. A dead end within a dead end. How did she ever expect to get out of there?

Hailey. Her name is Hailey, his bear grunted.

Christ, he never should have listened to the beast. Now that it had gotten its way, it would never back down.

Hailey needs us. Hurry up, his bear insisted.

He put on his straightest, most expressionless face — an art that had taken years in military hot spots to perfect — and stepped toward the last booth. Her feet didn't show under the curtain, but he could picture her huddled on the bench with her legs pulled up and a breath caught in her throat.

He inhaled, imprinting her scent in his mind. A flowery scent, like that of the highest mountain meadows in the early days of summer, when bees buzzed everywhere and berries were just beginning to show. But there was fear mixed into that scent too, and it made his bear rage.

When I get my claws on those guys. . .

Tim flexed his hands, reminding himself that wasn't the point. Helping the woman — Hailey? — get away from them was.

He stepped in front of the last stall and stopped, scratching his brow. He'd stormed plenty of buildings with his Special Forces unit, not to mention bunkers, military installations, and tunnels. But how exactly did one extract a single woman from a changing booth?

Briefly, it occurred to him that she could have a weapon. That *she* was the bad guy being chased by good guys, not the other way around. But a split second later, he dismissed the idea. The woman was the one with fear in her eyes, while the men looked as if they were out to kill. Which meant he'd better get moving with Operation Exit Shopping Mall, quick.

"So," he said, trying to keep his voice light. Failing miserably, because the deep rumble thundered through the silence of the changing area. "You can stay in there all you want. None of my business."

Except she *felt* like his business, damn it, although he had no idea why.

"But there are at least four guys after you," he went on. "And I reckon you've got five minutes, tops, before they figure out which way you went."

Something moved behind the curtain, and a second later, she spoke. "Only four guys?"

Tim grinned. Spunky little thing, wasn't she? Behind the snark in her voice, though, came the uneven scratch of fear.

"Call it approximate." He squinted at the curtain, wishing he could see through it because he'd forgotten what she looked like. Her eyes were the only part that had stuck in his mind — a pure, rich blue, like the spring sky over the Rockies. "Four guys, at least, on this level of the mall. And yeah, I'd say you have about five minutes, give or take."

"And you are...?"

He tilted his head. Even backed into a corner, she managed to keep her shit together. "Timber Hoving," he said. "You're Hailey, right?"

The air went very still. "How do you know that?"

He rolled his eyes. If she knew how much he could find out if he ever decided to really investigate, she'd freak out.

"I heard one of them say as much. The guy in a gray suit who's in love with himself — and possibly his phone."

The woman huffed. "Jonathan. Of course."

Of course? She sounded pretty fed up with the guy. Was he her boss?

He looked at the curtain then at his watch. "Listen, are you coming or not?"

A pensive silence ensued. "Coming... where? With whom?"

"Coming with me. Getting the hell out of here."

"You know a way out?" Her voice rose in hope. Hope he was already terrified of dashing if he somehow messed up.

He scrubbed his chin. Yeah, he did know a way out, but he doubted she'd like what he had in mind.

A hand appeared at the edge of the curtain, and she peeked then hid again, leaving him grasping at the details that had just flashed before his eyes. Blue eyes. Blond hair. Strong, sharp cheekbones covered with freckles he wished he had time to count.

"Why should I trust you?"

She was trying to sound tough, but her voice wobbled a little, and his heart ached at the loneliness in it.

He ran a hand through his hair. Why *should* she trust him?

He shrugged. "You just can. I promise."

And, he supposed, because she had no choice.

The thing was, it felt like he didn't have a choice either. He simply had to help her because... because...

Destiny, his bear whispered.

He took a deep breath and decided not to examine that sentiment too closely. Not now, with so much rushing through his mind.

For a few quiet seconds, time ticked by. Then the curtain opened with a metallic zing of rings over a steel rod, and the woman glowered at him. Hands on her hips, chin stuck up, eyes shooting bullets as if he were the guy who'd chased her into there, not the guy who wanted to get her out.

Don't let me down, those eyes blazed. *Don't you dare let me down.*

His chest tightened, and his shoulders squared the way they would when his unit got assigned one of those *Mission: Impossible* operations no one else had a hope in hell of carrying out. This felt just as life-and-death — and just as heavy on his shoulders.

Which was crazy. She was a perfect stranger. And yet her trust struck a bull's-eye in the one soft spot left on his heart.

She was lean — too lean, really — and a good five inches under his height. Still, she glared like he was the one who'd better watch out.

"Let's say I decided to trust you," she said. "What then?"

He sucked in a deep breath, trying not to get lost in those amazing eyes. Then he clicked his jaw a few times. *Focus, damn it. Focus on getting her out.*

His mind spun through the options one more time, and the same series of steps jumped out as his best plan.

"Wait here one second," he said. "I'll be right back."

Chapter Four

The woman — Hailey — squeaked in protest, but Tim strode back to the main area of the sports shop. His choices were limited, but hell. He grabbed a sweatshirt off one rack and several pairs of shorts off another, then hurried back to the changing area and thrust them at her.

"Pick something. Hurry."

She stared. "What?"

He stirred the air with his hands. "They're looking for a woman in white."

She scowled down at her dress and muttered, "I knew it wasn't cream."

What that meant, he had no clue, but he decided to let it slide. "Like I said, they'll be focused on finding one woman wearing white. Not two people in dark clothing."

She stared at the bundle of clothes. "You think that will work?"

He nodded. He'd done enough surveillance to know how hard it was to make that kind of mental leap. "Not guaranteed, but a good chance. What's your shoe size?"

By then, she had the clothes clutched to her chest like the world's flimsiest armor. "Um... eight."

A few minutes later, they were at the counter, pulling price tags off the clothes she'd already thrown on — a blue sweatshirt and pink sports shorts that were a size too big. But, hell. It worked.

"I'll pay you back," Hailey said firmly when he pulled out his wallet.

He nearly said, *That's the least of my worries right now,* but the words caught in his throat when she leaned over and

29

undid her bun. Long, silky, blond strands cascaded over her shoulders then bounced around as she finger-combed it all back and asked, "Better?"

He gulped. Worse, because how was he supposed to concentrate on extracting his target when he could just stand and stare at that?

He cleared his throat and stuck a pink baseball cap on her head. "That's better."

She took it off, grimacing at the big, loopy script on the front. "Aloha?"

"Aloha," he growled and stuck it back on.

The salesgirl bundled the white dress into a bag, ran his credit card, and waved them off with a hearty *Mahalo* before going back to her phone.

"I'm only trusting you temporarily, you know," Hailey whispered when he grabbed her hand and walked toward the doors.

"I'm only helping you temporarily," he shot back as a reminder to his inner bear.

He peeked down the hall. None of the men he'd spotted earlier was in sight, so he strode out, trying to amble and not rush. When they came out at the food court, Hailey moved closer to his side.

Nice, his bear hummed inside.

Well, it would have been nice under different circumstances, and his mind veered off into all kinds of fantasies of what those might be. Him and her out on a Sunday stroll, with nowhere in particular to get to and no one to get away from. Getting to know each other, laughing, having a good time.

Silverware clattered, and he yanked his attention back to the present.

Temporary, he hissed at his bear.

"Now what?" Hailey whispered in his ear.

So close. So nice. His bear closed its eyes, still dreaming away.

Tim pointed to the escalator. "Over there. Once we get down to street level, we can catch a cab or disappear into the crowd."

Which was a good plan, but as their escalator rolled down, the opposite one rolled up, cutting across at a diagonal. The moment Hailey looked down, she tensed.

"Oh God. . . "

Three reporters were coming up, cameras at the ready. What was that all about?

With no time to ask, Tim turned to block her body from view. Then he slid an arm across her shoulders the way a guy might with his girl and whispered in her ear.

"We got this. Don't worry. Just look down. See anyone else there?"

She nodded in short, choppy jerks and gestured toward the sidewalk. "Over there. And there."

The people she indicated were easy enough to pick out thanks to their fancy clothes and shiny shoes. Like church had just let out or a big gala event had just broken up.

He picked out a route with his eyes and tugged Hailey forward as soon as the escalator bottomed out. The sidewalk wasn't far, but he took a meandering path from storefront to storefront, pausing at window displays or touching items as if he were interested in buying them. His heart started beating faster because they were almost outside. A few more steps and—

Hailey pulled up short and made an abrupt U-turn. "Those two."

Tim looked for a new option, but damn. Three men and one woman stood behind them, scanning the crowd.

"Oh God," Hailey murmured. "That's Isabelle. . . "

Tim had no idea who Isabelle was, but clearly, the woman was bad news. He and Hailey were surrounded on three sides, with a store on the other. No way out. Except one. . .

"Don't take this the wrong way," he whispered before hustling Hailey over to a support column and leaning close.

Her eyes went wide as he closed in as if for a kiss. *Really* close, until barely a millimeter separated them. Her minty breath came out in shocked little gasps.

"Shh," he whispered, putting his arms on either side of her head, blocking anyone's view of her face. All anyone would see was a guy kissing his girl.

And it nearly came to that too. He was so close, and despite the urgency of the situation, his brain started to shut down. Her honeysuckle scent filled his ears, and his blood rushed. Their legs bumped, and with each deep breath, their chests touched. When Hailey tentatively slid her arms around his waist, he nearly sighed.

It wasn't a kiss, but it was close.

So good, his bear groaned.

Hell yeah, it was. So good that it took everything he had not to close that last millimeter and cover her lips with his. Hailey might not have even minded, judging by the way her eyes went from startled to dreamy and distant. His had to have been the same — or worse, glowing outright.

Mate, his bear murmured. *She is my mate.*

Behind him, two men swept past so quickly, one of them bumped the shopping bag that held Hailey's dress.

"Sorry," the man muttered, hurrying on without a second thought.

Go. Now, a voice screamed in Tim's mind. The exit was open; it was their chance to escape.

But he barely heard, what with the way Hailey looked at him and the effect of the word that kept echoing through his mind.

Mate...

He gulped. Every shifter knew what that meant. A chance encounter with a soul mate, all engineered by fate. A single look that could change a man's life.

But for that to happen to *him*? Here? Now?

Hailey's lips twitched, brushing his, and a heat wave rolled through his body along with a reckless sense of hope.

Yes, a voice rumbled from the depths of his mind. *She is the one.*

Her eyes flashed, and he wondered if she'd just heard the same thing, turned around to mean him. *Yes. He is the one.*

But, damn it. Behind them, people were barking orders and hurrying around.

"Try that way," one man hissed to another. "We have to find her."

Have to protect her, his bear snarled.

Tim nearly snarled too. He'd just found his destined mate. Couldn't the world let him process that?

Then another scent hit him, and he jolted.

Shifter? He grabbed Hailey's hand and led her toward the exit. Her first few steps were shaky, and he kept her close, resisting the urge to look around.

Was the man he'd seen chasing her first a shifter? Was he nearby?

Tim hurried forward. The exit was right there, and it was clear. A second later, they were outside, and Hailey blinked hard. Tim wanted to blink too. That feeling of being blinded wasn't just in his eyes, and it wasn't from the sudden change to broad sunlight. It was inside him, filling him with a warm glow.

Mate... his bear murmured, as blown away as he was by the thought.

"Go," he said, all but shoving Hailey into a cab. The traffic had parted just enough to let the cab squeeze through if they moved fast.

"Where to?" the driver asked.

Tim stared at Hailey, terrified she'd give an address where he'd have to leave her forever. But she stared back at him, looking equally blank.

"Um... Pearl Harbor," he said, throwing out the reference point that jumped into his mind. A mind rapidly cluttering with new options and ideas, because a bear always had to have a plan.

The driver had the radio on, and a cheery voice rattled off reports on Honolulu's sunny weather, miserable traffic, and an outrigger canoe race. Tim huddled closer to Hailey, keeping his voice down.

"Where are you staying?" he whispered.

She motioned behind them. "Back there."

He glanced out the rear window. No one had appeared in hot pursuit — yet.

"I have to get away," she said hoarsely. "Far away. I have to hide."

He thought it over. White dress. Reporters. Men in hot pursuit. What exactly was going on? "Listen, if you're in trouble with the law..."

She shook her head quickly. "It's not that. I swear I'll explain later." She shot a hard look in the direction of the driver. "Right now, I need to find someplace to hole up in for a few days. Someplace off the beaten path."

Tim sat very still, because he knew a place exactly like that. Koakea Plantation, his home on Maui, was about as far off the beaten path as anyone could get. But he couldn't bring a perfect stranger into the midst of his fellow shifters. They lived apart for a reason, guarding their secrets from prying human eyes.

Still, Maui was full of little hideaways. Surely, he could find a place for her to stay somewhere.

His bear nodded eagerly. *Someplace where we can guard her.*

He took a deep breath, fighting that spinning, out-of-control feeling that was rapidly taking over his neatly ordered life. He'd come to Oahu with a clear plan, and Hailey wasn't part of it.

She is now, his bear growled.

He looked at Hailey, unable to say yes, unable to say no.

"How does Maui sound?" he found himself whispering at last.

Hope brightened Hailey's eyes before doubt clouded them again. "Maui would be great, but how can I get there? My wallet is at the hotel. I have no credit card, no ID."

Tim felt a funny little stretch set into his cheeks. A smile? What the hell was he smiling about at a time like this?

Destiny, his bear chuckled. *It has to be.*

He leaned over the front seat and spoke to the driver. "Can you take us to the heliport, please?"

The driver nodded, but Hailey grabbed Tim's arm. "Heliport? As in, a helicopter? You have a helicopter?"

He grinned. No, he didn't. But his brother did.

"Do you trust me?" he asked, holding his breath. Even if her options were limited, she didn't necessarily need him. She could go to the police, call a relative for help, or find someplace to hide on Oahu until she sorted out her problem, right?

And yet he wanted her to trust him. Desperately.

His heart thumped as he watched her lips. Were they forming a round *no*?

She searched his eyes for a long time before nodding slowly. "Yes. At least, temporarily."

He broke into a wide grin. The *yes* part felt as good as the sun coming out on a cloudy day, no matter how *temporary* it might turn out to be.

"All right then," he said, trying to keep cool. "Maui." He pointed to the horizon.

Hailey looked. Maui wasn't actually visible from there, but the ocean sparkled between the buildings they passed.

"Maui," she whispered, and her throat bobbed.

She was quiet for the rest of the drive, but her fingers never stopped playing with the single pearl that hung from her necklace. A lumpy, oblong thing that didn't go with the fancy clothes she'd been wearing when he first spotted her. When they stepped out of the cab at the heliport, she clutched the shopping bag like her first line of defense. Which he supposed it was. The question was, what made a woman desperate enough to leave everything behind?

What the hell? a deep voice growled into his mind.

Tim whipped around and spotted his brother, Connor, standing beside a brown helicopter decorated with red and yellow stripes.

"Hailey, meet Connor," Tim said in his most uncompromising voice.

Connor shook politely and said, "Nice to meet you." At the same time, he grunted into Tim's mind.

Who the hell is this?

Tim didn't really have an answer, but he wasn't about to back down. The chopper had four seats, and only two of them were spoken for, right?

She needs help. And quit intimidating her.

I'm not intimidating anyone, Connor said as he glared.

Hailey gulped and eyed the distance to the parking lot.

You came to Oahu for your contractor's license, and you found some woman instead? Connor did not sound impressed.

Tim couldn't quite believe it himself. For the past few months, nothing had distracted him from his goal of getting that license. Now, all he could think about was Hailey. How exactly had that happened?

He replayed the first half of the morning in his mind. He'd gotten up early and flown to Oahu with Connor. The helicopter was due for inspection, so Tim had grabbed the chance to tag along. The Honolulu office of the Department of Commerce and Consumer Affairs had walk-in hours, which meant he could get his license faster than waiting for the monthly date on Maui. He'd been so excited about it too — the idea of checking off every requirement and walking out, ready to go into business for himself. Timber Hoving, general contractor. Bit by bit, the dream of running his own company was coming true. He could be his own boss and maybe even hire a couple of extra hands someday.

It had all gone to plan, right through the point when he had run a couple of errands at the mall and stopped at the food court for lunch. But then Hailey had blown into his life like a typhoon no one had spotted on the forecast.

I'm helping her. Temporarily, he told Connor. Then aloud, he added, "Hailey needs a ride to Maui, and we're it."

He hoped that would put her at ease, but Connor did the opposite when he crossed his arms and widened his stance.

"And what is Hailey going to do when she gets to Maui?"

Stay with me, Tim's bear nearly whispered. *Forever.*

Tim shoved the thought way, way back into the back of his mind. "We'll figure something out on the way."

36

"You'll figure something out?" Connor said in a dull, disbelieving tone. *A bear who never does anything without planning the next five steps is suddenly flying by the seat of his pants?*

His brother might have been glaring, but Hailey had gratitude pouring from her eyes. Then a car raced into the heliport parking lot, and her face fell. It was just some hot rod pilot late for his shift, but Tim motioned for Connor to hurry up.

"We'll talk on the way, okay?"

Connor didn't budge, though, and they glared at each other for the next minute. Really glared, fighting an inner battle so intense, he started to sweat.

We need to take her with us, he insisted.

Tell me why, his brother snapped. It was an order, not a request, making Tim clench his fists.

His brother was alpha of their little pack, and while Tim was used to speaking his mind, he rarely challenged a direct order. He'd never needed to. Connor was the oldest; he'd always been in charge. That was just the way it was.

Except his bear was suddenly rebelling, bucking rules that had never rankled him until now.

Hailey shifted nervously from foot to foot, watching them both.

Fine, Connor finally muttered. *But you'd better have a goddamn plan soon.*

Within ten minutes, they were all strapped into the chopper with headsets on and views of Pearl Harbor expanding rapidly beneath. Hailey laid a hand against the window, looking down at the memorial site with an inscrutable expression. Then Connor swung the helicopter around, and her eyes moved over the busy strip of Waikiki and the ridgeline that climbed toward Diamond Head. What could he possibly say to put her at ease?

Just in case you're crazy enough to think she can stay with us, she can't, Connor barked into his mind. *You know Cynthia will back me up on this.*

Tim stared straight ahead. Cynthia was the co-alpha of their shifter clan — a young dragon widow with a mysterious past, a young son, and an uncompromising leadership style.

But surely, she would have a heart for Hailey, a woman on the run?

Tim glanced back just as Hailey looked up at him. Those pure, blue eyes so full of fear and hope. Those full lips, quivering the tiniest bit. He barely noticed when his peripheral vision shut down, gradually narrowing his world to Hailey and nothing else. His mind was the same way. All his carefully laid plans and dreams became a blur, and everything ceased to exist except her.

Destiny, his bear murmured.

He gulped. Destiny? Could it really be?

Chapter Five

Hailey clutched her seat and peered out over the water as the craggy mountains of Maui grew closer and closer. The helicopter had already flown over the long, low hump of Molokai, and she couldn't believe the views. Of course, it would have been a hell of a lot easier to enjoy the stunning sights if it weren't for her current predicament.

Her eyes darted between the two men in the front of the helicopter. On the right was the man who'd helped her escape the mall. Tim — the one with mesmerizing eyes and a soft yet powerful voice that counted more on resonance then sheer volume to get a point across. She still couldn't believe she'd trusted him, but something about him put her at ease. Something she couldn't begin to explain. Plus, it was getting harder and harder to assume he had anything nefarious up his sleeve. There was no way Jonathan could have posted Tim in the mall as a trap, not when Jonathan had been so sure she would accept his proposal.

She swallowed a groan and bumped her head against the window. Jonathan. What had she ever seen in him? How could she have been so dumb?

"You okay?" Tim asked.

He was too far away to touch, but it felt as if he'd reached out and given her a hug. A hug that shouldn't feel that good because he was a perfect stranger. Yet something about him screamed honor, justice, and *You can trust me.*

Temporarily, she reminded herself.

She sighed and stared out over the mottled water. The ocean was a deep, dark blue in some spots, and a brighter, friendlier turquoise around the islands' shores.

"I'm okay. Just feeling dumb."

"Care to tell us what's going on?" Connor asked in his harder, edgier voice.

She glanced up. Tim had introduced Connor as his brother, and it showed. Not so much in the details but in the overall impression. They had the same hazel eyes, the same bristling sense of authority, and the same wary stance.

Did she want to tell them what had happened? Not really, no. But she owed these men an explanation after everything they had done for her.

"I came to Honolulu for a wedding. Turns out it was my own wedding." She rolled her eyes. "Or so Jonathan thought."

The men looked at each other in confusion, so she backed up.

"I've only known Jonathan for about two months. We were seeing each other off and on. More off than on, honestly. When he invited me to his sister's wedding, it didn't seem right to break up with him just then." She let out a bitter chuckle. "But it turned out not to be his sister's wedding. It was a surprise wedding he'd planned for us." Her voice rose as the appalling scene replayed in her head. "He got down on one knee in front of everyone." She shook her head. "He actually thought I'd say yes."

Connor's eyebrows tightened. "I guess he was wrong?"

Hailey uttered the same mirthless chuckle. "You bet he was wrong. Trying to pressure me into a wedding? No way." She gnashed her teeth. "But with everyone there, watching... I guess I panicked. His security guys were closing in on me—"

"Wait. What?" Tim broke in. "His security guys were going to force you?"

Hailey kept her eyes on the water because it was too hard to look him in the eye while explaining how naïve she'd been. How flighty, like a silly teen. But when she replayed the scene in her head, she saw Lamar coming toward her with those wide, mercenary eyes. And her mother – her own mother! – trying to pressure her to agree. So maybe she hadn't been so crazy to run. Maybe *they* were the crazy ones.

40

"Honestly, I'm not sure what Lamar would have done. But when I ran, he followed. He and the other security guys, coming after me like I was a criminal to say no." Her voice was shaking and her hands, too. "Jonathan joined them, and I couldn't stop running. All I wanted was to get away."

An uncomfortable silence ensued until Tim surprised her with a low, grumbled comment. "I guess I would have run too."

She nearly laughed out loud. She didn't believe for a second that Mr. *My Chest is a Mountain, My Arms are Tree Trunks* would ever contemplate any such thing. But it was sweet of him to say.

"So, what's the plan?" Connor shot a sidelong glance at Tim like he expected his brother to have an entire strategy plotted out in his mind. But Hailey had a feeling Tim was just as lost about what to do as she was, and he proved it by scrubbing a hand over his chin.

She spoke before he could. It wasn't Tim's responsibility to solve her mess. She would have to find a way out on her own.

"I haven't had time to think of a plan. But this is a good start – getting away from Oahu and Jonathan." *Not to mention the press,* she nearly added. But neither Tim nor Connor had seemed to recognize her, and things were already too complicated to mention that. "I just need to find a place to lie low for a few days."

"Lie low?" Connor stared. "Don't you have someone to call?"

She pursed her lips. All she had was her mother. No brothers, sisters, or close cousins to call for help. The one person she really would have loved to call was her grandfather, but he had died years before. And as for friends – well, she hadn't made too many in the fashion world. The friends she had grown up with, she hadn't seen in years.

She frowned at her reflection in the window. Had her mother been sheltering her from those friends all along?

Just doing what's best for you, honey, she could picture her mother saying.

41

Hailey thumped a fist against her thigh. Well, fine. She had a bank account, and there was plenty in it. She just had to figure out how to access it. Maybe she could call her lawyer. She did have her phone, and his number was on it.

She scowled. Her mother had that number too. In fact, her mother had all the numbers, having taken care of all the details, all the time. Too many details, in hindsight.

Hailey thought it over. Hopefully, she could go to a bank and prove who she was. Once she got access to her money, she could fly home. Then she could make that public statement she'd been planning about stepping away from modeling. And as for Jonathan...

She shuddered. He had never threatened her before, but the way his eyes had narrowed when she was getting ready to run... How far he would really go?

She took a deep breath. One thing at a time. She could get a restraining order if necessary. In fact, she could get one against her mother if push came to shove. Then she'd find herself some nice, quiet place far away from her old life and make a completely new start.

"Do you have money? A credit card? Someone to call?" Tim asked.

She gulped, trying to dislodge the lump in her throat, and shook her head. No, she didn't have any of those things.

"I'm sure we can figure out some way to help you for a couple of days," Tim said.

Connor's jaw hung open, and though he didn't say anything, she could read the words on his lips.

A couple of days? Are you crazy, man?

But Tim gestured forward, bringing her attention to the horizon.

"Maui," she whispered, gaping at the view.

Oahu was nice, but Maui was much more rugged. The mountains were higher and wilder. Surely, there was a place among them she could hide away in for a few days.

No one spoke after that, and Hailey tried to clear her mind for a while. She nearly succeeded, marveling at the emerald colors of the land and the turquoise hues of the sea. But the closer they got to the golden strip of shoreline, the more doubt welled up in her mind. Where would she go? What would she do?

Connor maneuvered the helicopter toward a concrete landing pad on what looked to be a hell of a nice estate on a quiet corner of the island. She caught sight of three or four roofs between the palms, but the rest was all neatly trimmed lawns and thick stands of trees. There was a big garage, too – a really long one with space for at least eight cars. Hailey looked from one of the men in the front seat to the other. They lived on an estate like that?

Her thoughts must have been spelled out on her face because Tim gestured. "The guy who owns the helicopter lives on this estate." Then he pointed farther right. "We live next door, working a little caretaking, a little security."

Security fit Tim and Connor to a T. But *little*? No way.

"Nice," she said, trying not to get her hopes up. Surely people with that much land would have a little corner she could hide away in. Maybe she could do some work in exchange.

Then she snorted softly. Her line of work was not exactly useful, not in any practical sense. Her best bet was to borrow enough money for a cab to a hotel where she could try to straighten the rest out.

The helicopter bumped down, and a man and woman stepped out of the line of palm trees, sheltering their eyes from the sun with their hands. Were they the owners? Hailey steeled her nerves, trying to think of what to say and how.

"They're the caretakers," Tim said, leaning in. "Looks like the owners are out right now, but don't worry. They're friends of ours."

Connor's pursed lips said he still didn't like it, but Tim jumped to the ground and helped Hailey out before his brother could say a word. The rotors slowed over their heads, and Tim led her to the waiting couple.

"This is Hunter Bjornvald," Tim said, introducing the big, burly man. "A fellow be— buddy from our Special Forces days."

Hailey started to wonder what the *be-buddy* stutter was all about, but then Tim got to the *Special Forces* part and blew her away. No wonder they all looked so badass.

The woman, on the other hand, was a gorgeous islander with long, silky hair. She should have looked fragile beside the big man, but she had her own understated aura of authority.

"Dawn Meli," Tim said, continuing the introductions. "Meet—"

"Hailey Crewe," Dawn said right away.

Hailey's stomach lurched as Tim stared. God, she hated when that happened. Some people recognized her; others didn't give a damn. Either way was fine with her, but she always felt like a liar for not mentioning anything up front. On the other hand, she didn't want to go around announcing, *By the way, I'm a successful model,* to everyone she met.

Connor's mouth hung open, and the man named Hunter looked just as confused. "Who?"

Dawn laughed and smacked Hunter between the shoulder blades. "Hailey Crewe, the model. I really have to get you out more often."

"Hailey Crusak, actually," Hailey said, as if that helped at all. "My agent thought Crewe would work better."

"And what brings you here?" Dawn asked.

Hailey looked at Tim, wondering how much to say.

"It's a long story," she sighed at last.

The men looked at each other for a moment, and Hunter scrubbed a hand over his chin, clearly unsure about what to do. But when a calico cat wandered by with a plaintive meow, Hunter broke into a huge grin and scooped it into his arms.

"Hey, Keiki," he murmured, nuzzling it under his chin.

Hailey smiled as the cat looked at her with an expression that said, *Don't I have it good?*

You sure do, she thought, glancing around at the grounds and at the obvious outpouring of love the cat received.

"Don't worry. We'll deal with this," Tim said with a firm look at Connor. "Come on over to our place."

He led the way down a long, snaking footpath that led to the neighboring land. It was obvious when they crossed the property line — not so much from the rickety old fence but from the way the manicured grounds of the estate gave way to the tangle of what looked to be an abandoned farm of some kind.

"We're still fixing the place up," Tim murmured apologetically.

Hailey looked around wistfully. Fixer-uppers had always appealed to her, but ever since her career had taken off, her mother had insisted on nothing but the best. When Hailey wasn't on the road for work, she lived in a state-of-the-art, cubical condo with no character at all. But this...

She gazed around, taking it all in. The focal point of the plantation was a grand old house that had been restored right down to the gingerbread trim on the eaves. A friendly, welcoming place, in contrast to the reserved woman who met them on the porch.

"Hailey Crewe, meet Cynthia... Brown," Connor said when they ascended the steps.

There was a tease to his voice, and the pause between the first and last name made the woman shoot Connor a pointed look. Cynthia had a regal air to her — not snobbish, but definitely aloof. At least, until a little boy with red hair and gorgeous green eyes ran up with an excited, "Mommy! Mommy! Who's here?"

That warmed Cynthia right up, and she took his hand. "I was about to find out for myself, honey."

Hailey shook hands with Cynthia then crouched down and offered the boy her hand. "I'm Hailey."

His eyes went wide. "Like the comet?"

She laughed. She had cometed into these people's lives, but other than that... "Not really, but I have seen the moons of Jupiter," she tried. "My granddad used to show me."

Her heart warmed then ached as it always did when she thought about him.

"Oh! I can show you my comet book." The boy ran back into the house.

"Joey..." Cynthia called, then gave up with a sigh.

"Hailey Crewe!" a spunky young woman exclaimed as she bounded up to the porch.

"Hiya, Jenna," Tim said.

Connor, who'd been gruff and reserved until then, broke into a huge smile at the sight of Jenna, and when they kissed, it was long and hard. Then along came a woman who looked a lot like Jenna, and it was time for Hailey's jaw to drop.

"Jody Monroe?" she asked.

The blonde smiled and took her by both arms. "Hailey Crewe. Wow. Another fugitive from the modeling world?" She said it with a laugh, and Hailey warmed. Maybe she wasn't crazy for wanting to leave that world behind.

"You know each other?" Connor asked.

"We modeled for competing ad campaigns," Jody explained to the others. "Hailey did *Boundless,* and I did *Elements.*"

"Yours came out really well," Hailey said, and she meant it. The modeling world had gone wild about the fresh new face in the industry. But Jody had dropped out of modeling as quickly as she'd started.

Smart girl, Hailey decided. Smarter than she was for getting sucked in so deep.

Jody laughed. "I discovered modeling wasn't exactly my thing. Surfing — and Cruz — are." She pointed to the dark-haired man at her side. "But *Boundless* did really well, too. From what I hear, the big boss of the company I was working for — Moira — was really angry. Like her fragrance was the only one that could succeed. Ha."

Hailey chuckled, but at the mention of the name Moira, the others frowned and exchanged hard looks. What was that all about? Moira LeGrange had quite a reputation, but still.

Cynthia cleared her throat. "All right, everybody. Settle down so Miss Crewe can tell us what this is all about."

Everyone took a seat around the huge table on the porch, and Hailey steeled herself with a deep breath. Then she told them the whole story from the time she'd met Jonathan two months earlier to the moment she set foot on the estate next door.

Two more men came along and quietly introduced themselves — an easygoing man with a golden beard named Dell, and another brother of Tim's — Chase, who quietly listened in. Cynthia tapped her fingers on the table, listening intently as Hailey continued with her story. Chase paced, and Dell wandered off to read the books Joey had brought down. Dawn and Hunter had come along, listening as intently as the rest. Long silences stretched out whenever Hailey paused, and she had the strange feeling that they were communicating somehow. The little nods and hand gestures matched those of people talking to one another — but no one's lips moved, and no one uttered a sound. Keiki, the cat, wandered under the table, rubbing against their legs, purring with love.

When Hailey finished, Jenna gave her a grim nod. "I was on the run once. I know how it feels."

Connor pulled Jenna closer to his side. "No running anymore," he whispered, gently tucking a strand of hair behind her ear.

Cynthia glanced over to where Joey sat inside, and a haunted *something* flashed through her eyes.

Hailey looked around. Hunter and Dawn were the kind of warm, loving couple you could spot from a mile away. Connor and Jenna, too. Tim, on the other hand, kept his eyes firmly on the ground as if uncomfortable around such open displays of love. Dell and Chase looked happily single, while Cynthia wore an air of sorrow around her shoulders like a cape. Each of them had a different story, but it was clear they were a tight-knit community as well.

Hailey looked down as Keiki wound around her ankles, purring to comfort her. She reached down to pet the cat's soft, tricolor tail.

"Unfortunately, you can't stay here," Cynthia said, more gently than Hailey expected. Still, Hailey's hopes plummeted, until Cynthia added, "But I believe I know where you *can* stay."

"Where?" Tim blurted before Hailey so much as peeped in relief.

Cynthia looked at Hunter. "What's the name of that place? Where you grew up?"

Hunter nodded immediately. "Pu'u Pu'eo. A small place on the other side of Maui."

Dawn's eyes sparkled. "Pu'u Pu'eo. That's perfect!"

"Pu'u what?" Connor and Tim asked at the same time.

"It's Hawaiian for Owl Hill," Hunter explained. "My foster mother's place. I grew up there." His eyes took on a wistful, faraway look.

"It's a great place," Dawn added. "Far from the road and totally off the grid. No one – and I mean, no one – would ever think to look for you there."

"Precisely," Cynthia said, giving Hailey the distinct impression she knew all about getting away from... something.

Hailey knotted her fingers nervously. *Off the grid* sounded like exactly the kind of place she needed right now.

"Are you sure? I'd hate to impose." Then she caught herself. "Shoot. I already have imposed. A lot. On all of you."

She looked at Connor and then trained her eyes on Tim. From the very beginning, he'd given her the benefit of the doubt. Not only that, but he'd put himself out on a limb by bringing her to his friends for help. But his steady eyes told her he'd do it all over again.

She gulped. She barely knew him, yet she already owed him so much.

"It would be our pleasure," Dawn assured her. "Believe me. We want to make more use of the place so the jungle doesn't swallow it up." Her grin faded and her voice grew hushed when she went on. "Besides, we're happy to pay our luck forward. We've been where you are, you know. And we came out of it stronger and happier."

Jenna nodded and wove her fingers around Connor's. Was she thinking about whatever dire circumstances had driven her here?

"It would be perfect," Tim said carefully. "But there's no protection there. If anybody managed to track Hailey down..."

Hailey grimaced. She could just picture the media spectacle that might ensue.

Cynthia scratched her head. "I don't see how. None of us will say a word. But you're right. It would be better not to leave Hailey totally alone." She looked around. "She'll need someone to stay with her, just in case."

Dawn must have sensed Hailey's alarm because she spoke up in a soothing tone. "Just to get you settled in. Like I said, it's off the grid. You have to haul water from the creek, use kerosene lanterns, all that. Oh — or maybe you don't like roughing it?"

Hailey laughed out loud. Roughing it? She'd been dreaming of roughing it for the last three years. Of heading out into the woods, pitching a tent, and staring at the stars. Living a simple life away from the glitz and glamour she'd been sucked into.

She caught herself there. That world had paid her handsomely, and she would never forget it. But she was ready to move on, for sure.

"Roughing it is no problem," she said as memories of her childhood came back to her. The couple of times the power had been turned off when her mother couldn't make the payments. That especially cold winter when they'd had to scrounge for wood. The thrift-store clothes and worn-out shoes.

And that was just what she'd experienced. She couldn't imagine how hard it must have been for her mother. No wonder the woman was so determined to get ahead.

Hailey closed her eyes. Surely, she could find forgiveness. After all, her mother only wanted to protect her from the kind of life they'd escaped.

"Tim can go with her."

Her eyes snapped open. What had Connor just said?

Tim looked just as surprised as she was. "Me?"

"Sure," Connor said with a wry grin. "You're perfect."

Hailey stared. *Perfect* was exactly the problem. Those warm eyes, that hard body. That knight in shining armor aura and willingness to please.

The dirty part of her mind ran away with all the ways he might be willing to please her, and she grabbed for her drink. She nearly missed her mouth, she was that rattled — and excited — about the idea.

"The place needs work, right?" Connor smacked Tim on the back. "Why not let Mr. Contractor here get to work?"

"Well, I guess..." Tim murmured.

Which might not have sounded too eager, but the shine in his eyes said something else.

"I could help," Hailey said quickly. "The least I can do is earn my keep."

"Perfect," Connor concluded. "Let's do it, then."

At least two different gruff voices replied with a firm *Roger*, and before Hailey could so much as say *boo*, everyone sprang into motion. A controlled kind of energy hit the place, giving the impression of a well-oiled military unit kitting out for action. Tim, Hunter, and Connor huddled like a trio of field marshals formulating a plan. Dawn and Jody wrote up a shopping list and set off for the supermarket in a Land Rover. Jenna clapped with the excitement of a great idea.

"We'll have to find you some clothes. I could lend you some of mine if you don't mind." She flashed a huge smile. "Then I can tell people I handed down my clothes to Hailey Crewe." She giggled. "Sorry. I'm the youngest in my family. Can you tell I have this complex about hand-me-downs?"

Hailey laughed. "No complex here."

"One thing," Cynthia said. "It probably makes sense to call someone." She held up a hand when Hailey started to protest. "Just so no one thinks you've been abducted or drowned, God forbid."

Hailey frowned, but it did make sense. Someone handed her a phone they insisted couldn't be traced, and she nervously tapped in her agent's number. Luckily, she got an answering machine, so a quick message was all it took.

"David? It's Hailey. Listen, I just wanted to say I'm fine. I'm taking some time off. I'll be in touch."

And *beep* — she disconnected with a heavy exhale then looked around. Lightning didn't strike her, nor did a plague of locusts inundate her. Of course, really quitting the business would be harder to pull off. But this was a good start. A tiny wave of relief went through her.

"All set?" Cynthia asked. "Good."

Everyone broke into action as if they'd been waiting for that command. Jenna took off across the property, promising to come back soon. Joey brought out an array of star and planet books — plus one on dinosaurs for good measure — and showed Hailey his favorite parts. Everybody was so nice, so eager to help, and no one asked the kind of probing questions Hailey wasn't ready to face. *How could you be so stupid? What did you ever see in Jonathan? Why didn't you get out sooner?*

It was as if a whirlwind was sweeping around her, not giving her time to think until all those forces collided and packed her into a car. A beat-up white pickup with bags of food piled in the back, a duffel bag of clothes on the rear bench seat, and a cold bottle of water in the cupholder. They'd thought of everything, it seemed. Hailey found herself climbing into the passenger seat while Tim slid behind the wheel. They both slammed their doors and looked at each other.

Everything went very quiet, and she gulped. Tim gulped too.

"Off you go," Dawn said, waving from outside. "Take good care of the place."

Hailey blinked a couple of times. Was this really happening? She'd found a place to hide away — along with her own private security guard. A hunky, if broody, security guard with massive forearms and a chest a mile wide.

She glanced over at Tim. When the man frowned, he was downright terrifying. When he smiled, it was like the clouds breaking up after a long period of rain. At that moment, he was pensive, and who could blame him if he was having second thoughts?

But when he looked at her, his eyes sparkled, and there it was again. That inexplicable feeling that everything would be all right. That whatever happened next was meant to be.

She swallowed hard. She'd trusted her mother. She'd even trusted Jonathan at first. Could she trust herself when it came to judging Tim?

Temporarily, she tried reminding herself.

"You okay?" he murmured as the pickup bumped down the unpaved drive.

Hailey bit her lip. Well, she'd find out soon enough. "I'm okay." *I think.*

Chapter Six

The drive to Pu'u Pu'eo took an hour, and the second Timber pulled up to the tiny cottage, Hailey sighed.

"Cute."

It was cute, he had to agree — one of those tiny cottages on a huge property hidden away in a lush section of rainforest. Hunter hadn't been kidding when he'd called it off the beaten track.

"Perfect." Tim nodded, driving through the open gate.

The front door was open, and he and Hailey crisscrossed each other, exploring the house. A big living room took up the front, with a wide picture window and a worn but homey couch. A long counter on one side served as the kitchen, with a stove, a fridge, and a few cabinets. A narrow hallway ran to the back of the house with two square rooms on the left and one long, narrow room on the right.

Our foster mother, Georgia Mae, had the room near the front, Hunter had said. *Kai and I shared one room, and Ella had the one in the back. It wasn't much, but it was home.*

A home that had been loved well, Tim could see, even if it begged for a fresh coat of paint. The outhouse was out back, and the shower was the creek, but Hailey didn't seem to mind one bit. She took the back bedroom — the one with big, shuttered windows that opened on to a swath of jungle bursting with giant red flowers. He took the one on the right. By the time they'd swept out two rooms, spread clean sheets on the beds, and wolfed down the sandwiches Dawn had packed for them, the sun had long since set.

"Well, I guess I'll turn in," Hailey said. Then she forced a smile. "This might be the earliest I've gone to bed in years."

"You sure you don't want to call anyone else?"

"No, thanks."

It killed him to see her paste on a smile and troop on. Did she really have no one to count on?

She can count on me, his bear said.

He watched her turn away. If he were in desperate trouble, he'd be able to call his brothers or Dell, and they'd come running. But Hailey...

"I guess I'll turn in too," he whispered, not knowing what else to say.

As she moved around, preparing for bed, he kept out of her way and thought it all through. The crazy events that had brought them together. The running. The fear. And above all, the trust Hailey had placed in him.

A hell of a day was right.

Destiny, his bear whispered. *What else could it be?*

Once Hailey had settled in, he got ready for bed too, spending a full minute rubbing his left shoulder against the doorframe of his room in an instinctive bear habit of marking his turf. He nearly ambled over and did the same to Hailey's door before he caught himself.

Would you cut that out? he snapped at his bear. *She's not ours. She's a human. She doesn't even know who we are.*

Not yet, maybe, his bear said dreamily. *But someday...*

Someday didn't fit with *temporary,* and yet it occupied his thoughts as he stared at the ceiling after going to bed. The door to Hailey's room was open, as was his, and he spent a long time straining for any sound. Wishing she were closer, hoping she was okay. Wondering about fate.

Tim tapped his fingers. His brother Connor had recently found his mate. Did the thought of her make Connor's chest swell and his gut roil with butterflies? Had he suspected from the very start, the way Tim suspected Hailey was his mate?

I don't suspect, his bear grumbled. *I know.*

He'd never wanted a mate. It didn't make sense. He had all the support he needed from his brothers and his buddy Dell. Why complicate life with all the emotions and compromises that came with a mate?

But out of nowhere, a hollow feeling had settled into his gut, and it wouldn't go away. An emptiness he'd never felt before. Like someone had knocked him all the way over from *perfectly fine on my own* to *desperate for a mate to share my life with*.

Which was dangerous — really dangerous, because destiny had a way of making a shifter's animal side rebel against the more rational human part of his mind.

When he finally fell asleep, the notion of *someday* spilled over into his dreams. Nice dreams — a far cry from the usual raw, edgy dreams in which he made long to-do lists, contingency plans, and equipment inventories.

On the contrary, his dreams were soft, slow, and a little blurry, but all of them were nice. Like rocking on the porch with Hailey or walking barefoot across the lawn. In another dream, he finished the almost-kiss they'd had back in the mall. Her lips were soft and full under his, her hands tight around his waist. And when she opened her eyes to look at him in wonder, her expression said, *Wow. I think you might be my mate.*

Which was silly, of course. Humans didn't know about destined mates. Plus, Hailey had just run from a man who had offered her forever. Why the hell would she want another guy proposing the same thing?

When he woke at dawn, his nose twitched, and his groggy mind slowly caught up with where he was. Then it all rushed back to him, and he sat up quickly, testing the air in alarm. But the scent tickling his nose wasn't the scent of trouble. It was the rich aroma of freshly ground coffee that came with a low, melodious sound. When he walked to the front room, Hailey was at the stove, humming under her breath. The orange sleep shirt she wore must have been a loaner from Jenna, and it hung to just above her knees.

Over the previous day, all he'd really noticed were her eyes. Now, his gaze stuck on her long, slender legs. Her hips swayed as she rocked in place, and the movement made her hair bounce and shine. He might have stared at her forever if she hadn't turned around and smiled.

"Good morning," she murmured.

"Good morning." His voice came out all rumbly the way it did when his bear wanted to be heard too.

"I hope you don't mind." She gestured at the supplies she'd set out on the counter.

He shook his head. "Hunter did say to make ourselves at home." He stepped closer and inhaled the heavenly aroma of fresh coffee mixed with Hailey's honeysuckle scent. "Wow. That smells really good."

She gave the coffee grinder another few turns, intensifying the scent. It was one of those old-fashioned coffee grinders, and she opened the little drawer at the bottom, revealing the fresh grounds.

"I hope you know how to use this stove." She laughed. "I haven't been able to get it started."

He shuffled closer to demonstrate, pulling a match from the big box on the overhead shelf. "You turn the knob to this position and hold it in."

The stove started clicking, and he lowered the match. A *whoosh* sounded as the flame zipped around the burner. When he raised the match, he discovered Hailey was close enough for either one of them to blow it out. And, *whoosh*! A second set of flames seemed to zip around his veins in exactly the same way. Instinct tugged on his soul, pointing to Hailey, and he felt like he was awakening for a second time. The slow, rumbling sense of a beast waking from a winter den.

Mate, his bear whispered. *She is our mate.*

He closed his eyes, not daring to move lest he disturb a rare moment of utter peace. The kind he'd never felt in his decade in the army, nor with another person crowding his space.

But Hailey didn't crowd him. She just made him feel alive and free.

He was a tick slower turning away from the stove than Hailey, and they ended up face-to-face. Hailey's eyes shone, and he held his breath, itching to cup her cheek. Or better yet, to finish off that almost-kiss.

Hailey looked like she wouldn't mind, and he nearly did it too. But then he came to his senses abruptly and sidestepped away. Damn bear, making him do stupid things.

"All set," he said, a little too quickly.

Hailey bit her lip and averted her eyes, then forced a quick smile. "So, put me to work, Sergeant. Like I said, I want to earn my keep."

He looked around. "What about breakfast?"

She held up a dry piece of toast, and he stared. No wonder she was so skinny. Too skinny, really.

So he talked her into a second piece of toast with butter and jam. She ate it with her eyes closed and a look of utter bliss that made his bear ridiculously satisfied — even more satisfied than he was with his own piece of honey-covered toast. But the second Hailey finished, she bounced back to her feet and looked around.

"Okay then — where do we start?"

That was an easy one, because one corner of his mind had been busy with that issue overnight, and he had a whole plan mapped out.

"House first. Then the cistern so we don't have to lug water all the time."

Hailey nodded, and boom — off she went, scrubbing windows and floors and hauling every scrap of upholstery out into the sun. She wasn't kidding about earning her keep. Meanwhile, he crawled under the house, tapping foundation posts, checking crossbeams, making a priority list and timeline for everything that had to be fixed.

At one point, he was backing up while eyeing the roofline, checking how straight it was. Hailey must have been looking over her handiwork, because she was out on the lawn too, and they backed right into each other.

"Sorry." He jerked around with his hands up, because that butt-to-butt bump hadn't been planned.

It was nice, though. His bear grinned.

Hailey whirled just as quickly and blushed an adorable pink. "My fault."

And for a second, they stood, lost in each other's eyes, speechless. Smiling. Daydreaming, almost.

57

Then Tim snapped out of it and backed away, stammering about roof tiles.

Cut that out!

Who, me? his bear said far too innocently.

Yeah, right. The beast had a way of subtly steering him toward Hailey whenever it could.

It's not me, his bear sighed dreamily.

His big, bad inner bear, who'd once declared itself immune to anyone and anything, was turning to mush, ambling around with its head in the clouds.

I swear it's not me, the beast insisted. *It's destiny.*

And hell, maybe it was, because around Hailey, he could barely see straight.

Hailey hurried away, still pink. A shade his face must have mirrored, because he felt his cheeks heat. It took a couple of kicks at the ground and a lot of blinking to get his shit together.

The whole day was like that, a roller coaster of perfectly comfortable and slightly awkward moments, one after another. They bumped another two times in the yard and once again on the way into the house. Hailey stepped forward at the same time as he, and they nearly got tangled in the doorway. Each time, their eyes locked, and he burned to stay close to her. Yet, each time, Tim came to his senses and stepped away.

Damn bear! The beast was subtly, sneakily rebelling, doing its best to wear down his resistance to the burning attraction he felt.

He muttered to himself, trying to remember the next job. But the mental list that was always clear and orderly in his mind had gone completely blank, and it took five minutes of wandering before he finally figured out what came next. Namely, clearing the clogged gutters. That took most of the afternoon, but the plus side was, it gave him a bird's-eye view of Hailey's comings and goings. She seemed to revel in the work, humming as she carried a bucket in each hand. Her hair was up in a sloppy ponytail, and she wore the sporty clothes and pink *Aloha* cap they'd bought at the mall.

A small barn owl had perched on a nearby branch, and it hooted in approval.

Yeah, Tim wanted to say. *She's something, isn't she?*

"Don't look so surprised," Hailey chided him, pausing long enough to look up. "No princess here. I know what real work is."

Oops. Caught red-handed.

"Don't doubt it," he called, bringing a little smile to her face.

Apart from a quick lunch on the go, they both kept at it until the sun sank low, marking the end to one of the quietest, nicest days Tim had experienced in a long, long time.

"I'll make dinner. You wash up." He waved her to the creek.

It was hard to keep his eyes off her as she walked across the yard with a bottle of body wash in one hand and a towel in the other. She swiveled her head as she walked, taking in the thick foliage. The owl hooted again, and Tim nearly replied.

Yeah, I think she's amazing, too.

The owl wasn't a shifter, just a friend of Hunter's foster mother who still kept an eye on the place. Tim went back to cooking before the bird caught him watching Hailey too closely.

Hoo. Hoo. It chuckled and fluttered off, letting him know it was too late for that.

He made lasagna — one of about three meals he could pull off without messing up — and while he was washing, Hailey made garlic bread and set out two places on the porch table. She'd even found a candle for a little ambiance, and the second he spotted it, she blushed.

"Nice," he said, making her blush harder.

Cynthia, the dragon shifter who ran the plantation house, was big on candles and fancy napkins and such, and he'd never seen the point. He was a practical, no-frills kind of guy, and if he'd been eating with one of his brothers — say, Chase, the world's quietest wolf shifter — they would have plonked down, eaten their grub wordlessly, and been perfectly happy. Who needed a candle?

But now, he got it. The candle gave the place a warm, familiar glow, hollowing out a space for two in the vastness of the surrounding forest. A nice, cozy, intimate space.

Definitely not here with Chase, his bear chuckled.

Hailey's hair was shiny from her bath, and her skin practically glowed in the candlelight.

"Garlic bread?" She held out the basket.

Her nails were a mess by then, and she'd been working hard all day. But she seemed at peace, like him.

He dug in, and within a few bites, he stopped and closed his eyes. He'd been on the go for so long, and the occasional glance at the sunset or a dunk in the water seemed like plenty of break time. But now he found something inside him unwinding. The peace that surrounded him seeped right into his soul.

His bear loved it too. The space. The trees. The rushing creek.

The company, the beast added, half drunk on her scent.

"That was so good," Hailey said, finishing off the tiny portion she'd allotted herself.

"That's all you're having?"

Her eyes strayed to the rest of the lasagna then darted away. "That's plenty."

He'd been taking huge, gulping bites, but she'd only nibbled. He doubted it had to do with nervousness — not after the number of calories she had to have burned that day. So he pushed the casserole dish toward her and nodded. "Go for it."

She pursed her lips and closed her eyes, clearly fighting temptation.

He laughed. "I'm not selling you drugs, you know. It's just food. You know, food?"

She laughed. "Not in my line of work, it isn't."

His brow furrowed. What was it like to have to starve to secure a new contract? Did her manager — or worse, her mother — look over her shoulder and count every calorie?

"Actually, it is." He waved around the tidy yard and much-improved house. "Your new line of work, at least."

She laughed and finally gave in, letting him heap a second helping onto her plate. She chowed down immediately, and he had to hold back a smile.

"Must be pretty different from modeling," he mumbled between bites of garlic bread.

She grimaced. "Yeah, it's pretty different. But this is the Ritz compared to the house I grew up in." Her eyes traveled over the worn floorboards and peeling paint. Then she covered her mouth with her hand. "Sorry — no offense. This cottage is great, and I love helping its character show."

His chest went all warm. He loved that too. Fixing up old places, making them come back to life. Maybe even making them better than they ever were.

"Where did you grow up?"

She smiled. "Montana. My mom worked in a diner in Fort Benton. My dad worked in forestry." Her face lit up for a moment before dropping in a way he didn't dare ask about. "As soon as I was old enough, I helped in the diner too. I started out bussing tables. You know, setting out the silverware, filling water glasses. My mom worked in the kitchen." Her eyes were far away, and her voice had a wobble to it that he wasn't sure how to read into.

That lifestyle, he could picture her in. *Supermodel*, not so much. Jenna had given him a quick peek at a magazine ad, and he'd hardly recognized Hailey. The woman in the picture looked so... painted. So removed. They'd photoshopped out her freckles, which killed him, and teased her hair all over the place. She looked nothing like the vivacious — if pensive — woman in front of him now.

Hailey took a deep breath and caught his gaze. "I can't tell you how much I appreciate—"

He cut her off with a brisk wave. "Maybe I should find runaway brides more often. The place looks great."

She flashed a huge smile. "It feels great to do real work for a change. Getting my hands dirty. You know..."

For a second, she looked worried that he wouldn't understand, but he just grinned. That asshole she had run from might not know about hands-on work, but he sure did.

"Oh, I know, all right. Believe me, I know."

They smiled at each other for a minute, and his grin only faded when the achy feeling started up in his chest again. Like a rusted-over gate to a secret compartment was slowly creaking open, ready to let her in. A door he wasn't sure he wanted to open, because there were sure to be all kinds of forbidden feelings in there.

"Oh, look!" Hailey pointed as a lightning bug blinked in the yard. Another joined it, and between that and the bird calls coming from the surrounding woods, the serene feeling intensified. Serenity even deeper than that at Koakea, a place he'd come to love.

The place doesn't matter, his bear said. *It's the person. It's her.*

"So peaceful," Hailey whispered.

They didn't exchange more than a few words in the next half hour, but it didn't feel awkward. It just felt nice. Watching the jungle grow dim, letting the day wind down. Even washing the dishes didn't seem like a chore, not when he got to do them with her. And finally, when the night was dark as ink and the crickets chirping at full blast, they headed to bed.

"Good night," Hailey called softly, pausing at her bedroom door to look back.

"Good night," he whispered.

Did the crickets actually sing louder at that moment, or was that his imagination? Had the starlight somehow found a way inside to make her eyes shine so brightly? And that warm, happy feeling in his gut — that was just the lasagna filling him up, right?

He cleared his throat and nodded quickly before stepping into the darkness of his room. "Good night."

Chapter Seven

The next days followed in a similar way — hours of work divided by moments of sheer bliss whenever Hailey came close. Hailey brewed coffee with a different finishing touch each day, always beating Tim to the kitchen. He'd wake slowly, trying to place the aroma each time.

"Coffee with a hint of cinnamon," she said, handing him a mug on the second day.

Other times, she used a splash of cream, a touch of maple syrup, and his favorite, a drop of honey. Every sip slid down his throat like an elixir, and he'd end up smacking his lips like a bear over a honey jar.

"So, where do we start today?" Hailey would ask once they'd both had breakfast — which in her case had become toast with jam *and* butter, and that was progress, for sure.

She loved to dig in and work, a lot like him. But he was doing penance for years as a military engineer — more demolition than construction. What was Hailey compensating for?

The big job of day two was clearing out the cistern that collected water off the roof, and it was a doozy. He stood in the shoulder-high cement cistern, shoveling muck from the bottom into buckets he handed to Hailey, who emptied the slop into a wheelbarrow. Once the wheelbarrow was full, he would trundle it down to the compost heap in the woods. If he didn't act fast enough, Hailey would take off with the wheelbarrow, insisting she could do it. When she came back, she'd be sweaty, and her face would be smeared with dirt, but her smile was wider, her face fresher than before.

Which brought him back to the same question: what burning need did the work fulfill for her? Was there something missing from what she'd done before?

"How did you go from a diner to modeling?" he asked as they worked.

She frowned like it wasn't the best memory. "After high school, I started waitressing full time, hoping to save up for college. I had a plan and everything," she said with a little smile. "How much I needed to have saved by when to be able to do community college on the side. But one night, some out-of-towners came through, and one of the guys kept looking at me. *Really* looking at me. It creeped me out at the time. The woman he was with called me over and asked if I'd ever modeled. I nearly brushed them off, actually." She laughed. "They stayed until closing time and talked to my mom. One thing led to another and. . . " She stirred the air with one hand. "Eventually, we quit the diner and left Montana." Her voice grew sadder and sadder with each sentence. "We moved to LA, and. . . yeah. That's how it went."

He looked at her over the edge of the cistern. Her tone wasn't exactly enthusiastic.

"What's it like?"

"Modeling?" She snorted. "Lots of waiting around for the light to be perfect or for props to arrive. Hundreds of shots, over and over until I couldn't even remember what product I was representing. Thank goodness I had my mother to keep me away from – shall we say, all the bad influences?"

For the first time, Tim found a reason to want to hug Hailey's mother instead of strangling her.

Then Hailey sighed and motioned toward his feet. "Better get moving, mister. We have a lot of work to do."

The cistern took a full day, and odd jobs around the property took another. And in no time, they fell into a nice routine. Each day started with a mug of Hailey's amazing coffee, and Tim had even taken to staying in bed for a few minutes with his eyes closed, relishing the smell. He hadn't lounged in bed for years, and God knew the guys would ridicule him if they found out.

He and Hailey grew more and more comfortable around each other – almost too comfortable at times, making it all too easy to forget how *temporary* their arrangement was. Once, he'd come up behind Hailey as she was brewing coffee and put his arms on the counter on each side of her without thinking. She'd gone right on humming like having him there was part and parcel of a perfect morning for her. As for him, he'd gotten so drunk on her scent, he nearly planted a kiss on the side of her neck.

Kiss, his bear had murmured at the time. *Good idea.*

He'd snapped away just in time. Hailey turned in his arms, and she wasn't surprised in the least to find him so close. In fact, her eyes dropped to his lips, and he wondered whether she was imagining a kiss too. His skin tingled the way it did when he shifted into bear form. His heart thumped harder, and he swore he sensed Hailey's do the same.

"Do you feel that?" she whispered.

If she meant that feeling of two tectonic plates sliding into position beside each other, lining up for some huge stroke of fate, then hell yes.

"I do."

Her eyes strayed up and down his body, warming him as they moved.

"I've never felt that before," she said as if she had just experienced her first live earthquake.

But it was no earthquake, and he knew it. It was destiny. The question was, what the hell should he do? Was it best to leave destiny to unwind at its own pace, or did you grab your chance while you could?

"Never felt that before either," he said.

But then the scent of something burning wafted through the air, and Hailey fluttered her hands.

"Oops. Better not burn the toast this time," she murmured, and that was the end of that.

Except it wasn't the end. The work, the heavenly coffee, and Hailey combined in some magical way to loosen up all kinds of hidden doors in his soul, and Tim found himself laughing, thinking, and dreaming more and more. *Feeling* more, too, because he'd turned off emotion for a long time. He'd turned off hope, too, but now, it was welling up in him.

Maybe he and Hailey could spend longer together. Maybe they could fix up his place at Koakea. Maybe even make that *their* place instead of just his, because everything was better with Hailey around. The way she stared off into the distance wistfully sometimes made him drift off and think about *someday* kind of things. The way she savored every bite of her food made him slow down and relish it, too. And when she paused and looked back at the house, he'd do the same. The cottage was coming along in leaps and bounds, and he couldn't help but imagine his place at Koakea improving the same way. He even imagined a vase of flowers on his patio and candles on his table, which *really* showed how far gone he was.

That and the fact that he'd started to memorize a hundred little bits of Hailey trivia and couldn't wait to stock up on more.

Had she grown up with pets?

"No chance." She laughed. "My mother is allergic to animals. She can't even be in the same room."

Siblings?

"Only child." She sighed.

Favorite pastimes?

She held her hands up in a fighting stance. "Watch out. I do kickboxing. You know what that means?"

"What? Whoa!" He ducked as she demonstrated.

"I can kick the air really well. And punch too."

She was joking, but she really was good. Still, he hated the idea of a tall, muscled private instructor guiding her through every move. That image, he didn't need to entertain.

"I'll watch out not to make you mad, then," he murmured and went back to work.

Eventually, another nice day wound to a close, and they lingered on the porch a long time after dinner. He pulled his stool a little closer to her rocking chair that evening so that their feet touched. Hailey looked over, smiled, and—

The owl hooted just then, and Tim scowled into the night. Having a couple extra sentries was always a good thing. But chaperones, he really didn't need.

On the other hand, there was no denying the fact that reality was out there, just beyond the tangled curtain of vegetation around the house. So when Hailey insisted on doing the dishes, he strode just far enough down the road to get reception on his phone. He'd been checking it less and less often, not really wanting that connection to the outside world. But Hunter and Connor had been quietly investigating Hailey's case. And the more they discovered, the more Tim was vindicated in feeling that Hailey wasn't nuts for what she had done.

Jonathan Owen-Clarke, Connor's text read. *A real asshole, if you ask me.*

Tim had figured that much, and he couldn't help wondering what a nice girl like Hailey was doing with a guy like that. But once he'd thought it over, it did make sense. A young woman thrust into an intense, isolating career with an overprotective mother. Then along came Jonathan, who had probably put on a good guy act at first. Good enough to try out for a date or two, he supposed.

Jonathan Owen-Clarke comes from big money, Connor's text continued. *California oil money that goes back several generations. The father is Richard Owen-Clarke — the guy who ran for governor. The older brother is gearing up for a run at a Senate seat, and I'm guessing Jonathan isn't far off. That ranch he bought in Montana establishes residency. So who knows what he has planned?*

Tim didn't like that one bit, but it wasn't exactly grounds for a criminal investigation. So Jonathan was an asshole. So Hailey had made a mistake. So what? Hailey had shown guts — and brains — for leaving the jerk.

Meanwhile, Lamar Dennison, his head of security, is much harder to track, Connor reported. *We know he's been working for Owen-Clarke for two years, but he's got virtually no record before that. It might be an assumed name. Still investigating, though. In the meantime, you two sit tight. The newspapers are full of the story, and everybody is talking about it. Hailey was right about lying low for a while.*

Tim was about to click the phone off when one last text came through.

PS - Smart girl for dumping that shithead. Take good care of her.

Tim glared at the phone. Oh, he'd take care of her, all right.

"Any news?" Hailey asked when he walked back into the house.

He turned off the phone, not wanting to lie, but not wanting to alarm her either.

"Not really. The story is in the papers, so we ought to stay out here another three or four days."

She arched an eyebrow in a tease. "You don't have it planned exactly?"

He grinned. "Call it approximate."

She smiled back, then went serious. "I'm good with that, but are you?"

He looked up. Of course, he was good with that. The last few days had been... Different. Special. Important, somehow.

"I mean, you must have work you need to do," she said. "Contracting, right?"

He smiled. At a time when her life was in shambles, she'd remembered that detail about him.

Funny how the urgency he'd felt about setting up his business had faded away despite the fact that he'd been planning it for months. Securing a loan, pricing equipment, investigating the best ways to advertise — all according to a detailed schedule he'd drawn up. He'd even traveled to Oahu to expedite his license. But in the past few days, that didn't seem as important anymore. Nothing did.

"Call this practice," he said, waving around.

She smiled. The ensuing silence stretched out, though not in an uncomfortable way. Both he and Hailey looked over the yard, watching the lightning bugs glow. There were so many fucked-up places in the world. So much struggle and conflict. He'd come to Pu'u Pu'eo to give Hailey a time-out, but it seemed he needed one too.

So he relished every slow morning, drew satisfaction from every sweaty workday, and drank his fill of quiet evenings on

the porch. The only part of the day he didn't enjoy was bedtime, because it meant parting with Hailey. Like on the sixth
night when they were both turning in to their respective rooms.
Hailey paused beside him as he stood in the doorway to his
room.

"Hey," she whispered.

"Hey," he echoed, holding his breath while his heart
pounded away.

"I had a really nice day," she said, flushing a little.

"Me too," was all he could manage.

He thought that would be it, but Hailey looked down at
his feet, then up at his eyes, and finally, with a what-the-hell
shrug, she leaned in to give him a peck on the cheek. A tiny,
barely there kiss that made his blood rush.

She pulled back and paused.

Please do that again, he wanted to beg. *Please.*

And miracle of miracles, she did. She leaned in for another
kiss, locking eyes with him the whole way. And that second
kiss didn't go for his cheek. It landed square on his lips.

The second they connected, fire zipped through his veins,
and his hands cupped her waist. His entire body sighed with
weary pleasure as he moved his lips gently over hers.

It was a soft, steady kiss. The kind that didn't have to get
hotter or hungrier, because it was just right the way it was. A
first-time kind of kiss that gave him plenty of time to savor the
way Hailey's body melted against his.

When they finally broke apart, they grinned at each
other. Hailey's eyes shone, and her cheeks flushed. Tim's
chest swelled, because the barrier of awkwardness that always
seemed to spring up between them was finally gone. Really
gone.

Slowly, he cupped her face and drew his thumb along her
cheek.

"Nice," he whispered.

Hailey broke into a huge grin that just about knocked him
out. Not supermodel gorgeous, because models always seemed
to have pouty looks. More like girl-next-door, joyous and gen-

uine at the same time. And before he knew it, he was grinning too.

"Nice," she agreed.

They stood without speaking for a moment, because words weren't the only way to communicate, and her eyes were filled with so many messages. Then she took a deep breath, and he did too.

"Good night," she whispered, stepping toward her room.

He nodded slowly, watching her go. "Good night."

Chapter Eight

Hailey tried to keep her eyes forward as the pickup rattled down the coastal road, but her gaze kept wandering back to Tim. Or more precisely, his arms. The man had to have the thickest, most muscular forearms she'd ever seen. His hands were huge too, with veins that ran close to the surface as if there was no room among all that muscle underneath.

She jerked her eyes away. She'd done far too much covert peeking over the last six days. Six of the best days she'd ever had. So unrushed. So peaceful. The last few years of her life seemed like a constant blur of activity — meetings, photo-shoots, training sessions. On Maui, time ticked by at a totally different pace.

Part of it was the place, but the rest was Tim. The man was steady as a rock. Quiet and introspective. Thoughtful, too, like in the way he made sure to give her the least lumpy chair, the one unchipped mug, and first use of the sink. If she'd let him, he would have done the cooking *and* cleaning, and all the hauling of water from the creek, too. He was ridiculously tidy — so much that she started aligning pillows on the battered old couch at exact angles to each other the way he did.

And, wow — what a kisser. Her chaste little goodnight peck on the cheek had turned into the most electrifying kiss she'd ever had — and Tim hadn't even been trying hard. What would it feel like if he kissed her with wild abandon?

Her cheeks flushed, and she looked out the car window so he couldn't see her blush. It was crazy how the man messed with her mind — and body.

"You okay?" he asked.

She turned even redder and reached for her water bottle. "Perfect."

"Sleep okay last night?"

She nearly spat the mouthful of water all over the cab of the pickup. After that kiss? She'd spent half the night touching herself, pretending he was there with her.

"Good, thanks. And you?"

She risked a look over and — wow. Was that a blush spreading on her tough soldier's face?

He scrubbed a hand over his unshaved chin and nodded quickly. "Fine, thanks."

She hid a grin. Maybe she wasn't the only one feeling the attraction. Then she sighed, because of all the times to lose her head...

He tilted his head at her. Not asking *What?* outright but asking all the same.

She motioned vaguely with her hands. "You're like Mr. Action Plan. Meanwhile, I don't have a clue what to do with my life."

He laughed. "Ten years in the army leaves plenty of time to make plans, let me tell you."

She pictured him leaning against a tank, staring off into a desert sunset. Or him lying on a bunk in his barracks, staring at the ceiling and tapping his thumbs.

His voice dropped. "It's not always good, you know. Kind of a compulsion at times."

His hands tightened over the steering wheel, and a totally different image zipped through Hailey's mind. One of Tim sprinting through a combat zone that shuddered with deafening explosions and shouts.

She swallowed hard. Maybe the man wasn't as unmarked by combat as he let on. Maybe all that planning was a way to seize back control after one too many close calls.

She touched his arm, and the smile he'd forced gradually grew looser. His eyes went from dull brown to a bright, shiny hazel, and the muscles of his forearm went from rock hard to... okay, rock hard, but not quite as tense as before.

He drove on for a quiet, companionable minute while Hailey looked at Maui with new eyes. It was easy to take the views for granted, but when she reminded herself of other areas of the world...

Her fingers reached for her pearl, then stopped. She'd left it under the mattress in her room before showering and hadn't had time to slip it back on. Which was a pity, because there was something comforting about that pearl.

"Architectural design," Tim said out of the blue.

"What?"

"Architectural design. Ever think of that? You have an eye for it." He waved over his shoulder. "Like your idea for a gazebo up at the house."

"I just kind of threw that out," she protested. They'd been looking from the porch toward the creek one evening, discussing Tim's idea for a covered picnic spot out there. In no time, she'd grabbed a pencil and sketched an octagonal gazebo.

"That's what I mean," he said. "My idea would have come out looking like a hut at a state park. Yours would look great. Do you do that a lot?"

She laughed. "Believe me, my artistry is limited to doodling on napkins. It never amounts to much."

"Who knows? Maybe someday it will." He said *someday* with such conviction, it warmed her soul. Then he laughed. "And, if all else fails, you could make coffee. What is that called — a barista?"

She laughed. "Are you saying I'm bound for Starbucks?"

He laughed — really laughed — because they'd gotten over the hump of that awkward moment the way they had gotten over so many others in their first days. "Nothing wrong with that, but no. Something upscale. Your coffee is way too good."

"Glad you like it." She grinned.

For the next few miles, she took in the scenery and chewed over the image of a *someday* a lot like this. Busy days. Honest work. A good man to share it all with.

The curving road straightened, and the cliffy coastline gave way to long stretches of beach. Tim made a left turn at a light then parked and motioned to the building on their right.

"Hardware store's right there. It might be better for you to wait in the truck, though."

She pulled her baseball cap low — the pink cap he'd gotten her that day in the mall — and shook her head. "Are you kidding? No one's going to recognize me now."

Her hair was matted, her legs scratched, her nails a disaster. She was the polar opposite of the made-up, perfectly put together puppet she used to turn into on the set of any photo shoot. And the best part was, nobody frowned or hurried to fix all those terrible flaws.

Tim looked her over dubiously. "You still look too good." She laughed outright, and he turned pink. "I mean..." He grumbled a little and fished around behind his seat. "Here. Put that on."

It was a checkered flannel shirt. *His* flannel shirt. She pulled it on slowly, inhaling deeply in the little cave it formed. It was nice, being wrapped in Tim's scent. Safe and secure, where the world couldn't find her.

"How's that?" she asked, pulling the shirt the rest of the way down.

Tim stared without saying a word. His eyes flashed, and she had the distinct impression of him holding an entire conversation with himself. He did that sometimes, as if he were part Boy Scout, part bad boy, and the latter was struggling to break free.

He slid out of the truck a second later, muttering, "You still look too good."

Hailey hid a smile as she followed him into the hardware store. The way most men ogled her creeped her out. But Tim looked at her the way a person might look at a waterfall or an especially striking landscape. Like she was something special, something he'd never seen before.

Of course, she was out in public, and she had to be careful. So she kept her chin down and stuck close to Tim. It was childishly exciting to be out after so many days in her hideaway.

She'd loved the peace of the remote little cottage, but it was nice to get out too. Really nice — until her gaze caught on the newspaper rack, and she froze.

Runaway bride holed up in island hideaway? the headline screamed.

Hailey stared. There was an image of her facing Jonathan at the wedding on Waikiki, and another image of some kind of estate with a huge wall. At first, she panicked. Was that Koa Point, where Tim's friends lived? But when she got herself together enough to read the caption, she exhaled.

Witnesses report seeing Ms. Crewe on an estate owned by celebrity actress on Kauai...

At least there was that. The reporters had the wrong island and the wrong estate — not to mention the wrong friend, because she didn't know any celebrities. She hurried after Tim and stayed a step behind him the rest of the way.

"What do you think of these?" he asked, holding up two cans of paint. "Dawn said she thought the hall would look good in yellow."

Slowly, Hailey relaxed. A hardware store was just about the last place anyone would recognize her, right? She considered the paint cans.

"That one. It's softer."

He squinted at the label. "Softer? They both look yellow to me."

She nearly laughed, imagining what her makeup artist would have to say about *that*.

"Believe me, that one's much better."

He looked at both cans one more time, perplexed, and finally put one back. "I'll take your word for it."

Ten minutes later, they had everything they needed — plus an issue of *Architectural Digest* Tim handed to her with a stern look that said, *Someday, remember?*

She took it and even threw in a second magazine — an amateurish gazette called *Hawaiian Horticulture.*

"Who knows?" she joked at his inquiring look. "I might just grow my own coffee someday."

That was a joke, but Tim nodded so earnestly, she couldn't help but mull over the idea. She was looking for a career change, after all.

She started leafing through the magazines on the drive back, but the sun was setting, so she put them aside and looked up. The sky was a purplish blue, and the clouds turned orange and pink.

"Beautiful," she murmured.

Tim glanced over. "The sunset is really amazing from over at Koakea. But, yeah. This is nice too."

She snorted. "You're getting spoiled."

He laughed. "Maybe I am." Then he tapped his fingers on the steering wheel and pointed left. "Spoiled enough for dinner out, maybe. Takeout, I mean. Okay with you?"

She nodded eagerly. Anything that drew out this beautiful drive with Tim worked for her.

"According to my friend Boone, the best lunch truck on Maui is on this beach." He swung the vehicle off the road, into the parking lot of a beach park. "Hopefully, we're not too late."

"Hopefully," she echoed, not the least concerned. That was another thing about Tim — that sense of *everything will turn out all right*. That rock-steady, *I have a plan* and *nothing is a problem* outlook she wished she could emulate.

The beach showed through the trees, and the surf was up — way up, from the look and sound of it. A big silver truck was parked in the nearly deserted parking lot. A family was moving toward a car with their rolling cooler and beach toys in tow, and two young men loaded kiteboards into a battered old station wagon.

"You ever try that?" she asked.

"Kiteboarding? Not my kind of thrill."

She laughed, having quickly learned that about him. The man seemed at his most content with long days of hard labor and quiet evenings by a crackling fire. Had he always been that way, or had his time in the military taught him to cherish the little things?

"What about you?" he asked.

She shook her head quickly. "I'd love to try surfing, but I doubt I'd be coordinated enough to kitesurf."

He shook his head. "Don't underestimate yourself."

It wasn't the first time he'd said that, and the words stuck in her mind. Did she really underestimate herself? Was it a by-product of having her mother nag at her all the time? Either way, she'd started to make his words her mantra. When the time came to face the world again, she'd make sure to keep that message at the front of her mind.

The thought of venturing back into the hustle and bustle of LA nearly turned her stomach, so she pushed the thought away. She'd given herself a few more days to clear her mind before making any decisions, and dammit, she was going to enjoy every minute of that time.

"Jenny's Mixed Plate?" She read the painted letters on the side of the truck.

"That's the one."

The second Tim parked and they both slid out, the Asian woman behind the raised counter of the lunch truck called out.

"Last call before I close up for the night. What will it be?"

Hailey hurried over and studied the menu. She'd never had a fish taco, and she had no idea what a *poke* bowl might be.

"Um...what do you recommend?" she asked Tim.

He shrugged and whispered, "I'm not sure. First time out in Hawaii."

Something about that made her glow. His first time out, and it was with her?

"Whatever's easy for you," she told the woman behind the counter, knowing all too well what it was like to clean up a restaurant only to have a last-minute customer rush through the door.

Tim nodded, and the woman in the lunch truck gave her an appreciative smile. "I can do a *poke* bowl and a *luau* plate. Fine with you?"

Hailey nearly laughed. If only the woman knew how fine she felt. For years, her mother had kept her on a short leash, shielding her away from nice, down-to-earth guys like Tim. So a night out — even a modest night out to a takeout truck —

with a sweet construction worker type felt like an evening at a royal ball. Better, even, because no one fussed over her hair or clothes. No one counted her calories. She was free to be herself — and in charge of herself — for a change.

They took the food out to the top of a sand dune and ate with their fingers — another plus. The marinated fish was delicious, and while Tim kept apologizing for being on the wrong side of the island for the sunset, she couldn't have cared less. Surf rolled up on the beach in endless breakers, and they stayed long after the last of the kitesurfers had gone home.

"The park must be closing soon," Hailey murmured, although she didn't want to go.

Tim didn't seem too concerned. "Yeah, but I'm pretty sure no one is going to come along and kick us out."

And so they sat there, watching the surf as the color slowly faded from the sky. The sun was setting somewhere behind them, but facing east was symbolic, somehow. Facing the future instead of dwelling in the past.

Hailey hugged the flannel shirt around herself and turned to Tim, about to thank him yet again. But before she could speak, their eyes caught as they had so often over the past few days. And not just *caught* but *locked* together, and she never wanted to let go.

"You've got a crumb," he whispered, brushing her cheek with his thumb.

He kept his hand there afterward, cupping her cheek. She closed her eyes and leaned into his hand. She couldn't help it. For the first time in years, she felt grounded. Confident that whatever she chose to do, everything would be all right.

The wind played with her hair, making it toss over Tim's hand. When he combed it back, she nearly hummed with delight. She opened her eyes to find Tim that much closer. His gaze had dropped to her lips, and his eyes seemed to be glowing a faint yellow-green as they had a few times over the past days. A trick of the light?

When Tim looked up, she could read the question in his eyes.

Can I kiss you? Please?

They'd been sitting close, with her knee bumping his and their arms crossed behind their backs, propping themselves up as they'd taken in the view. But the only view she wanted now was a close-up of Tim.

Could he kiss her?

Hell yes. She was dying for him to.

Chapter Nine

Hailey nodded and leaned closer, focusing on Tim's lips.
Round, soft lips that parted the slightest bit. Tim guided her
closer, and time slowed, letting her inhale his leathery scent.
Then they kissed — a light, tentative kiss. They broke apart
for a quick breath then came together again, and that second
kiss was heaven. She nestled closer, brushing the backs of her
knuckles against his cheek.

If she rubbed her hand one way, his skin was rough with
stubble. But if she stroked the other way, the scruff was soft
and springy. Her body warmed, and now that she had her eyes
closed, her other senses piqued.

Slowly, ever so slowly, he pulled back, and Hailey found
herself puckered up, stretching out the kiss.

"Nice," she whispered.

He nodded and whispered back, "Really nice. Can I do
that again?"

She grinned. Old-fashioned manners. Why had it taken
her so long to find a man like him?

"Sure, you can."

His lips quirked, and then he was kissing her again, cupping
both cheeks in his huge hands and leaning closer. Not close
enough to quell the desire that rose in her like a bonfire, but
it was a good start.

She slid her hand across his ribs, wanting more. Lots more,
with lots less clothing in the way. Her body cried for his, and
her mind filled with heated images. Like him leaning her back
and coming down over her. Her wrapping her legs around his
waist. Him touching her. Wanting her. Taking her...

She was just about to shuffle closer when Tim's cheek twitched under her hand, and he pulled away. *Yanked* away, actually, and she gasped at the abrupt change. What was wrong?

Tim scrambled to his feet, dragged her up by one hand, and pushed her behind his body. His nostrils flared, testing the air.

"Shit," he muttered, staring inland.

Hailey's jaw dropped as a dog trotted out of the shadows, its nose to the ground. A huge, scrappy dog with upright ears and a gray coat. When it looked up, it bared its teeth, and a long string of saliva dripped from its lips.

Shit was right. The beast was big enough to be a wolf. Wait — it was a wolf. She knew; she'd seen plenty in Montana, though never so close. Most wolves barely glanced up before loping for cover. This one strode boldly out of the shadows, coming straight for them, snarling under its breath. Was it rabid?

Tim took firm hold of her hand as he backed her toward the water, the only path of escape. When he spoke, his voice was tight. "No sudden moves."

Hailey gulped. She wasn't planning on it. But Jesus — a wolf? In Maui?

"Whatever brought you here, you need to get the hell out," Tim hissed. "Maui is our territory."

Hailey stared. Most people shouted or clapped to startle a wolf away. Tim was talking to it as if that were another person.

"Tim..." she whispered.

He silenced her with a quick hand squeeze that begged her to trust him.

Well, of course, she trusted him. But what the hell was going on?

"Let's walk to the car. Slowly," she whispered as her heart raced. Most wolves looked wary; this one had a predatory gleam in its eye.

But Tim stood his ground and waved the wolf off. "I'll tell you one last time. You are not doing this. Get out of here, and leave her alone."

The wolf snorted then looked back at a pair of headlights. The food truck was long since gone, and a new arrival was taking its place. Hailey exhaled, thinking that might be the police. But the two burly men who slid out of the SUV didn't exactly give off helpful vibes. They jogged up behind the wolf, close enough to catch it like a stray dog. But they didn't make a move to trap the beast, nor did it flinch. They just crossed their arms and glared at Tim.

Hailey stared. The only thing that kept her from bolting was having Tim there, so steady and broad.

"Please tell me one of you has more sense than he does," Tim said in that same controlled, even voice.

Hailey wanted to tug his hand and run. What was he talking about?

One of the men held out his hand. "You need to come with us, Ms. Crewe."

She stared, recognizing one of Jonathan's security men. How they had found her, she had no clue. But a second later, her mind served up the image of Jonathan offering crisp $100 bills to anyone with information as to her whereabouts. Had he found the cab driver, tracked her to Maui, and had the wolf follow her trail?

She shook the notion away. Even Jonathan wasn't that crazy. Was he?

"Get your dog on a leash," she spat. "And back the hell away. I am not going with you."

The wolf gave a low, threatening rumble, and Tim stiffened.

"I'm telling you, you'd better get him under control. If he so much as shows... Crap." Tim cut himself off. "Don't do this. I'm telling you not to do this." His voice was urgent — almost pleading — and his eyes were locked firmly on the wolf.

"Jesus, he's really going to do it," one of the two security men muttered to the other, looking at the wolf.

Hailey stared. What did they expect the wolf to do?

"Don't do this, boss," the other security man said, reaching for the wolf.

But the beast snapped at him and started pacing back and forth, eyeing Tim in open challenge.

"Jesus," Tim muttered. "How crazy are you?" Then he turned to Hailey and spoke in an urgent whisper. "Close your eyes. Don't look."

How could she not look? The wolf let out a strangled howl and reared up on its back legs, clawing at the air. A moment later, it came down on all fours and hunched, grumbling under its breath.

"What the..." Hailey gasped, backing away.

Its fur thinned, and its shoulder blades pulled back until they were square across its back instead of along its sides. The tail grew stubbier, and its feet flattened and stretched out. If Tim hadn't had such a firm hold of her hand, Hailey might have run in terror.

"Oh my God," she whispered. "No."

Her knees trembled, and she shook her head, unable to believe her eyes. The wolf slowly transformed into a shaggy, dark-haired man who stood stiffly and rolled his shoulders like a boxer getting ready for a fight. He was naked, but that didn't shock Hailey half as much as the sight of his face.

"Lamar?" The name barely moved past her lips, she was that shocked.

Tim glanced at her, even more troubled than before. He kept firm hold of her hand, backing her away from the dunes.

Lamar grinned and cracked his knuckles, one by one. "Now, now. What do we have here?" His nostrils flared like an animal's while he studied Tim. "Ms. Crewe and her new friend, who just happens to be a—"

"Watch it," Tim growled, cutting Lamar off.

Lamar chuckled. "Oh, is that how it is? I see now. She doesn't know."

Hailey wanted to scream. No, she didn't know what the hell was going on. She just wanted to get out of there, ASAP.

"We've been looking for you, Ms. Crewe," Lamar sneered. "Wondering where you might have gotten yourself to."

Hailey clutched the back of Tim's shirt and peered into the shadows behind Lamar. Would Jonathan appear next? Or was all this a hallucination?

84

"And here you are on Maui," Lamar continued. "Kissing a man who ain't the groom. Now what kind of woman does that?"

"A bride without a groom, from what I hear," Tim said in a low, dangerous voice. "That's what the jackass gets for not asking ahead of time."

"Oh, he asked, all right." Lamar insisted.

"Yeah, at the wedding, not before," Hailey cried out. "And I said no."

"What part of *no* don't you understand?" Tim growled with a note of finality that would have sent any other man packing.

Hailey's heart pounded, and her mouth was dry. But it seemed dangerous to show weakness, so she clenched her fists and held her ground. She could have her mental breakdown later. Right now, she had to keep herself together.

"Forget it, Lamar."

"You're trespassing," Tim added in a perfectly even voice.

Lamar laughed out loud. "This beach ain't your territory."

"All of Maui is our territory," Tim snarled.

Hailey glanced at him. *Our?* Did he mean his friends at Koa Point? No one could own *all* of Maui. So what did he mean?

"We just stopped by to pick up what's ours," Lamar spat.

Hailey's cheeks heated. "Yours? I don't belong to anybody, least of all your boss. So, get the hell out of here. I never want to see you or Jonathan again."

Lamar broke out in cackling laughter. "Not for you to decide, sweetheart. Not when the boss has his mind made up."

Her jaw dropped. Who the hell did Lamar think he was?

Tim beat her to a response. "Last chance to get your ass out of here before I flay your hide."

Lamar laughed. "Do you mean that literally?"

Hailey winced. God, was he going to transform back into a wolf?

Even Lamar's men looked uncertain. "You know the rules, man."

Hailey wanted to scream. What rules? They had to be breaking just about every law in the books.

Tim's hands were so tight around hers, she winced, but his voice stayed even and commanding. "Not going there, asshole. Not you, not me. Now, back down. Don't do something we'll all regret."

"You're the one who'll be regretting this, asshole," Lamar sneered. Then he turned to his men. "I'll take care of him. You grab her."

Hailey couldn't believe her ears. Did they think they could kidnap her? Force her to marry Jonathan? Where did this nightmare end?

Tim turned slightly and whispered, "I can hold them, Hailey. You run when I say go."

Hailey wrung her hands, not knowing what to do. It was her old nightmare all over again.

Run, Hailey! Run! her grandfather had cried that awful day when she was fourteen. A day that started so well — like this one — and ended so horrifically, with a pack of wild animals taking her grandfather's life. She'd locked herself in his truck and crouched in the back seat for hours before the state police had happened by and brought her home, a mess.

She couldn't have helped her grandfather, but the shame of leaving him behind still haunted her. So now, with Tim?

"Not going anywhere," she said.

The three men bristled, and Tim did too. Hailey was terrified they would break into a fight – or worse, that Lamar would turn back into a wolf and tear out Tim's throat. But Tim held his ground, keeping perfectly cool.

"Don't make a mess out of an already botched job," he told Lamar. "You're not taking her. Now get out of here."

Lamar scowled at the suggestion of failure, but before he could retort, a car rumbled into the parking lot, and everyone turned around. It was a big, boxy car, and Hailey shook, imagining Jonathan stepping out with another couple of guards.

But Tim's cheek twitched, and his hand loosened slightly around hers as a big man stepped into view. "Connor."

Hailey exhaled but didn't stop sweating one bit.

Connor strode up, circling around to his brother's side.

"What do we have here?" Connor murmured, crossing his arms.

Tim alone was formidable, but the two together were downright scary. Hailey could barely see over them as they stood shoulder-to-shoulder, forming a protective wall. She expected Tim to tell Connor about the lunatic who could change from wolf to human form, but all he said was, "What we have here is a fool. A stupid son of a bitch and his two even stupider men."

Connor huffed. "You have one minute to get back in your car and fifteen to fly your sorry asses off Maui. And when you get to Oahu, you'll catch the first flight to the mainland. Any delay, and you're dead."

His voice was dark and deadly, scaring Hailey. Connor meant it, she was sure. Tim backed him up with a deep, guttural growl.

The man on the left clapped a hand on Lamar's shoulder. "Come on. Let's get out of here."

Lamar shrugged him off, and Hailey worried that he would resist. But finally, he showed his teeth and stepped back.

"You haven't seen the last of us, asshole."

The three turned on their heels, and Connor followed them all the way to the car. When the SUV started up and reversed out of its spot, Connor backtracked to Tim for a last, rushed exchange.

"I'll make sure they go." His eyes jumped to Hailey, and his voice was grim. "You take care of her."

Tim nodded. "I'm bringing her to Koakea." Connor looked like he was about to protest, but Tim insisted. "I have to. It's safer there."

"Hang on—" Hailey started.

But Connor just muttered and ran to his car. Seconds later, he peeled out of the parking lot, following Lamar's SUV.

The crickets that had gone deathly still went back to chirping, and the park slowly returned to its earlier peace. A deceptive kind of peace, because what creature might jump out of the shadows next?

Hailey didn't realize her hands were shaking until Tim clasped them and pulled her closer. She stared into his eyes, stuttering as a dozen questions formed a logjam in her mind.

"Tell me that didn't happen. Tell me I didn't see that."

For a long, petrifying minute, Tim didn't say anything at all. Then he rubbed his hands over hers and kissed her knuckles.

"Let's get out of here. I'll explain in the car."

Chapter Ten

Tim slid into the pickup, slammed the door shut, and scrubbed a hand through his hair. Then he cursed under his breath for the hundredth time. Any sane shifter knew not to show his animal side in front of a human. That Lamar was one cocky — or psychotic — son of a bitch to shift in plain view. Worse, he'd done so in front of Hailey.

Tim clamped his hands over the steering wheel while his bear growled in his mind.

When I get my claws on him...

Yeah, no kidding. It had taken everything he had not to shift and rip Lamar to pieces on the spot. A bear against a wolf – it wouldn't be easy, but Tim had no doubt who would come out on top. In any other circumstance, he and Connor would have killed Lamar and the other two — a bear and a wolf shifter, judging by their scents — on the spot. But Hailey had been there, and her safety came first.

She's safe now, his bear murmured.

Yeah, she was safe. But, shit. How would he ever explain?

I'm a shifter too. And all those nice people you met at Koakea? Hunter is a bear like me. Chase is a wolf, but I swear he's nothing like Lamar. Dell is a lion...

Hailey hunched over in the passenger seat, burying her face in her hands. Every wracking sob she took tore at his heart.

"Shh. Hailey..." He leaned across the front seat and wrapped his arms around her.

Her sobs turned into mumbled questions he couldn't make sense of.

"It's okay now. I promise it's okay," he whispered again and again.

When she looked up, her face was smeared with tears, and her eyes shiny with fear. "What was that? God, what kind of monster is he?"

Monster made Tim's heart sink, because he was a shifter too.

"Shifter," he muttered after a deep breath. He couldn't lie to her, after all.

Hailey's eyes went wide, and her hands gripped his. So trusting. So totally innocent of the fact that he was that kind of monster himself.

"Shifter? You mean, like a werewolf?"

He nodded. "Sort of, I guess. But different."

"Different how?" Hailey's hands shook in his.

When he started the vehicle and drove off, his heart might as well have been dragging along the ground behind them.

"They can change back and forth, but not the way legends say. Like, not only under a full moon."

"No, they just change when they want to scare the shit out of someone," Hailey snorted. Then she shook her head. "How is that even possible?"

Tim figured it wasn't the time to explain how good it felt to be able to shed his human skin and disappear into the wild from time to time.

Hailey's eyebrows drew tight, and she stared at him. "Wait. How do you even know about them?"

For a second, his mind went blank. Jesus, what to say?

Tell her not all shifters are bad, his bear growled, jumping up and down inside, rebelling against the authority of his human side. *Tell her about me.*

It took everything he had to keep the beast under control. Explaining to Hailey about shifters would never work, so he went for a watered-down version of the truth.

"My mother told me."

His bear grimaced when Tim insisted it was to protect Hailey.

You're protecting yourself, idiot. Just tell her.

"I grew up in the Wasatch mountains. There are lots of guys who keep to themselves out there in the woods." *Like me,* he wanted to add, but the pickup was speeding along by then, and Hailey would probably throw herself out the passenger-side door if he did.

"Have you ever seen one before?" Her lips trembled.

God, his mother was right about small lies turning into quagmires that sucked you in.

"Yeah. A few."

His bear snorted.

"A few?" Hailey shrieked and gripped the door handle so hard, he was afraid she really would bolt.

"They're not all bad," he said, far too late. "Most just keep to themselves the way bears do."

"Bears?"

He closed his eyes for a split second. Shit. Why did he mention that?

"There are all kinds of shifters. Wolves, bears..."

His bear made a face. *You going to tell her about lions and dragons, too?*

No, he was not. This was already enough of a mess.

Hailey crossed her arms. "Lamar wasn't exactly keeping to himself, was he?"

Tim looked at her out of the corner of his eye. At least there was that — Hailey was tough enough to face that shock. But what would she think of him if she knew?

Hailey's face went white. "Oh my God. He works for Jonathan. Does Jonathan know? Wait — what if Jonathan is one too?" Her voice filled with horror.

Definitely not the time to tell her about us, he told his bear before it could so much as peep.

"I don't know. But you're safe now, okay?"

She bit her lip and nodded quickly, which just about tore him apart. Holding back the full truth meant he was betraying her trust, and that gutted him.

He tapped his fingers on the wheel, trying to think straight. "Right now, we need to get you to a safe place. Even with Connor making sure they leave Maui, we can't take any chances."

She looked around desperately. "Where?"

"Back to Koakea." The guys would kill him and he knew it, but what choice did he have?

"Cynthia said I couldn't stay, and you said she was in charge."

Tim frowned. All true, but when it came to Hailey's safety, *he* was in charge, damn it. "That was before we knew there were shifters involved."

The quiet, scrubby side road turned into a lane that cut through an industrial area, and eventually, he connected to Highway 37, heading to West Maui.

"Wait a minute," she protested. "Where are we going?"

"To Koakea, like I said."

"We're not going to pick up our things?"

He looked at her. "We can send someone over for that. Jenna and the others can loan you some clothes."

She didn't say anything, but her hands fretted the whole time, and her fingers clutched at her neck. What was so important at Pu'u Pu'eo that she needed to have?

A tense, too-silent minute passed before she spoke again. "You told him this is 'our territory.'"

His mind spun. Shit. How the hell would he explain that? The best he could come up with was, "I meant human territory."

He hid a wince. That was his first full-out lie, and it burned.

She studied him closely. Too closely. "How many of your friends know about shifters?"

He pinched the bridge of his nose then quickly let go lest she catch that little tell. "We all know."

She stared. "How? I mean, I never knew. I still can't believe it's possible."

He tossed out the first thing he could think of. "We came across some in the military."

"In the military?" Her voice hit a new high.

He touched her arm, which seemed to help. "Not all shifters are bad. But it's very hush-hush, and we have to keep it that way."

That was the tricky part — explaining to her why.

"Oh, you mean people will freak out if they find out?" She huffed. "Can't say I'd blame them."

He tried a different tack. "Well, no one would believe you, and you're the one who would come across as crazy."

That made her pause.

"And second, some humans wouldn't understand. They would hunt every one down — the good shifters along with the bad. Most humans have come across lots of shifters without knowing it. Good shifters who wouldn't hurt anyone."

"How can you be so sure?"

Because you're my mate, and I'd do anything for you, he wanted to say. *The women who lent you clothes are shifters. My friends are all shifters. They're good people, Hailey.*

He tried a softer version of that as he drove, constantly checking the rearview mirror. "Let's say someone you know well — someone you lived close to, even — was a shifter, and you didn't even know it." A flurry of all they'd done in the past few days paraded through his mind. "A person you trusted. Worked with. Laughed with. Shared meals with. Everything."

She snorted. "What, like a roommate or something?"

No. Like me, he ached to say.

"Yeah, like a roommate. Someone who was always there and you never thought twice about. Let's say you suddenly found out they were... maybe a different religion or something."

"What would that matter?"

He nodded, reinforcing his point. "Exactly. It wouldn't matter, because you know who they really are and what they're like. That they're good inside. So, little details don't matter."

"Turning into a wild animal is not a little detail. Lamar was a wolf." She shivered. "And he hid it all this time..."

That bastard didn't hide it long enough, his bear snarled.

Hailey shook her head and crossed her arms, resolute. "Anyone who hides a secret like that can't be up to any good."

Tim kept his eyes straight ahead and his lips tightly sealed.

"Do the police know?" Hailey asked a moment later.

He worked his jaw from side to side. Forget about the police — what would Hailey say if she knew the shorts she was wearing had been loaned to her by a bear shifter who was a cop? He could just see it now — driving by Dawn's patrol car, giving a casual wave.

"No," he said. "At least, most don't, just like most humans."

"So, no one can help me," she mumbled quietly.

"I'll help you. We all will."

She turned to him with a grateful smile that nearly broke his heart. "Thank God for you. I mean it. I don't know where I'd be without you."

Tim pursed his lips, and for a long time, the only sound was the rush of the pickup's tires over the road.

∞∞∞∞

"He what?" Kai bellowed.

It was an hour later, back on the plantation. The second Tim had gotten Hailey set up at his place with Jenna for company, he'd called a meeting with Cynthia and Kai — one of the dragons of Koa Point — at the main house. Connor was on the way, having escorted Lamar and his men on to the first flight to Oahu with the formidable backup force of Hunter and Dawn, who'd raced over immediately to assist.

"Lamar shifted right in front of Hailey," Tim repeated, running his hands over his face. "She saw everything."

Cynthia's eyes blazed. "He puts every shifter at risk doing that."

She looked up toward the second floor, where Dell was reading to little Joey. Chase was on patrol, and the shifters of Koa Point were on high alert, too. All were under strict orders not to show themselves in animal form anywhere near Tim's place that night.

"Who is this Lamar?" Cynthia added.

Tim shook his head. "I wish I knew."

Kai looked every bit as furious. "By the morning, we'll know everything there is to know about that bastard."

They were sitting in what had once been the first-floor parlor of the plantation house. Most of the time, the porch served as Koakea's meeting place, but more private conversations took place indoors — especially with a human on the property.

"I would have killed him on the spot if it weren't for Hailey," Tim growled.

Torn the bastard to bits, his bear agreed.

"Who were the others?" Cynthia asked.

"A bear and a wolf shifter," Tim said. He recounted everything he'd picked up on during the confrontation on the beach, including Lamar's ties to Hailey's would-be fiancé.

"So we need to question her," Kai murmured, looking as dark as ever.

Tim jumped up from his chair so fast, it fell over in a crash. "Not tonight, you're not."

Kai and Cynthia stared at him long and hard enough to make his cheeks heat.

"I didn't mean tonight," Kai finally said. "She needs a break. Maybe you need one too."

Tim glowered. What the hell was that supposed to mean?

"Is your house really the best place for her to stay?" Kai went on. "We could put her up at the Kapa'akea Resort with full security. Might be more up her alley, you know."

That was a dig at Tim's roughing-it shed of a house, and he knew it. Yes, Hailey was probably used to fancy places like the five-star Kapa'akea Resort. But she seemed genuinely at home in smaller, cozier, fixer-upper places like the house they'd just spent a week in. The moment he'd shown her his home, her tension had eased a notch or two.

"She's fine here," he muttered.

He was pushing the limits, and he knew it. Cynthia was in charge of the plantation, and Kai oversaw her. Both dragons ranked higher than Tim, and he'd never thought to question their authority before. But here he was, practically staging a one-bear rebellion.

It's not about rank, his bear insisted. *We have to keep Hailey safe and close.*

He closed his eyes. *Safe* was one thing. *Close,* on the other hand, probably wasn't a good idea. But it was too late to resist his attraction to Hailey. Which pretty much put him in purgatory now that Hailey had made her feelings about shifters clear.

"Three days," Cynthia said, looking at him and then Kai. "We give her three more days, and then she has to go. Agreed?"

Tim was about to protest when Cynthia cut in.

"I understand her predicament, but she can't hide here forever."

"If the press finds out she's here..." Kai muttered.

Tim went cold. It was bad enough harboring one human on the property. If the press tracked Hailey to Koakea, there would be dozens more. The snooping, inquisitive kind, armed with cameras and microphones. How could he and his shifter brethren possibly guard their secrets under that kind of scrutiny?

"Three days is plenty of time for Hailey to arrange for her own security and decide on her next steps," Cynthia said decisively.

She might as well have banged a gavel, and Tim could barely refrain from glaring. But if anyone understood about moving on after a traumatic event, it was Cynthia. No one knew exactly what had brought the young dragon widow to Maui with her son, but it was perfectly clear Cynthia knew all about being on the run.

"Three days," Kai agreed, giving Tim a hard look. "You got that?"

Tim barely concealed his inner bear's growl. *No way.*

He cuffed the unruly beast into place in a way he'd never had to do before. Keeping his clan safe had to come first, no matter how it gutted him.

"You got that, Hoving?" Kai repeated, glaring this time.

Tim gave a curt nod — the most he could get past his unruly bear. Yeah, he got it. Three days was all he had left with his mate. Some shifters were lucky and got a lifetime. Connor and Jenna had already enjoyed months together and still had years to come. Kai and Tessa were doubly lucky, what with rumors of a baby on the way. But him...

Tim nearly let out an angry roar. Three days weren't enough, damn it.

It will have to be, Kai's stern look said.

And, hell. The dragon shifter was right. Destiny was finicky that way. Some shifters won the *forever* lottery; others only got a day pass for a brief foray into love and luck. That was the problem with falling for a woman who would never accept his shifter side.

No, his bear pleaded. *There must be some way...*

He looked out over the midnight ocean. So vast, so emotionless. Much like his soul before Hailey had come along and added all that light and sparkle, like the moon did to the sea.

He stuck out his jaw. Three days were better than nothing, right? It would hurt like hell to give her up, but maybe it was better this way. He wouldn't have to tell Hailey about his bear side if they only had three days. They could just make the most of their time together. Saying goodbye would kill him, but at least he would have something to look back on for the rest of his long, lonely life.

So he stood and moved stiffly to the door, making a plan as he went. He'd pack a lifetime into the days they had. He'd make her understand how special she was and what she meant to him.

And then? his bear cried.

He stared into nothingness. Then he would have to find the strength to let her go.

Chapter Eleven

Hailey spent a long time fretting that evening, no matter how Jenna tried to put her at ease. It was only when Tim returned that she stopped twirling her hair and pushing her cuticles back with her nails.

"Hang in there," Jenna said on her way out. "However complicated things seem, they always work out."

Hailey wanted to snort. Her grandfather had been mauled to death by wolves. That hadn't exactly worked out. And Jesus, this was a whole different level of terrifying, what with a werewolf tracking her for an egotistical maniac who wanted her as his bride.

Hailey couldn't see how the mess of her life could possibly work out, but with Tim taking up most of the doorway, the impossible seemed slightly easier to believe.

He stood there a long time after Jenna went, rubbing his shoulder along the doorframe in one of many quirky little habits she'd come to love. His expression was heart-wrenchingly sad for some reason, and she fished for words to comfort him.

He opened his mouth first, but she held up her hand.

"If you don't mind, I'd rather just... pretend tonight," she said. "I know it's childish, but sometimes, you just have to turn things off and make believe everything is fine. I swear I'll face up to things tomorrow. But, tonight..."

Surprisingly, he looked relieved. Really relieved, like there was something he would rather not face up to either. "Never tried that before," he admitted. "But, yeah. Pretending works for me."

She bit her lip. He could have lectured her on making a mess of her life, especially getting involved with the likes of Jonathan and his thugs. He could have said enough was enough and cast her out to fend for herself. But he didn't. He just looked at her and smiled, like having her there was all he needed.

"So," she said, forcing a light tone. "Interesting place you've got here."

He ran a hand along the doorframe. "You like it?"

She turned pink. One little gesture shouldn't ignite the dirty part of her mind, but she couldn't help fantasizing about his hands on her instead. Rubbing up and down. Touching. Possessing. Protecting.

Maybe she was suffering from some kind of rescuer complex. Or maybe it was the way his chest stretched the fabric of his shirt, because what woman couldn't notice that? Either way, around Tim, a long-neglected sensual corner of her mind revved into overdrive.

Did she like the house? She cleared her throat, because saying *I love it* in a hoarse, needy voice just wouldn't do.

"I do," she managed.

She'd wandered around the outside already, and it was neat as a pin. Cute, too, what with an old-fashioned water pump and a coffee drying shed around the back.

Tim stepped forward, and her blood rushed, even though he only advanced as far as the next supporting beam. He thumped it and motioned around. "This whole place was a coffee plantation, and this was one of the sheds."

The walls were rough wood, and starlight showed through gaps between the beams. Crickets chirped all around, and a huge tree sheltered the west side. The roof sloped at different angles in different spots as if the building had been added on to over time. Inside, the structure split into two levels — well, two-plus, because the place had all kinds of cellars, towers, and side wings stuck onto it.

"Dell calls it the shoehouse. You know that story with the old woman who lived in a shoe?"

Hailey laughed, because that fit the structure perfectly. There was a big living room in front, with a kitchen niche to one side. Three narrow stairs went up to an open second level that stood at about the height of her chest — like a loft, but a low one. There was a double bed up there set on short legs, plus a small reading light and books stuck into the open framework of the walls. She could already picture curling up there after a long day of work.

"I love that quilt," she murmured, stepping over for a closer look at the appliqué work. The motif was an abstract pineapple pattern stitched in tiny, parallel lines.

"Dawn found it at a flea market. She makes some great finds." Tim smiled a little and looked off into his memories. "She and Hunter gave it to me as a moving-in present, from one bear—" He stuttered and started again. "From one buddy to another."

She looked around. Yes, the place was pretty bare. But all in all, it was more rustic than ramshackle, and homey as anything.

"How long have you lived here?"

"I've been on Maui for about two months, but I only moved in to this place a few weeks ago. It still needs a lot of work."

It did, but he'd already made it into an inviting, cozy home. It was small and a little dark, like a log cabin, but the air was fresh, and she could imagine sunlight pouring in by day. With a few nice decorative touches, it might even make the pages of a lifestyle magazine.

"Your own little man-den," she joked.

His smile wavered slightly as he mumbled his reply. "You could say that."

The loft looked barely high enough for a man of Tim's height to stand in, but the left side had a raised roof like a church belfry. Beneath the loft was a cellar that was too dark to see.

"You sure you'll be okay here?" He motioned to the bed that Jenna had covered with fresh sheets.

She gulped, fighting images of curling up with Tim on that bed. Not for steamy sex like she'd daydreamed about for the past few days — just to cuddle up for the night.

"It's perfect, but what about you?"

He motioned to the cellar.

"You can't sleep there!" she protested.

"It's fine. Seriously. Like you said, it's my den."

His voice was just as steady as ever, but there was something vulnerable in his eyes. Some terrible sadness where she'd seen hope shining before.

"But it's dark. Cave-like. I can't make you sleep there."

"You're not making me do anything I don't want to do," he said softly. "Plus, I guarantee once I get down there, I practically hibernate."

She laughed. "Ha. Hibernate. That's what I need to do. Then I can wake up a couple of months down the line and get my life back together again." She took a deep breath and shook her head. "Just kidding. I swear I'll only impose on you for one more night. Tomorrow, I'll make a plan and move on."

"Tomorrow?" He snapped his head up in surprise.

She gulped. Did he hate the idea as much as she did? In so many ways, she wanted to stay. Not just for safety but to feel as alive and free as she had over the past few days. And, damn. It would be nice to explore her feelings for Tim, too. But she was painfully aware that her attraction to him could be a function of being on the run. After all, she'd misjudged Jonathan in her desperation to gain some freedom from her mother and career. Was it just her desperation to get away from Jonathan that made her fall for Tim?

Her heart said no, but she'd already decided. "Tomorrow. I can't possibly ask you for anything more."

"Stay a few days." *Stay as long as you like,* his eyes added. "And you don't have to ask," he said, so quietly, she nearly melted all over again. "I'm happy to help."

The room was small enough that it only took her two steps to come right up to him, and when she got there, she slipped into a hug. "Hope you don't mind."

Their first touch was awkward, and she thought she might have made a mistake. At first, his arms were stiff and uncertain, but within seconds, he'd cinched her nice and close, just as he had on the beach. Even closer, if that were possible, and he held her tight. His body heat chased away the chill of fear, and his arms, circling her so carefully, created a wall no enemy could breach.

"I definitely don't mind," he mumbled, reminding her of his kiss. A kiss that had lit every on-switch in her soul until Lamar had appeared.

She kept her face buried in his shoulder, determined to shut Lamar and all evil away for the night.

This is all temporary, she tried reminding herself, but it was getting harder and harder to do.

"I don't know where I'd be without you," she mumbled.

"Aw, you'd be fine," he said, sounding breezy. But his arms tightened in a promise, and she closed her eyes.

"Sleep with me," she whispered. A second later, she pulled away and slapped her hand over her mouth. "I mean — that came out wrong."

He tilted his head, letting a hint of amusement show for the first time. "How did you mean it, then?"

Her cheeks burned. "I mean, sleep beside me. I mean... Oh, God..."

He laughed outright then pulled her into a warm hug. "I think I know what you mean."

She closed her eyes, ready to crawl into that cellar of his and die of embarrassment. "I'm going to blame that on being a little mixed up tonight."

His arms rubbed up and down her back, putting her at ease. "Being only a little mixed up is pretty amazing, considering what you've been through."

She laughed. *Plenty mixed up* was more like it, and not just from the scary parts of the day. Her lips were still tingling from the kiss they'd shared earlier, and her blood was much too warm for a woman who ought to feel chilled to the bone.

She forced herself to pull away. "I'm sorry. I have no right to ask so much of you."

The right side of his mouth curled up. "I think I can suffer a little more." His eyes clouded for a moment, like he'd just remembered a very good reason to say no. But then he nodded firmly. "Seriously. I'm happy to help."

She took a deep breath. "Okay, so — the bathroom is..."

He pointed, and she skittered away to get ready for the night. They'd agreed to pretend, right? So pretend she would. That it was perfectly normal to sleep beside a man she'd only known for a few days. That she hadn't been hunted down by a werewolf — correction, wolf shifter — earlier that day.

God, *mixed up* didn't begin to capture how she felt.

But, wow. Once she was ready for bed, sliding between the sheets had a certain thrill, and when Tim slid in behind her — slowly, carefully, like he was afraid she'd bolt — sparks ran through her veins.

She lay on her side, facing the wall, wearing nothing but panties and the T-shirt he'd loaned her. Tim tucked in behind her, leaving a half-inch gap between them as he drew the sheet and quilt over both of them.

"This okay?" he whispered as he rested his arm over her side, careful to keep his hand in the neutral zone around her belly.

"Sure." Her voice had a forced lightness to it, but every muscle in her body was taut.

She lay still, telling herself that feeling safe was all she wanted. That she hadn't been fantasizing about Tim every night for the past week.

"Goodnight." His deep rumble vibrated through her back and joined in with the sparks exploring her veins.

"Goodnight," she whispered.

For the first few minutes, Hailey listened to the chirp of crickets and the distant sound of the sea. She stared at the shelf where she'd left her watch and phone, wishing her pearl were beside them. The phone she could do without. But the pearl... Ever since her grandfather had given it to her years ago, she'd never been without it.

My father and mother met when he was stationed at Pearl Harbor at the end of World War II, her grandfather had once explained. *Love at first sight, he always said.*

Hailey closed her eyes, tuning in to the sound of Tim's soft breath.

My mother was a beautiful Hawaiian girl who followed him all the way to Montana. They were that in love. This pearl was her family's wedding gift.

Hailey had always wished she could have met her great-grandparents, but her grandfather's stories made up for that in part.

The pearl might not be perfect, but that just makes it more honest, as my mother always said.

Hailey closed her eyes. To her, the pearl had always been perfect. The dimples and oblong shape made it that much easier to hold when she needed it most. Like now, when her fretting mind was all over the place. But she'd left the pearl at Pu'u Pu'eo, and she hadn't had the chance to pick it up before they left.

I'll tell you a secret my mother told me. Her grandfather's warm, scratchy voice echoed in her mind. *This little pearl holds all the love in the world. Love that will keep you company wherever you go. Love that gives you strength to carry on.* Her grandfather would always pause there, and his smile would turn bittersweet. *I think my mother needed that, so far from home. She always wished she had a daughter to pass it on to. You know how happy she would be to know it's yours now?*

Hailey found herself curling her fingers in thin air, imagining the pearl in her palm. She could use some extra strength after the terrifying events on the beach, not to mention everything else. Jonathan. Her mother. The mob of reporters she was going to have to face when she emerged from hiding.

She nearly shuddered, but Tim curled his hand around hers as if he'd read her mind.

"Everything will be okay," he whispered, kissing her shoulder softly. Just a chaste little kiss, but still, her soul fluttered around in glee.

She wrapped her hand around Tim's and tugged it closer to her heart. Not close enough to seduce the poor man, just to settle herself down a bit. The next day, she'd make a quick plan of action, and step one would be retrieving her pearl. But for now...

Tim pulled her closer, erasing the distance between them, and she just about sighed. With a quilt, a comfortable mattress, and a huge, hulking bodyguard literally at her back, she had everything she could want, and before she knew it, she was drifting into sleep.

Pretend, Hailey. Pretend. That it was fine to have her rear snuggled into Tim's lap and her fingers laced through his. That the world was as peaceful and safe as it felt just now, and that everything would be all right.

Funny how pretending wasn't all that hard in the end.

∞∞∞∞

To her utter surprise, Hailey slept like a rock, and when she woke, the pink light of dawn streamed through the gaps between the cabin's beams. She stretched then froze, suddenly remembering how she'd gone to bed. This was supposed to be the awkward part, right?

But Tim murmured from over her shoulder, soothing her all over again.

"I think pretending is allowed for a little longer. Coffee's on me this time," he whispered, kissing her on the shoulder and rolling away.

She turned and watched Tim, keeping the quilt close in the chill of daybreak. Every move the man made was powerful and controlled, from the easy way he swung down the loft stairs to the exactitude with which he placed the kettle on the single-burner stove. He was wearing black boxers and nothing else, and the soft morning light glowed over every chiseled muscle on his broad frame. He scratched his chest in the absent-minded gesture of a man who was a little sleepy and totally at home.

When he pulled on a shirt and wrestled it down over his torso, she tried not to stare at the way all the different layers of muscle rippled. It wasn't just his looks that drew her in, though. She'd modeled alongside enough finely chiseled body-builder types to know a great body didn't always come with a sharp mind — or a pure heart. Some of those men had made lewd jokes; others had all but assumed she would follow them off the set and into bed. Few men so much as held a door open for her, let alone bent over backward to help her the way Tim had. And no one had that amazing mix of a soft touch and iron will that Tim had.

She stared at the shelf where her pearl ought to be and shook the thought away. She wasn't falling in love. She couldn't allow herself to. Not at a time like this, and not with her record of making mistakes.

So she took her phone off the shelf and clicked it on, bracing herself for the onslaught of messages that were sure to be there. Pretending was all well and good, but she had to face the music at some point.

Sure enough, her inbox was packed with dozens of messages, and she cringed.

"Milk?" Tim asked, holding up a mug. Looking at her with those deep, undemanding eyes. Begging her to stay in his world for a little longer.

She put the phone down, happy to delay unpleasant realities for a while.

"Milk would be great," she whispered, sliding out of bed and away from the phone.

He waited, quiet and patient as ever, while she slipped off to brush her teeth and change into the clothes Jenna had brought over the previous night. She would have preferred wearing Tim's oversize shirt all day. Unfortunately, that wouldn't do — not on the day she'd sworn to finally get a move on with her life.

But Tim said she could pretend a little longer, and damn it, she did. She sipped her coffee, looking into his eyes the whole time.

"Perfect," she breathed when she was done, though she'd been busier drinking in the sight of her companion than appreciating the flavor of that particular brew.

When he licked his lips, she had to yank her eyes away, and she swore his breath hitched. Hers did too, and an invisible energy field started swirling around them again, wrapping her in its spell. All kinds of crazy visions zipped through her mind, like waking up to an infinite number of mornings with Tim. Spending every night with him. Before long, a whole, happy future was playing out in her mind, with kids and summers and Christmases. Birthdays, weekends, and the occasional dinner out. Laughter, silky touches. There were tears too, but none were brutally dark and desperate, not if she could face sorrow with Tim.

She bit her lip. Was that a vision — the kind she'd be a fool to ignore — or was it mere fantasy?

Tim's eyes glowed, making the beautiful brown irises turn caramel. He whispered, reaching for her hands.

"Hailey, I really have to tell you something."

She held her breath. Had he seen what she saw? Did he want it, too?

His Adam's apple bobbed with a heavy gulp, signaling something momentous. Something that could change her life.

She nodded eagerly. But he paused, and the moment stretched on and on.

A shrill, piercing ring broke the silence, and they jumped apart. Hailey looked around and spotted her phone, vibrating and flashing with an incoming call. The urgent ring hammered at the silence of the rustic house until she couldn't stand it any more. She hurried over, looked at the display, and grimaced as it rang again.

"My mother."

Guilt sliced through her. How heartless had she been, cutting off her mother like that? The poor woman was probably worried out of her mind.

Hailey's hand froze halfway to the phone as it hit her. If Lamar could threaten her, he might threaten her mother. She snatched the phone up to answer.

"Mom? Are you okay?"

Tim tilted his head, listening, and she wished she could hold his hand. It sure would help her get through the call.

"Hailey? Goddammit, where the hell have you been?"

She held the phone away from her ear. No *Are you okay?* or *Oh my God, I've been so worried about you.* Just that shrill, cockatoo voice. Scolding. Demanding — no, issuing an order Hailey didn't want to hear.

Tim's brow knotted. "Everything okay?"

Hailey made a face, covered the phone, and held back a sigh. "Yeah. Totally normal."

Chapter Twelve

Hailey pressed the phone back to her ear. "Where are you, Mom?"

She nearly shrieked when she heard the reply.

"On my way to Maui, no thanks to you. What is in your brain, girl?"

If it weren't for Tim touching her hand just then, who knew what she might have replied?

"Why are you coming to Maui?"

"To shake some sense into you, of course. Now, tell me where you are," her mother snapped.

"Sounds like you know where," Hailey answered, trying to understand what was going on.

"Would you stop playing games? I know you're on Maui. Jonathan's security team tracked you down. I don't know what you were thinking."

Hailey's blood went cold. "Is Jonathan with you? No? Good, then listen, Mom. Listen carefully. You can't trust him. More than that, you can't trust Lamar. He's a monster."

Tim's hand dropped away from hers, and he turned away.

"Don't be ridiculous, Hailey. You're the one who ran away from your own wedding."

"It wasn't my wedding. It was Jonathan's. If he'd bothered to ask—"

"If you'd bothered to think, none of this mess would have happened. Lucky for you I talked Jonathan into giving you a second chance. Now, tell me where you are."

Hailey's hand shook, partly in anger, part in fear. "Where is Lamar, Mom?"

Tim stepped closer, listening in.

"What do I know? What's important is that I'm on my way to Maui. Now, stop playing games."

Hailey's immediate instinct was to board the first flight to Timbuktu, but she managed a level reply. "I am not playing games, Mom. I am taking back control of my life."

Tim gave her a firm nod, bolstering her nerves. Her mother had a way of making her feel like she was the crazy one, but Tim set her compass straight every time.

Still, it was time she faced the music, so she couldn't run, and within a minute, she'd grudgingly agreed to a meeting place.

"I'll meet you at the Kapa'akea Resort," Hailey said into the phone, following the words Tim mouthed. "Call me when you get close."

"But—"

"Call me when you get close, and come alone," Hailey said firmly before disconnecting the call. She sank into a chair and covered her face with her hands as the peace she'd gained over the past few days evaporated.

"It'll be okay," Tim whispered, crouching in front of her.

She forced a smile. "Seeing a werewolf didn't shake me as badly as the thought of seeing my own mother."

Tim's face went from warm to inscrutable. Then he cleared his throat. "The Kapa'akea Resort is a good place to meet. Security is already high, and we can get there early to scope out the place."

Hailey made a face. "Maybe I should call in the press. Make a preemptive strike." Then she shook her head. "Can you believe I'm talking about my mother that way?"

He shrugged. "From what you say about her, yes. I can believe it."

She stared out the door and forced herself to her feet. Reality had just caught up with her. She'd better go out and face it before it got any more out of control.

"Okay, so I guess I'd better make a plan."

Tim nodded but didn't say anything, letting her make up her own mind.

She thought it over. "So, I'll meet my mom and make it clear it's over between Jonathan and me." Easier said than done, and she knew it. "But that preemptive strike might actually make sense."

Tim grinned. "You have a military mind."

She laughed. "Well, you know how it is. Desperate times call for desperate measures." She frowned. "Is your mom this bad?"

He shook his head quickly. "I think we were the ones who drove her crazy, not the other way around. But I'm sure your mom...um..."

He was trying to find something nice to say, and she loved him for it.

"Um...I'm sure she means well," he finished a little lamely.

Hailey laughed — mainly because that was better than crying — and set about making a plan. She scrolled through the contacts on her phone, making a list in her mind. Tim walked off to make a few calls of his own. Apparently, Dawn knew a local reporter who sounded like the perfect person for Hailey to give an exclusive interview to. Meanwhile, Hailey called her agent, and though he was just as angry as her mother was, he did agree to overnight her a new credit card and ID.

The rest was still shaky in her mind. She couldn't leave Maui without some kind of security, because what if Lamar came along again?

She found herself watching Tim pace back and forth as he spoke into his phone. Too bad she couldn't stay with him. It was perfect in every way but one — the sinking feeling that she might be using the only honest person in her life. She didn't mean to use Tim, but he'd done so much, and she was so mixed up. How could she possibly trust herself at a time like this?

"Ready to go?" Tim asked a few minutes later.

She looked down at herself, checking her appearance. Her mother would have a fit at the sight of her in borrowed clothes. Which made it awfully tempting to put Tim's T-shirt back on, because that would really make a point. But, no. She wouldn't stoop that low. Jenna's clothes were perfectly fine.

He must have taken her hesitation for nervousness — which wasn't far off the truth — because he leaned in and kissed her. Just once, and just on the cheek, but wow. Her heart did a happy flip, and fire blazed through her veins.

She did her best to nod casually. "Ready to go."

Tim led her across the property. "Nothing like Montana, huh?" he said quietly, gesturing around.

She nearly laughed in relief. Tim was giving her the chance to pretend a little longer.

"Nope," she agreed. "I like it, though."

In truth, she loved it. The peace. The privacy. The prospect of getting the grounds back in shape. A tangled-over plantation was exactly the kind of project she would love to dive into once she stepped away from modeling.

But as beautiful as it was, everything Hailey saw reflected her mood. Scrappy rows of coffee plants strained to peek out through thick chokeholds of weeds. The hopeful pink color had long since seeped out of the atmosphere, leaving a clear blue sky.

A clean slate, she tried telling herself, but all she really saw was a huge void.

They paused on a rise, and she turned slowly, taking it all in. There were a few more houses sprinkled here and there, and a figure stepped out of one and stretched. She watched as a man raised his arms, facing the sea. Was that Dell? He doubled over, stretching and moving with feline grace. Soon, he was in a plank position and then a cobra pose.

She stared. "Dell does yoga?"

Tim nodded. "Yep. Every day."

The first few moves he'd done were familiar, but then he crouched, planted his hands on the ground, and eased into a handstand. *Not* the kind of yoga she'd ever tried. As she watched, he brought his feet together over his head and bent his knees, forming a diamond shape. Finally, he raised one hand off the ground and stayed there, perfectly balanced.

"Wow." She nearly whistled. A one-handed handstand? "Maybe I should have done some yoga this morning," she sighed, turning back to Tim. "Though I'm not sure it would help."

He wrapped his hand around hers and flashed that mini-smile. The one that said everything would be all right. But even that seemed a little thin, like he wasn't so sure himself.

When they reached the barn where his pickup was parked, Tim walked right past it and handed her a helmet instead.

"A motorcycle?" she squeaked, staring at the black Harley.

He grinned. "Yep. Connor — er, inherited — some money, and this was one of the few things he splurged on. Good get-away vehicle, I figure."

That was a joke but not a joke, and when she slipped on behind Tim, her hands shook. Was she really ready to face the outside world?

He revved the engine and sped off, telling her, *Yes, you are.* Wrapping herself around his hard body helped too, and when they got halfway up the driveway, a Land Rover with tinted windows pulled in behind them.

"That's Connor and Hunter," Tim shouted back above the noise of the engine. "Our backup."

She hid her face in his back. God, she owed so many people so much. How was she ever going to thank them all?

The Kapa'akea Resort was only a short distance down the coast — one of those ultrafancy places with a long, palm-lined drive and security guards who bristled as they approached. But Tim must have had some kind of contact there, because security waved the motorcycle and Land Rover right through. As they cruised down the private drive, Hailey watched polo ponies thunder over the green on the right. A golf course stretched out to the left, and pots of exotic flowers lined the porch of the resort. Tim parked beside the main building and walked Hailey over to an octagonal building on the edge of the polo field.

"This is the teahouse," he said, all matter-of-fact.

Connor and Hunter fanned out behind them, looking every bit as menacing as presidential bodyguards, and she gulped.

"You can meet the reporter in there," Tim said. "I'll wait out on the porch. Okay?" He squeezed her hands.

She gulped. Not okay, because wow — he'd gone to incredible lengths to organize all this for her. All she'd ever done was brew coffee for him.

"Perfect. Thank you. Again," she whispered, giving him a peck on the cheek.

His face was just as inscrutable as Connor's or Hunter's, but his eyes sparkled before he let her go.

Hailey took a deep breath. Someday, she'd find a way to say thank you properly. Right now...

She stepped inside the teahouse, extending her hand to each of the two people inside. The reporter turned out to be a friendly local woman in a flower-print dress who tut-tutted sympathetically at everything Hailey had been through — not at all the nosy shark Hailey was expecting. The photographer was a small Asian man who smiled and asked permission before taking Hailey's picture. She'd nearly done a double take at that. Tim, she noticed, made sure to slide out of the background of each photo, no matter what angle the photographer took.

Interviews were nothing new to Hailey, but this one just flew. There was something liberating about being the one to call the meeting and to tell her story in her own words. She went to lengths to make Jonathan sound better than he was with sound bites like *We just weren't meant for each other* and *I needed more space*, and she didn't mention Lamar. She did the same about her mother and the modeling industry, but the truth must have shone through, because the reporter scribbled away on a notepad and exchanged looks with the photographer that said *Holy shit. I'd be out of there too.*

Finally, Hailey signed an agreement granting the reporter exclusive rights to her story in exchange for the reporter swearing not to reveal her location, and that was that.

Meeting the reporter was the easy part. Then Tim's phone beeped out on the porch. When Hailey looked up, his grim expression warned her to brace herself. A long, black limo swept down the drive, coming to a halt right outside the teahouse.

"Good luck, honey," the reporter whispered on the way out.

The photographer winked at her with an apologetic, *You'll need it* look and followed the reporter away.

Hailey straightened her shoulders and forced herself not to cross her arms — classic defensive posture — when the limo pulled up. Nothing happened right away, and Hailey tapped her foot. Finally, the driver — a big islander who didn't look too comfortable in his suit and tie — stepped out and circled the vehicle, rolling his eyes with a look that said, *This lady really wants me to open the door for her?*

Hailey hid a frown. Yep, that was her mother in there, all right.

The driver opened the door, and a hand extended.

Hailey snorted. Her mother didn't need help to get out of a car. She'd seen the woman stomp and shove aside extras on a set if they got in her way. But her mother loved making a grand entrance and getting all the attention she could.

Hailey nearly laughed when the driver applied a little too much force and nearly launched her mother into the air. Her mother appeared exactly the way Hailey imagined the woman had been born — scowling, red-faced, and flailing. She shook a finger at Hailey like *she* was the one who'd done something wrong.

"Just you wait until I get started with you—" Hailey's mother began without so much as adjusting the red and white polka dot kerchief tied around her head. She wore a white blouse, red pants, and giant white sunglasses. A new outfit, in other words. Apparently, she'd been worried enough about Hailey to squeeze in some therapeutic shopping time in Waikiki.

"Nice to see you too," Hailey murmured.

Tim stepped forward, completely expressionless, letting his bristling shoulders do the talking.

"For God's sake—" her mother snapped.

Hailey opened the door of the teahouse. "We can talk in here."

Her mother marched past, chin high, arms swinging like a boxer's, her face nearly as red as her pants. Hailey held the door open long enough to show Tim she'd appreciate his support, and he filed in quietly behind them.

When the door closed, Hailey's mother spun and jerked an accusing finger at Tim. "Who the hell is that?"

Hailey glared. Really *glared* at her own mother, because that man — a perfect stranger — had shown more kindness and understanding than her own mother had in the past five years.

But she couldn't exactly say *he's the man I spent last night curled up with.*

"My bodyguard," she blurted, shooting Tim a look that said, *I hope you don't mind.*

He didn't move, didn't blink, but the corner of his mouth twitched, telling her he was okay with that.

There was no way her eagle-eyed mother missed that look, but all she said was, "Hmpf." Then she sniffed at a vase full of gorgeous irises and rooted around in her purse, muttering, "Jesus, all these flowers, all the time. Don't they ever give it a break?" Then she eyed Hailey's shirt. "God, what are you wearing?"

Hailey sucked in her lips and counted to ten.

Her mother blew her nose like a trumpet then thumped her purse onto a table, rumpling the sheer white tablecloth. "I can't believe how childish you've been. How selfish."

Hailey gaped. "It's selfish to refuse to marry someone? This isn't the eighteenth century, Mom. We're not destitute, and we don't need a title."

She winced at her own words. Maybe she shouldn't give her mother any ideas. Her mother was perfectly capable of hatching a scheme to marry her off to the next in line to the throne in one of those tiny principalities that still existed around the world. Or worse, to a sheik.

But her mother just went on as if she hadn't heard. "I've never been so embarrassed in my life. You walked out of your own wedding!"

"Not my wedding," Hailey shot back, trying not to scream. "A setup. A trap."

"A trap? A trap?" Her mother grew shrill. "I'll tell you what a trap is."

Hailey closed her eyes, knowing exactly what her mother would say next.

"Trapped is being a widow with a mountain of debt and a kid to feed. Trapped is flipping burgers day after day. Trapped is living in a house with a leaking roof, not knowing how you'll ever make ends meet."

"Mom—"

"So when a man comes along, and you fall in love—"

Hailey threw her hands up in a stop sign. "I don't love Jonathan, Mom. I never did. I think it was all a subconscious need to escape."

"What could you possibly want to escape?"

You, she nearly said.

"I'm an adult now, Mom. I need space."

Her mother smacked the table and didn't so much as flinch when the vase tipped over. Hailey tried to catch it, but she was too late. Water sloshed across the perfect tablecloth, and the flowers fell into a heap.

"Everything I ever did for you," her mother snapped. "All the sacrifices I made..."

Hailey cupped a hand and did her best to scoop the water back into the vase. A losing battle, because as much dripped through her fingers as landed back in the vase. She stuffed the flowers in next, but several petals remained strewn across the tablecloth. The whole thing was a mess. The story of her life.

"You did all that, Mom, and I appreciate it," she said as gently as she could. "But we're not stuck any more. We have money. More than we ever dreamed of."

"Maybe more than *you* ever dreamed of," her mother muttered.

Hailey wanted to hang her head. How high was her mother aiming? How much would be enough?

"You've never been practical, Hailey. Without me, you'd still be back at the diner."

Without me, Hailey wanted to say, *you would still be at the diner.* But she refused to stoop that low. And anyway, she couldn't get a word in, because her mother was on a roll.

"You're just like your father. Impractical. Romantic. Like holding on to that piece of land."

Hailey stared. Her mother was still going on about the land her grandfather had left her? It was a tiny plot way out in northern Montana where her great-grandparents had lived when they'd first moved there in the 1950s. The place wasn't worth much, but it had a lot of sentimental value, and she'd hung on to it through thick and thin.

"Marrying Jonathan has every advantage, and you know it," her mother went on. The only thing that cut her off was a series of sneezes that seized her next. "Jesus, is there a dog in here or something?"

Hailey ignored her. "What advantage, Mom? I don't love Jonathan. There's nothing there. No magic, no chemistry." Hailey couldn't keep her eyes from roving to Tim. *Not like the chemistry I feel with him.*

"Magic? Chemistry? Those don't pay the bills."

"No, my modeling does. We haven't had problems paying the bills in years. We don't need Jonathan's money." Why couldn't her mother get that into her head?

Her mother frowned through another violent sneeze. "He can take you places you've never dreamed of, Hailey. First the Senate, then who knows? Maybe even the White House."

Hailey gaped. The White House? Her mother wanted her to marry an arrogant ass because he had a long shot at running for president someday? Was she crazy? Hailey couldn't even imagine herself living that kind of life.

Her mother somehow mistook her disgust for interest, because she flashed a wild smile and gushed on. "Just think about that, Hailey. You and me, in the White House. And thanks to me, Jonathan is willing to give you another chance."

Hailey slapped her hands over her eyes. It was all so surreal. Then she straightened quickly, determined to make her point and get out.

"I'm not going back, Mom."

"Thanks to me, you don't have to go anywhere." Her mother grinned, motioning outside.

The few resort guests in Hailey's line of sight were all looking up, and palm branches waved madly in a sudden burst of wind. The sound of rotors filled her ears, and even Tim looked up in alarm.

Hailey's stomach folded in on itself, making her feel sick. That was a helicopter out there, and she already knew who was in it.

"What have you done, Mother?" she cried as the helicopter touched down.

The door flew open, and Jonathan stepped out, looking every bit the harried corporate executive ready to close the deal of his life.

"Only what's best for you," her mother snipped.

Hailey's lips moved, trying to form a protest, but it was too late. Jonathan was already striding toward the teahouse like he owned the place. Like he owned Hailey, in fact.

"No," she whispered miserably. "No."

Chapter Thirteen

Stop him, Tim barked to his friends outside.

Unnecessarily, as it turned out, because they reacted as quickly as he. Tim blocked the door while Connor and Hunter intercepted Jonathan just outside the whirring perimeter of the helicopter's spinning blades. Both men crossed their arms and pinned Jonathan with cold, hard looks that stopped him in his tracks.

Tim looked at Hailey. "You don't need to talk to him if you don't want to."

He sure wouldn't want to. If the arrogant attitude hadn't already made him hate Jonathan, the way the guy touched his tailored suit and slicked-back hair would.

"Of course, she needs to talk to him. He's her fiancé," her mother squawked.

Tim ignored her, as did Hailey.

"I don't want to, but I need to. This needs to end." Hailey's voice wavered, but her eyes were fierce.

You're amazing, he wanted to say. But he couldn't, not with her mother there.

Her mother, meanwhile, let out a sneeze so loud, his ears rang. Then she sniffed and rubbed her eyes. "I swear, someone must have let an animal in here at some point. My allergies..."

Tim rolled his eyes but held back what he was dying to say. *Yes, there is an animal in here. Me.*

Instead, he turned to Connor and Hunter and grunted, *Let him through. Just keep an eye on the others. Any shifters out there?*

Negative, Connor replied. *The pilot and the bodyguards are all human.*

At least there was that — Lamar was following their orders to stay the hell away from Maui.

Jonathan started to argue with Connor, insisting that the pale, portly man beside him ought to be allowed through too.

Tim looked at Hailey. "Who's that?"

She sighed. "His lawyer."

Tim stared. What kind of man brought a lawyer to make up with his girlfriend?

Ex-girlfriend, his inner bear growled.

"Everything is business to Jonathan," Hailey muttered, reading his mind.

"Nothing wrong with business," her mother sniffed.

Tim resisted the urge to shake the woman. Mothers were supposed to love their children. Guide them. Scold or praise as the situation demanded. God knew his poor mother had done a lot more scolding than praising with all the trouble he and Connor had gotten into, but she'd never held back her love. But Hailey's mother?

Too bad she's too old for Jonathan, his bear muttered. *They'd be perfect for each other.*

Connor looked toward Tim, who shook his head. *No lawyer. One asshole is enough for today.*

Jonathan strode forward, smoothing over his tie, obviously preparing his words. Hailey's mother checked her hair as if angling to hook the guy herself. Hailey, meanwhile, set her stance a little wider, bracing herself.

You can do this, Tim wanted to cheer to her as he stepped away from the door. He had to allow Jonathan in, but if the bastard so much as made a move on Hailey...

"Hailey, sweetheart! I was so worried about you!" Jonathan declared the second he came through the door. "Are you all right?"

At least he bothered to use the right words, even if Tim could smell the lie. Hailey could too, and she backed away from Jonathan with her arms firmly crossed.

"I'm fine," she snipped while her body language ordered Jonathan to back off.

Jonathan threw up his hands the way guilty men did to declare, *Who, me?*

Tim wanted to throttle the guy already. He was too slick. Too rich. Too sure he'd get whatever he wanted, regardless of the means.

Jonathan gave him a disdainful look, but Tim turned on his fiercest grizzly glare, and the man withered under his gaze. Jonathan looked between Hailey, her mother, and Tim, then finally aimed his question at Hailey's mother.

"Who is this?" he demanded, not man enough to face Tim himself.

"My bodyguard," Hailey shot back.

Right on cue, Tim turned on that blank stare that said he wasn't listening even though he was right there. People rich enough to have security guards always fell for that.

And sure enough, Jonathan turned to Hailey and picked up his charm offensive where he'd left off. "I can't tell you how worried I was."

Hailey wasn't buying one word, and it showed. "You've wasted your time, Jonathan. It's over. And if you'd ever bothered to ask, you would have known it was over a long time ago."

Jonathan tut-tutted as if Hailey were an unreasonable child. "Baby, I—"

"Don't call me baby." Her eyes blazed.

Jonathan tried a different tack. "Now, I realize it might not have been a great idea to surprise you like that—"

"*Now* you realize?" Hailey barked.

"—but I love you." Jonathan went on without skipping a beat. "When Lamar found you—"

Hailey shoved her hands on her hips. "And how exactly did he do that?"

Jonathan stopped, looking genuinely surprised. "He doesn't ask about my work. I don't ask about his."

Hailey's eyes narrowed. "Maybe you should."

Tim sniffed the air, using his keen bear senses. Did Jonathan know his head of security was a shifter? The air around him had the faintest whiff of shifter in it, but nothing fresh enough to cause alarm.

"What is that supposed to mean?" Jonathan asked.

"Lamar creeps me out," Hailey said.

"He creeps out a lot of people. Kind of useful at times." Jonathan grinned.

Tim scowled. Would Jonathan be amused to discover his head of security could turn into a wolf?

"Anyway, what counts is that we're together again." Jonathan held out his hand, showing those manicured fingernails again. "I want you to be mine, baby."

"I am not a baby, and I am not yours. I never was, and I never will be."

Tim wanted to give her a little fist pump. Hailey was being tough as anything, but she had to be near her limit. The sooner she got this over with, the better.

Jonathan's eyes hardened, but a moment later, his voice was sticky-sweet. "Hailey, honey. I promise to make it up to you."

When he reached inside his jacket, Tim nearly slammed him into the serving counter of the teahouse. But Jonathan saw him coming and threw his hands up. "Whoa! Take it easy. It's just this."

Tim kept his arms three inches from his sides, ready to pounce as Jonathan slowly pulled out a square box. His preying eyes shifted back to Hailey as he opened the box, revealing a necklace strung with huge, shiny pearls.

"Remember these, princess? They're for you. A symbol of my love."

A symbol of my wealth, he might as well have said.

Hailey didn't move. Her mother clapped her hands to her chest and glowed as if to demonstrate how rich-people courtship went. "Why, Jonathan. They're gorgeous."

Jonathan grinned. "Pink pearls. The very best. You know what pink represents?"

Hailey looked like she couldn't care less.

"Fame, fortune, success," Jonathan said, answering his own prompt.

"Of course," Hailey muttered.

Her fingers went to her throat but then fell away, and Tim remembered the single bead she usually wore. It was pink, too. Had she left it at his house?

Jonathan leaned toward Hailey and shot a pointed look at Tim. "I'd rather speak privately, honey."

I bet you would, asshole. Tim amped up his scowl, making Jonathan eye the door.

"I'd rather not talk at all," Hailey said. "The answer is no. The answer will always be no."

Hailey's mother stopped sniffling and sneezing long enough to chime in with her two cents. "Just hear Jonathan out. You owe him as much."

"I owe him?" Hailey turned pink. "What would I possibly owe him?"

"More than you know." Hailey's mother shrugged, suddenly coy.

Jonathan grinned in a way that made Tim look twice. What was he so satisfied about?

"What is that supposed to mean?" Hailey demanded, looking between the two.

Tim looked, too, as a sinking feeling grew in his gut. Those two had definitely colluded on something — something beyond the deceit that had lured Hailey into that wedding in Waikiki.

"Just the biggest contract of your life," her mother said, looking more vindictive than any mother ought to be.

Hailey narrowed her eyes. "What are you talking about? The *Boundless* campaign? I only got that contract when the other model dropped out at the last minute."

Jonathan went right on smiling, and Hailey's mother did too, letting some realization slowly sink into Hailey's mind.

What? Tim wanted to yell. *What happened?*

Hailey's mother laughed. "Dropped out? You think Joelle Parks dropped out of the *Boundless* job?"

Hailey's brow furrowed. "She was forced to when that drug bust went public. No advertising agency would touch her after that. But..." Hailey trailed off, slowly turning white. "No.

127

You didn't." She looked from Jonathan to her mother. "Tell me you didn't have anything to do with that."

"We didn't have anything to do with that," Jonathan said, letting his shit-eating grin grow.

Hailey backed away, covering her mouth with one trembling hand. "Oh my God. You did, didn't you? You found out about her problem and made the story go public."

Hailey's mother broke out laughing. "Made the story go public? Honey, we made the story in the first place."

Tim gaped. Hailey's mother had arranged for drugs to be planted on some unsuspecting young woman to eliminate the competition and let her own daughter win the contract? How sick was she?

But it wasn't all the mother. Jonathan had played a role in that as well. One glance at the two of them exchanging smug looks said it all.

Hailey looked ready to cover her ears. "You destroyed Joelle's career for—" She slapped a hand over her mouth, and her mother filled in the rest.

"For you, Hailey. There. Now you know what to be grateful for."

"Mother, how could you?" Hailey shrieked.

"I did what I had to do. That contract was ours."

Hailey gestured helplessly. "Ours?"

Jonathan waved casually. "All water under the bridge."

Tim nearly socked him. Hailey screeched. "Water under the bridge? You ruined her life!"

Jonathan shrugged. "Business. Stars come, stars go. You got your chance, and that's all that matters. Now everyone knows your name."

Tim formed a fist. He really was going to sock Jonathan now.

"Why does that matter?" Hailey half yelled, half cried.

"Because it makes you perfect," Jonathan said. "Don't you see?"

All Tim saw was a vision of Jonathan flying through the glass door of the teahouse. If he had to listen to another second of the sick bastard's talk, he'd be ready to do just that.

"See what?" Hailey cried.

"We're perfect. My money and connections. Your face and fame. We'll make the Senate in no time!" Jonathan crowed.

"*We'll* make the Senate?" Hailey protested.

Jonathan shrugged. "I'll make the Senate. Just you watch. Give me a year or two after we're married, and then I'll be ready to make my bid for that Montana seat."

Hailey turned her head in a desperate *No, no, no!* motion. "This was your plan?" She turned to her mother. "And you were in on it?"

"Baby, just think," Jonathan said in that overly confident voice of his. "You'll be Mrs. Jonathan Owen-Clarke, Senate wife. Maybe even First Lady someday. And with my brother in the Senate for California, we'll be the new Kennedys. Everyone will love you." *Everyone will love me,* his expression said as he added, "You'll never have to work again."

Hailey's eyes bugged out. "Why would I want any of that?"

"You did say you wanted to stop modeling," her mother pointed out.

Tim scowled. Apparently, the woman had been listening, just not admitting as much.

"I want to stop modeling, but I don't want to stop working. Why would I want that? I want to earn money," Hailey said. "Honest money. I want control of my own life. Can't you see?"

Tim sure as hell could see. Jonathan wanted to control Hailey as tightly as her mother had, but Hailey was fighting back.

He stepped forward a tiny bit. This was her battle, and he was just there to support. But damn it, he'd make his support clear.

Jonathan sneered in his direction, then reapplied his smile when he looked at Hailey. A smile he probably practiced in the mirror while he imagined his illustrious political career.

"I swear, I'll take good care of you."

"I don't need to be taken care of." Hailey stomped. A moment later, her expression changed as she studied Jonathan. "Or do you mean *take care of* the way Lamar takes care of things for you?" Her voice dropped to a low whisper.

Jonathan's eyes flashed ever so briefly, making Tim bristle. Yeah, Jonathan was perfectly aware of the strong-arm tactics his head of security used. But the businessman went on talking, smooth as can be.

"Baby, all I want to take care of is you."

Hailey's mother exploded into another sneezing fit and dabbed at her nose. "Does this place allow pets or something?"

Or something, his bear muttered.

He was sorely tempted to let his fangs out and give her and Jonathan a good scare. But Hailey would be terrified too. Worse, she'd be repulsed.

He clenched a fist hard enough for his nails to cut into his palms. Sleeping next to Hailey had given him a hint of heaven, but hell wasn't far off. Not if she discovered he was a shifter.

A young waitress appeared from the back room. "Can I get anyone a tea?"

Jonathan slammed his fist on the table so hard, the silverware jumped. "Do I look like I want some goddamn tea?"

The waitress scurried off, and a second later, Jonathan was back to his fake smile. "Hailey—"

Tim wouldn't have thought it was possible for Hailey's face to pinch any tighter, but it did, and he knew why. Once upon a time, she had been that waitress. That nobody — at least in the eyes of men like Jonathan. Which meant the jerk had just nailed his own coffin shut.

Hailey looked at Tim and gave the faintest possible nod. He nodded back. Yeah, he'd had about enough too.

"I've said everything I need to say. Goodbye, Jonathan." Hailey strode to the door then whirled. "And I mean goodbye."

"You'll regret this," Jonathan snarled, stepping in front of her.

Tim would have tossed the asshole out the nearest window if Hailey hadn't shoved him aside first. "Regret meeting you? Yes. But you'll be the one regretting things soon. I'll get a restraining order if you or any of your wacko security guys come anywhere near me, and I'll go to the press with every detail of your sick wedding plan. I'm sure that will look good on your record when you run for office."

Jonathan opened his mouth in horror, but Hailey flicked her eyes away from him and looked at her mother in a mix of sorrow and disgust. "I'll call you, Mom."

"You'll call me?" Her mother's eyes widened in outrage.

Hailey nodded firmly. "Sometime. Whenever I'm ready to talk to you without screaming. Goodbye."

Then she walked out, leaving her mother and Jonathan staring as if they'd didn't know Hailey had it in her.

Tim followed immediately. Well, he wasn't the least bit surprised. Hailey had a hell of a lot more than a pretty face going for her. She had guts and more soul than both of those two crooks — yes, crooks — combined.

The door to the teahouse swung shut behind him, making the glass panel rattle. Of course, Hailey's mother snatched it open a second later and called out, "Now, you listen to me. . . "

Hailey didn't listen, though, and neither did Tim. Hunter and Connor were waiting outside, ready to escort Hailey's mother and Jonathan onto the helicopter.

"Hailey!" Jonathan yelled.

"Miss Crewe?" the portly lawyer murmured as Hailey swept by.

"What a goddamn circus," Connor muttered.

Tim rushed to catch up with Hailey, but she didn't stop until she reached the motorcycle at the far end of the lot. There, she closed her eyes, huffing and puffing like she'd just blown a house down. A big, ugly, brick house she'd probably never dreamed of demolishing until then.

"That circus is my life," she whispered.

Tim took her hand and kissed her gently on the knuckles. "Not any more, it isn't." He handed her a helmet and nodded toward the motorcycle. "Can I offer you a ride?"

Her smile was weak and weary, but it was still a smile. "Yes, please."

Chapter Fourteen

If it hadn't been for Tim's reassuring bulk right in front of her — or the powerful roar of the motorcycle engine he gunned down the road — Hailey might have burst into tears. Instead, she nestled her head between his shoulders, letting the scenery blur in the periphery of her vision. The helmet muffled sound, giving her even more of a cocoon to hide away in. And instead of breaking down, she fumed.

Her own mother, an accomplice to a crime. And Jonathan — the arrogant bastard. Had he really thought she would embrace his plan?

Apparently so, because he had turned a shade of red she'd never seen before and stormed out of the teahouse after her. Too bad Tim's friends had stopped him. She'd missed the perfect opportunity to kick Jonathan in the balls.

She dug her fingers into Tim's leather jacket and rocked her head from side to side. Connor was right. Her life had become a circus.

Tim let go of the handlebar long enough to cover her right hand with his, and his words echoed through her mind. *Not any more, it isn't.*

She smiled, if only briefly. The truth was, that circus had at least one more hoop she'd have to jump through when the press found her — the nasty, prying Hollywood press, not that sweet woman from the Maui Times. But after that, maybe there was a light at the end of the tunnel.

"Want me to go faster?" Tim shouted over his shoulder.

She laughed. Was that man-therapy for times like this? Well, she was ready to give anything a try. "Yes, please."

He revved so hard, the front tire nearly peeled off the ground, and she shrieked. A good kind of shriek, which she followed up on by clamping onto his back as tightly as a baby baboon.

She couldn't actually see Tim grin, but she could feel it, and it made her smile too.

"Thank you," she whispered. Too softly for him to hear above the whipping of the wind, but heck — maybe he could sense it the same way she could sense things about him.

"Too bad," she sighed when he finally parked at the plantation barn.

He turned to look over his shoulder. "Too bad?"

"I was enjoying that ride. Feeling free," she admitted.

He grinned, and a tiny bit of the bad boy showed. "Want to go back out?"

She did, but she shook her head. "Time to face the music, I guess."

He took her hand. "You already did, and you were amazing."

She snorted. He was the amazing one. She was the one with dysfunctional relationships and a mess of a life.

Her eyes strayed over the property. Lucky Tim. Smart Tim. He kept to himself way out in this quiet corner of Maui. Would she ever find a way to do the same?

She slid off the back of the motorcycle, reluctantly releasing her grip on him. It was time to make some plans and get on with her life.

"Hey," he called as she walked off. "Where are you going?"

She stopped, looked around, and gave a bitter laugh. "Good question. I have no idea. But you've done so much for me. It's time I stopped imposing and moved on, don't you think?"

Her heart beat a little faster, and she strained for the protest she was dying to hear. Something like, *No. Please, Hailey, don't go. Stay a little longer so we can see where things between us go.*

Their chemistry was undeniable, and she'd give anything for a chance to get to know Tim more intimately — ideally, when her mess of a life calmed down. She was sure he wanted that, too, but something always seemed to put on the brakes.

Tim's eyes grew so bright, she could swear they glowed, and he opened his mouth to reply. She leaned forward, stiff as a board, telling herself not to wish or hope too hard. But then Tim froze and hardened up all over again. When he spoke, his voice was gruff.

"I guess so."

Hailey swallowed hard, but the leaden feeling of disappointment still pressed on her chest. Okay, he didn't want her. Or he did, but he wasn't ready to go there. Had he been burned by some heartless woman in the past? Was he turned off by the realities of who she was?

She was about to force her chin up and breeze away when Tim took her hand and smiled that bittersweet *I wish things were different* smile. Then he murmured, "Come on. Coffee time."

He waited, giving her every opportunity to resist. But she didn't have any resistance left in her — especially not for him.

"Coffee sounds good."

They walked side by side to his house, where he led her around the back. There was a little lean-to there that he'd turned into a patio, with one chair, a rickety table, and a gorgeous view of the dips and rises of the plantation, all leading to a triangle of incredibly blue ocean visible between the slopes.

He waved around apologetically. "Someday this will be a nice terrace, with sliding doors to the living room. But for now, I have to walk around."

She stepped to follow him, but he shook his head. "You sit. Relax. Think. I'll be right back."

Seconds later, he returned, carrying a second chair that didn't match the first, yet somehow fit perfectly. Like the table, which looked like a recycled strip of fence laid sideways over a sturdy frame. Obviously, Tim had a penchant for repurposed woodwork.

"Just one more second..." he said, disappearing again.

Hailey stood at the edge of the patio, fingering the leaves of a coffee plant that grew near the roof post. She leaned over, sniffing its sweet scent. Small green beads were starting to form amidst the tiny white flowers. Someday, Tim would be able to pluck coffee beans right from his patio.

"Cool," she whispered into the wind.

If only she could stay and watch those buds grow.

A finch flew over the bushes, showing a rose-colored belly and pink beak. Hailey watched, trying to relax and not think.

When Tim came out with two steaming mugs and coffee cake, her eyebrows shot up, but he just shrugged. "My mom did this when I was little. When she'd had it with everything, including us." He flashed a half smile as he set the mugs and plates on the table. "Connor and I were kind of a handful, in case you didn't guess. So she would order us to go outside and give her ten minutes of peace. And she'd just sit there, holding a mug of coffee. We'd sneak over to watch her, and neither of us got it. She didn't drink the coffee — she'd just hold it with both hands and watch the steam swirl in the air. And she barely touched the cake." He laughed. "That's what we found totally crazy. But sometimes, I catch myself doing the same thing. Every time we lost a guy on a mission—"

His eyes clouded over, and his face turned dark.

Hailey's throat went dry. She'd been so wrapped up in her own troubles, she'd forgotten to put things into perspective. She looked down, studying Tim's callused hands, if not his face. What awful experiences might he have endured? What memories still cropped up in his dreams?

Tim cleared his throat. "Anyway, I do it now too. I get the coffee and cake out, just like her. Not as good as your coffee, of course." He faked a smile, trying to lighten the mood.

Hailey smiled, hiding the sadness inside. Both of them needed to start a whole new chapter in their lives. Too bad it wasn't in the cards that they could try that together.

She cupped her mug in both hands and took a sip. "It's great," she said, looking deep into his eyes. Then she set the mug down and picked up the coffee cake. "But there's no way I'm just looking at this cake."

He laughed and picked up his own, watching her. Daring her, almost.

She took a huge bite and nearly moaned at the taste. "See?" she mumbled through the crumbs. "You're corrupting me."

He shook his head. "Nah. Just helping you find freedom again."

Finding freedom for the first time was more like it, but she wasn't about to spoil the moment with those details.

A minute ticked by peacefully, and she wished it were an hour. Life was so much clearer from a place like this. A modest place in peaceful surroundings with a huge view. Her eyes slid over to Tim, already regretting the future she would never have with him. Her mouth filled with a bitter taste — not the coffee, but the memory of Jonathan.

"You okay?" Tim murmured, tuned in, as ever, to the slightest change in her mood. Hurrying to make things better if he could.

She made a face. "Just wondering what I ever saw in Jonathan."

A few quiet seconds ticked by before Tim spoke. "Freedom?"

She sighed. "Obviously, I was kidding myself. But, yes." She closed her eyes, remembering. "I think I saw a way back to a quieter, simpler life. He has a ranch in Montana. Two thousand acres of peace and quiet. Kind of a play ranch, but still. It was easy to picture myself there."

"Why not buy your own ranch?" Tim asked softly.

She frowned. "And live way out in the middle of nowhere alone?" She shook her head. "I like the idea of settling down in a quiet, out-of-the-way place with someone special." *Someone like you,* she nearly said. "But not alone. Besides, a ranch is a lot of work." She smiled faintly. "I do have a little land way out in northern Montana. My great-grandparents lived there for years. Just a little cabin." She laughed out loud as a new realization came to her. "My mother was always pushing for something bigger and better, but I guess all I really want is a small, cozy place. Like my great-grandparents' cabin."

"Like the house at Pu'u Pu'eo," Tim added with a smile.

She nodded and waved around. "Like this house."

Tim's eyes caught hers, and she saw an entire happy future unwind in them. A future she'd love to share, but oops. He'd already made it clear the answer was no. And if she didn't respect that, she'd be no better than Jonathan.

"Anyway," she said, moving on quickly. "Maybe that's where I'll start. That place in Montana. I could fix it up and finally do it justice." Then she frowned. "What does it say about me that I love the idea partly because my mother hated the place?"

Tim shook his head. "It just says you've had enough. Nothing wrong with that."

She took another bite of coffee cake, moving it slowly around her mouth with her tongue. She'd had enough, all right. Enough of strict diets and harried schedules. Enough of other people running her life.

A footpath led down the center of the property, and the sight of Dell sauntering toward the main house brought back the memory of what she'd seen that morning.

"That," Hailey said without thinking. "That's what I want."

Tim looked skeptical. "You want Dell?"

She play-kicked his foot. "No, I do not want Dell." *I want you.* "I want to be able to tune everything out. To concentrate on me."

Tim laughed. "Dell is good at that, all right." He put his elbows on the table and rested his chin in his hands. "What else do you want?"

She snorted. "Where do I start?" But then she caught herself. "No, that's not fair. I already have so much. Shouldn't be greedy, you know."

But Tim insisted. "Seriously. Run with it. What do you want?"

She stirred her coffee and licked the spoon, watching the liquid swirl. "Peace, I guess. Quiet. Time to think."

Tim nodded her on.

She considered. "I want to be normal. Meet normal people. Do normal things."

He tilted his head. "Like what?"

It was funny how fine company and fresh air got her thinking. "Going out for a meal. Just something simple, like we did on the beach. Before Lamar came along." She frowned then pushed away the bad parts of that memory. "I'd go for a walk through town, just because. Window-shop. Maybe even look at the stars."

"The stars, huh?"

She sighed. "Yeah. Kind of hokey, huh?"

He shook his head. "No. Not in the least."

Licking one finger, she collected the last of the crumbs from her plate and held it up. "See? Greedy."

He laughed. "If everyone used your definition of greedy, the world would be a better place. Want another piece?"

She did, but she'd already overindulged and was about to say as much when Tim spoke.

"One more day."

She blinked. "What?"

"Stay. Please. Just one more day. It will give you a little more time to figure things out, and it will give me time to...uh..." A sly look came over his face as he trailed off.

"To what?"

He shook his head and stood quickly. "Not telling. Not yet."

She stared. What was he up to?

"Do you trust me?" he murmured.

She snorted. "Do you have to ask?"

He grinned. "Okay, then. You stay one more day and figure out what you'll do next. In the meantime, I have some planning to do too." He checked his watch. "Two hours, maybe three. You okay with that?"

She stared. "And then what?"

He flashed a mysterious smile. "Leave it to me."

Chapter Fifteen

"Not sure that's such a great idea, man," Dell said, scratching his ear.

Tim grimaced. He knew perfectly well that planning a day out for Hailey wasn't a good idea. But still...

"She deserves it, damn it."

She did. A little normalcy made special because she'd missed all the little things for so long. Things he could relate to, having hankered for them after so many tours of duty in dusty corners of the globe.

"Not sayin' she doesn't." Dell's voice slowed to a concerned drawl as he continued. "But it's gonna be awfully hard to let her go after." Tim scoffed, but Dell pressed on. "I've seen the way you look at her."

Tim scowled. "What?"

"The way you look at her. And not just because she's gorgeous, even if she is."

"Bet your ass it's not about that," he snarled. Hailey was so much more than a pretty face. She was like... like one of those caged animals he'd always yearned to set free.

Dell stuck his hands up in defense. "That's the scary part, man. It's exactly the way Connor looked at Jenna all that time he tried to resist her. Do I need to remind you he failed?"

Failed? Tim's bear protested. *He succeeded. He won his mate in the end.*

But that was different, and Tim knew it, because Hailey would never accept his shifter side.

Yes, it would hurt like hell to let her go. But he wanted to give her this one last gift. It had taken everything he had to tame his inner grizzly's urges to claim her outright, but now, he had the upper hand. At least, he hoped he did.

Dell leaned closer. "Better to cut your losses while you're ahead, man. Let her go."

Inside, Tim's bear roared and raged, but Tim held perfectly still. "Just do it," he barked, then caught himself. "Please. I need to do this, and I need your help."

Dell sighed and ran a hand over his stubbly chin. He'd shaved that morning, but thick blond scruff had already grown in. By evening, he'd have a pretty decent beard. Typical lion shifter, in other words.

"I'll do it, but I only have until six. Same with Chase. We have to work tonight."

Tim nodded curtly. "Thanks."

Dell sighed. "Not sure you'll be thanking me later." Then he slapped Tim on the back. "Love hurts, man. Better you remember that."

Tim would have snorted if Dell's words hadn't had a flat ring of pain. Whatever had happened to Dell, it happened before they'd met, and Dell had never talked about it. Tim guessed the Casanova act had to do with Dell protecting his heart. The lion didn't mess around with as many women as his reputation suggested, but even when he did get involved, he refused to open his heart.

"Dell! Dell!" Joey ran up, waving and grinning.

"Heya, Joey," Dell called, brightening immediately.

"Want to play tag?"

"Tag? Hell yes. I'm it." He roared and sprinted at Joey, who squealed and ran as Dell made one exaggerated leap after another, purposely missing the boy each time.

Tim watched them go. Refusing to grow up was another one of Dell's self-defense mechanisms. The lion shifter practically made irresponsibility an art form. But he would follow through on his promise, Tim knew. Which meant Hailey would have double the security for the first half of what he had planned.

And that meant everything was falling into place. Hunter had assured him that Hailey's mother and Jonathan had left

Maui. And he'd already met with Connor, who'd done background checks on both. The mother was an open-and-shut case, but Jonathan...

"I'm telling you, those people are bad news," Connor had said. "Should have known by the double last name."

"Known what?"

Connor wrinkled his nose. "Old money. Oil money. Pure snobs."

Yeah, you could say Connor still had a chip on his shoulder about that kind of thing, even with Jenna's influence to file down the rougher patches of his soul.

"The dad is a major player, like you guessed. The oldest son is running for Senate, and all indications are that he'll win. The third son is in rehab, not that they're calling it that." Connor paused long enough to shake his head before going on. "There's a sister who's engaged to another oil baron, and word has it they're looking to expand the empire."

"So what's with running for public office, then?" Tim had asked.

"Think about it. There's not much new oil left to discover. It's all about getting access to protected land. And with a couple of sons in the Senate..."

Tim nodded slowly. "They could push through new laws making it easier to drill."

The very thought of pristine lands opened up to oil concerns made him sick. The last refuge for so many bears and other free-roaming mammals would be destroyed.

"The bastards are slick enough to pull it off, too," Connor added. "They have contacts in all the right places, not to mention the ability to lie with a straight face, even if it's on their mother's grave."

Tim's bear claws pushed toward the surface when he thought of Jonathan dragging Hailey into that world. But he'd harbored enough anger for one day. Jonathan was gone, as was Lamar, who was being watched by Kai's contacts on the mainland. Hailey would be safe, so he could concentrate on giving her what she needed most.

Freedom, even if it was just a taste.

Freedom, his bear murmured as he strode across the property.

"Don't forget this," Connor said, coming up with an envelope addressed to Hailey from a lawyer's office, delivered care of the Kapa'akea Resort.

Tim felt a couple of ID and credit cards inside, and Connor grinned. "Good news. Now she can go home."

Tim nearly growled, but Connor softened his expression and added, "Better for both of you, you know."

Yeah, he knew. But damn it, he was trying out pretending for a change.

Connor froze, studying him closely. *Really* closely. "Or maybe not better," he concluded. "You serious about her?"

Tim kept his lips in a tight, thin line. If he let one or two of his feelings out, the rest might follow, and that wouldn't do.

A faint smile formed on Connor's lips. "I guess you are."

Tim frowned. No, he wasn't. He couldn't be.

Yes, I am, his bear insisted. *It's destiny.*

Connor leaned in and spoke in a hush. "Sometimes you got to fight for what you want, you know? If you really want it, that is."

Tim stared at the ground. He'd never shied away from fighting for a just cause, no matter how slim the odds. But the odds of Hailey accepting him — a shifter who could change into a wild beast — were damn near impossible after what Lamar had done.

"What if it's a losing battle?" he muttered, kicking the ground.

Connor tipped his head one way then the other and finally backed away. "Your call, man. All I'm saying is the heart doesn't lie."

Tim closed his eyes. A lying heart wasn't his problem. The fact that he was a shifter was.

"Gotta go," he murmured, turning away. There was no use torturing himself. He had an evening with Hailey — one evening to squeeze a whole lifetime into. And damn it, he'd make it good.

So he took off, concentrating on putting the rest of his plan in place. Then he forced himself to stretch his usual five-minute shower to fifteen and took out the straight-blade razor he saved for important occasions. Which meant he was using it for the first time in years, because nothing had ever felt quite as important as this.

Joey wandered by the back of the barn where the men's showers were and stopped at the sight of the blade.

"Wow. Can I touch it?"

Tim grinned. Cynthia would have a fit if he let her son anywhere near that razor. Which made it awfully tempting to do just that. Cynthia needed to loosen up — a lot. But he wasn't about to get in hot water with the dragon shifter on an evening as important as this.

He held out the tin cup of shaving cream. "Sorry, kiddo. No razor. But do you want to whip this up?"

Never in the history of mankind had anyone whipped shaving cream as earnestly as Joey did. When he was done, Tim turned a bucket over as a seat and let Joey watch as he moved the blade over his neck and chin. Somewhere in the distance, a bird sang, and a truck rumbled by on the distant road. Otherwise, the plantation was quiet enough to hear the dull scrape of the blade.

"What do you think?" he asked Joey after finishing one side.

Joey pointed. "You missed a spot."

He dabbed a bit of cream on Joey's nose and had a closer look in the mirror. "You're good at this, kiddo."

Joey nodded eagerly. "Daddy used to shave like this."

Tim's jaw clenched. Shit. No wonder the kid was so fascinated. But, damn. What exactly did a guy say to something like that? Tim didn't know squat about Joey's father other than he'd died not too long ago in a dragon fight.

"Oh, yeah?" He forced himself to continue. Deadbeat dads like his own, he could write a book about. But losing a devoted father...

"Yep," Joey said. He was smiling, which was good. "But his hair was red."

145

Tim stopped long enough to tousle Joey's. "Like yours, huh?" The kid grinned from ear to ear. "I guess that means you'll be a mighty dragon someday, too."

"Someday," Joey said, nodding earnestly.

Tim swallowed away the lump in his throat and got to work on the other side. "So I guess I can teach you how to shave like this someday."

Joey practically jumped off the bucket in glee. "You will?"

"You bet." Tim wiped the cream off his face and turned so Joey could see both sides. "How do I look?"

"Nicer," Joey said promptly.

Tim laughed. "Nicer? What do I look like most of the time?"

Joey shrugged. "Like a bear. A really strong one."

Tim ran a hand over his chin and checked the mirror. He supposed that translated to menacing. Well, *nicer* worked for him, especially tonight.

He took the mug and swirled the brush on each of Joey's cheeks, making him giggle.

"Here," Tim said, lifting Joey so he could look in the mirror. "Now you can practice." He took Joey's index finger and ran it along each cheek like a blade. "Oops. Missed a spot." Then he covered the boy's head with the towel and gave him a good rub. "All set?"

Joey popped out of the towel, beaming. His hair was a mess, but what the heck. The important thing was, a conversation that could have gone either way had wrapped up on a good note.

"All set," Joey replied.

"Well, I gotta go. What are you doing tonight?"

Joey jumped off the bucket. "Mommy and I are watching *Jurassic Park.*"

"Not too scary?"

Joey shook his head, then looked around and whispered, "I cover my eyes on the scary parts."

Tim laughed and patted him on the back. "I do that too. Have a good time."

And off the kid ran, leaving Tim to dress in his best jeans and his only polo shirt. He walked home, lost in thoughts of mothers and fathers. Of families that stuck together through thick or thin. Of resilience and the joy to be found in little things.

He slowed, sniffing the breeze.

Little things, his bear murmured, nodding him toward the right side of the path.

He plucked a perfect white plumeria and twirled it in his fingers the rest of the way home. The closer he came, the faster his pulse skipped. And when his nose led him around the back to where Hailey sat on his makeshift patio, he stopped. She was cupping a fresh mug of coffee with her eyes closed and her head tipped back. Her hair shone in the afternoon sun, and a sheet of paper lay on the table before her, full of notes, circles, and cross-outs. Her plan for the future, he supposed. There was even a sketch of a house in the corner. Her cabin in Montana, maybe?

He was seized by the urge to grab that piece of paper, crumple it up, and throw it away, as if that would prevent Hailey from leaving. But he got himself under control and went back to pretending — a habit that had more going for it than he'd ever appreciated before. Hailey was right. Pretending was okay every once in a while.

He cleared his throat and watched her eyes flutter open. The sky-blue color intensified as she took him in.

"Hi. Oh, wow." Her eyebrows jumped up, and she scrambled to compose herself. "I mean, you look nice. Special occasion?"

He grinned and held out a hand. "Yep."

The moment Hailey slipped her hand into his, he warmed, and he had to work hard not to pull her into a hug. When he tucked the flower behind her ear, she smiled, and his bear chuffed at her trust.

"And the occasion is...?" she asked.

"You okay with a surprise?"

She laughed. "As long as it doesn't include a wedding or a visit from someone I don't want to see."

He shook his head immediately. "No weddings. No visits. Just me."

He hadn't intended for the last two words to come out so husky, but they did, and that energized, crackling feeling set into the air again. That whisper from the depths of the mountains, telling him she was the one.

Hailey caught her bottom lip with her teeth and leaned closer. Her gaze fell to his lips, and when she spoke, her voice was husky too.

"Sounds like a good surprise."

He nodded. "I promise."

Which was a little scary, because how could he be sure she'd like what he had planned?

Her eyes drifted up and down his body, taking their time. "Is there a dress code for this surprise?"

He shook his head. "Nope. You're perfect just the way you are."

Yes, he meant that in more ways than one. And yes, watching her blush made his blood rush.

He took a deep breath, because this was it. "Okay, then. Ready to taste freedom?"

Hailey's smile stretched, and her eyes shone. "You bet I am."

Chapter Sixteen

Tim led Hailey to the barn and motioned around, pretending he was as cool on the inside as on the outside.

"So, lady's choice. Do you prefer the stylish comfort of the Toyota..." He pointed to the battered old pickup he shared with the other guys. "Or the — what's the word? — exhilaration of the motorcycle?"

Hailey didn't hesitate. "If we're talking freedom, it's gotta be the motorcycle."

A little shot of adrenaline went through him. He couldn't agree more, plus riding the bike meant he got to keep Hailey nice and close.

"Perfect," he said, pulling two jackets from hooks on the wall.

The Harley was one of Connor's few splurges, and whenever he and Jenna weren't going for a joyride, the others were welcome to use it.

"I bet Joey loves this thing," Hailey said.

He laughed. "Cynthia hates it, but she did let Dell take Joey for a ride around the grounds. They were going like five miles an hour — barely fast enough to stay upright — but Cynthia was still white as a sheet. Joey was thrilled, though."

"Lucky kid." Hailey winked.

Well, yes and no, but it wasn't the time to elaborate. Tim handed Hailey his leather jacket and took Connor's for himself. No way was he going to allow another man's scent to envelop Hailey all evening, even if it was his happily mated brother's.

The satisfaction he got from watching her nonchalantly zip it up gave his bear all kinds of dangerous ideas.

Keep her. Tell her. Make her ours, it growled.

He ignored it, busying himself with folding extra sweaters and a blanket into the saddlebags.

"Whoa. We are staying on Maui, right?" she joked.

He grinned. "Yep. But it gets cold where we're going. Or so I've heard."

"You've never been there?" He shook his head, which seemed to make her even happier. "Cool. So it's kind of a surprise for both of us," Hailey decided.

Laughing had never come easier to him than it did around Hailey. "You can say that."

When he handed her a helmet, she only hesitated to remove the flower tucked behind her ear and place it on a shelf on the wall.

He pulled on a helmet, threw a leg over the seat, and kicked the engine to life. Then he did his best James Dean and nodded Hailey onto the back. "Hop on."

"Yes, sir."

Hailey laughed and slid smoothly into place like they went for joyrides every day. The ride to meet her mother had been all about business, but this. . .

It really was a joy, cruising up the highway with her, even if the speed limit kept him to a mere forty-five. All those scents rushing his bear nose at once — scents he could pick apart and enjoy since they weren't riding off to another confrontation for a change. The earthy smell of the mountains mixed with the sweet fragrance of gardenia. The spicy smell of ginger, and the duller scent of the tall grasses growing on the mountain slopes. The motion was enjoyable too, like riding a horse. He leaned into each curve, and Hailey did too, both of them moving in perfect harmony. Even on the straightaways, she kept her hands firmly around his waist.

He could have whooped with joy — and that was just the first part of their evening out.

Hailey tensed when they zipped past the turnoff to the Kapa'akea Resort, but by the time they slowed to cruise through Lahaina, she was swiveling her head left and right. It was almost a shame to pull over, but they had a lot of riding yet to come, so he rolled into a parking spot and turned off the engine.

"Are we there?" Hailey asked, leaning over his shoulder.

Tim fought off the temptation to turn and kiss her. "This is just our first stop." He motioned around the historic town.

It was midweek, and not a cruise ship day, which made the streets quieter than usual. Still, parking would have been a nightmare if they hadn't come on the bike, and it was a good thing he'd told Hailey to bring her cap, too. With the bill pulled low and her hair mussed from the helmet, the likelihood of anyone recognizing her was slim.

She chuckled, running her hands along the hat's bill. "This is turning out to be even handier than I thought."

He laughed. It was the pink cap he'd bought for her back on that fateful day in Waikiki.

Fate, his bear murmured. *You know it is.*

Yes, it was, but some things weren't meant to be.

"You okay?" Hailey asked, touching his arm.

He faked a smile and motioned down the street. "Yep. Right this way."

As they walked, he scanned the streets, checking for any sign of trouble — and for his backup team. Within a block, he caught sight of Dell, shadowing them from across the street. Chase appeared a few steps ahead of them on the sidewalk, slowing whenever Hailey did to check out a shop's T-shirts or wood carvings.

"This is great," she gushed, motioning around.

He took her hand. It was great, and not just for the centuries-old, whaling port feel of the place with its swinging store signs and long, covered balconies overhead.

"Oh." She stopped, noticing Chase for the first time. "Look. Let's say hi."

Hi and bye, Tim nearly grumbled, grateful for his brother's support but greedy enough to want to keep Hailey to himself.

Chase waved, making a pretty good show of pretending he just happened to be there. A small miracle in itself, because Chase still hadn't mastered all the nuances of human behavior, not even years after coming in from the wild.

151

Dell ambled up, all cheery and innocent, like he just had happened to stumble along.

All clear? Tim grunted into his friend's mind.

Dell nodded. *Roger. Not an enemy shifter within miles, and I mean within miles of Maui, not just Lahaina. You can enjoy your date.*

Not a date, Tim protested. It was just a nice night out for Hailey's sake.

Dell raised one fair eyebrow. *You sure about that?*

Tim scowled, but hell. It did feel like a date. Hailey stood nice and close, warming his side, and her hand felt so right in his. The sun was slowly sinking toward the horizon, and the sound of a street musician drifted down the block.

"Hi, Chase. Oh, Dell. You're here too," Hailey said.

Chase gave his usual shy smile, while Dell swooped right in to kiss Hailey on both cheeks, ignoring Tim's growl of warning.

"Hey! Good to see you. Enjoying town?"

"Sure am." She nodded and pressed back into Tim's side.

He smirked at Dell. *See? Mine.*

Dell smirked back. *All too evident, buddy. Just remember not to fall too deep.*

Like Tim needed a reminder.

"You guys on the way to work?" Tim asked as if he didn't know.

"Yep. Right over there. The Lucky Devil." Dell pointed out the bar to Hailey.

"We're making one stop first," Chase added, sounding more insistent than usual.

Dell rolled his eyes. "Of course. Because we really need a drink before going to work at a bar."

But it didn't turn out to be that kind of drink, as Tim discovered when Chase led them another two blocks to a truck standing at the edge of the seaside park. Chase's steps grew faster and his face more hopeful with every step.

What's this all about? Tim asked Dell.

Dell grinned. *I'll let you see for yourself.*

"Best smoothies in town," Chase said by way of explanation.

Tim stared. "Smoothies?"

Chase was a wolf shifter — a carnivore to the core. A guy who salivated over steaks and burgers while shunning just about everything else.

"I love smoothies," Hailey chirped, reading the menu.

Two tourists stepped away from the ordering window of the food truck, and Chase stepped up, bright and shiny as a kid at his first circus. "Hi."

Chase had never been much of a talker, but he didn't need to, not with his body language filling in the rest. He was as excited as a golden retriever. Tim could practically see his inner wolf wag its tail.

"Hi," the brunette in the smoothie truck breathed.

For a long minute, nothing happened except those two staring at each other.

"Hi," Chase murmured again.

Behold, Dell chuckled into Tim's mind. *A wolf in love.*

Tim blinked a few times. Chase was in love with the woman in the smoothie truck?

"Can I get you the usual?" she whispered to Chase in a tone more suited for something like, *Would you like to go out with me tonight?*

Not that she would ask him that outright. The woman seemed just as shy as Chase and just as quiet. A cute bookworm type with her hair done up in two simple braids.

Chase nodded eagerly. "Yes, please."

"Make it four," Dell said then looked at Hailey. "Okay with you?"

"Okay with me," she said cheerily.

The smoothie girl blinked a few times, noticing the others for the first time. "Oh. Right. Four."

"We'll just wait here," Dell said loudly, motioning Tim and Hailey off to the park.

"How long has that been going on?" Tim whispered.

Dell sighed. "A couple of weeks now. She's new in town."

Puppy love or the real thing? Tim threw the question directly into Dell's mind.

Dell laughed. *Pun intended?*

Hailey smiled, peeking back. Chase hadn't budged, watching the woman's every move. "They're cute."

Dell rolled his eyes. "Yeah. Cute. It's sickening."

Tim shot Hailey an apologetic look. "Dell isn't exactly a romantic."

"Of course I am," Dell protested. "Candlelight dinners by the water. Slow dancing. Champagne — the works. I just don't drag things out past their expiration dates."

Hailey chuckled, nestling closer to Tim, making him stand straighter, prouder. "I guess that works for some people." *Just not for me,* her tone said.

Me neither, Tim nearly said.

"Yeesh. Look at them," Dell muttered. The smoothie girl had handed Chase the first two cups, but they'd gotten stuck staring into each other's eyes all over again, each of them holding the cup as if that almost-contact was the highlight of their day. "I'll go pay, or we'll never get anywhere."

He headed over, leaving Tim and Hailey on their own.

"They are cute," Hailey insisted. "But that's kind of sad." She motioned to a man lying on a scrap of cardboard in the park.

Tim laughed. "He's not homeless. Just taking a siesta. It's an islander thing." He hadn't been in Maui that long, but he knew that much. "See?"

As he spoke, a woman in a flowing muumuu walked by. She arranged another square of cardboard on the grass and settled down on it, looking out over the ocean.

"Like a beach towel?" Hailey asked.

He nodded. And before he knew it, Hailey was skipping off toward a trash can.

"What are you doing?" he called.

"Tasting freedom." Hailey laughed, taking the sheet of cardboard propped beside the trash can. Left for that very purpose, Tim supposed. She dragged it over to the seawall, plonked down, and patted the space beside her. "Come on."

His cheeks stretched enough to hurt, out of practice after what had seemed like weeks of tension.

"My mother would be shocked," she murmured happily. "I might even try surfing."

He laughed and scooted a little closer until they were hip-to-hip. "That might have to wait. Red flag day tomorrow, according to Jenna. Dangerous waves, in other words."

She waved a hand breezily. "Horseback riding, then. Or maybe skateboarding."

He laughed outright at that one, and she laughed too. Even her eyes laughed as they locked with his, and his body warmed.

He dragged his eyes over to the ocean, and Hailey did too. Another quiet minute ticked by before either of them spoke.

"So, explain to me about your brothers," she murmured.

"Connor and I grew up on the Utah-Idaho border. Chase is our half brother from my dad's side."

He decided not to go into details about his deadbeat dad, a myriad shifter who could take any form he wanted. That explained why Tim was a bear shifter, like his mother, while Connor was a dragon, and Chase a wolf born to an all-wolf mother. Where their father was these days, Tim had no idea.

"We enlisted right after I graduated high school and re-upped a few times. All of us together. And then, we came here."

He looked out over the glittering ocean. Maui. His new home?

Hailey let a second skip by before asking in a hushed voice, "Is it hard?"

He looked over. "Is what hard?"

She made a vague gesture. "Transitioning back. Coming home."

The palm trees along the waterfront cast long shadows, and Tim stared off into the distance. Honestly, he hadn't given the subject much thought. Coming to Maui had been a lot like taking up a new post in the military. A much looser branch of the military, granted. He lived with the core of his old unit — his brothers and Dell, though his heart still ached for the buddy they'd lost in the last days of their service.

He yanked his mind away from that dark, slippery path and focused on the present. With the security work — not to mention Cynthia's strict leadership style — it didn't feel that different from the military, really.

"Not that hard," he murmured.

His bear snorted.

Okay, so he had done a good job of locking his emotions away for a long time. So long, he'd started to forget what many of them felt like. And anyway, it made more sense to keep himself removed. Logic worked. Logic got the job done without all the doubts and heartache that came from getting overly involved. And if he'd had that inner armor engaged for a little too long – nothing wrong with that, right?

But it feels good, his bear whispered. *Feeling feels good.*

He frowned, pulling up a few blades of grass. Feelings were fine as long as the emotions were good ones. But *bad* usually followed on the heels of *good*, and that was better avoided altogether.

Something warm and soft touched his shoulder, and the tension that had crept into his muscles eased away again. He glanced up to find Hailey touching him.

Nothing happened for the next minute. Well, nothing on the outside. But on the inside, he went all warm and mushy. His breathing slowed, and his pulse evened out. The sound of the surf filled his ears, and his heart swelled.

Mate, his bear sighed. *She's my mate.*

He took a deep breath, not wanting to believe it. But what other than a destined mate could calm his inner bear like that?

Hailey drew her hand back slowly, glancing at her fingers with an awed look, like maybe they were tingling or something. He sure was.

"Now, who's cute?" Dell teased, coming up with their smoothies.

Tim whipped around and growled. "Don't you have to get to work?"

Dell laughed. "Touché, my dear bear — er, buddy." He covered up with a laugh and turned away, dragging a reluctant Chase with him. "Have a nice evening."

"See you soon?" the smoothie lady called to Chase.

"See you soon," Chase said, as earnest as a knight taking a vow on one knee.

Someday, Tim would have to figure out who that woman was and how serious Chase was about her. But he could barely guard his own heart right now, let alone his brother's.

"Bye," Hailey said. Then she took a long, slurpy sip of her smoothie and smacked her lips. "Wow. That is good. And you know what?" she murmured, nice and close to Tim's ear.

He leaned in, determined to enjoy every second he had with her.

"I'm already having a nice evening," she whispered.

He smiled. "That was the plan. And it's not over yet."

Hailey looked about as excited as Joey had been at the prospect of shaving. "It's not?"

Tim sipped from his smoothie, shaking his head. "Nope." Then he ticked a list off his fingers. "So — being normal, doing normal things — check. Meeting normal people..." He faked a frown. "I'm not sure Dell and Chase count as normal—"

Hailey stuck an elbow in his ribs. "They're very sweet."

"Right. Sweet." Tim thought some more. "We've covered window-shopping too, which leaves dinner and stars, right?"

Hailey's eyes shone.

Tim knew he ought to have nodded and done something trivial like tapping his paper cup against hers in a toast. Giving her a jaunty *Yep* and leaving it at that. But the earth was humming under his body, and his heart was thumping hard. Hailey's lips were just inches from his, her scent calling to him.

"Dinner..." he murmured, leaning in, though food was the furthest thing from his mind.

Hailey leaned too, and her eyes dropped to his lips. "Stars," she whispered.

A whisper that melted into silence when his lips closed over hers in a soft kiss.

Chapter Seventeen

Hailey closed her eyes, tuning out everything except the soft touch of Tim's kiss. A kiss that was a lot like the sunset forming on the horizon — full of light and promise, like the best was yet to come.

Tim's lips moved in a silent whisper, and she cupped his cheek to stay close. Her thumb stroked his skin. Baby-soft was hardly the word for Tim — not even for his freshly shaved chin — but that's what she sensed. Soft skin, a gentle touch, and his leather-and-pine scent.

She couldn't care less about dinner, and stars were already shooting through her mind. So really, she could have spent the rest of the evening kissing on that scrap of cardboard in that oceanside park. But Tim gently pulled back and stopped a hair away from her lips. His eyes were closed, his jaw suddenly tense.

"Hey," she whispered in protest. "I liked that."

His lips curled into a faint smile. "I liked that too."

So why did he stop? She went on stroking his cheek, keeping him close. Feeling greedy because everything about him made her want more. Of course, he'd been the one telling her to *run with it* before, right?

She licked her lips, tipped her hat back, and leaned in. Their shoulders bumped as they kissed a second time, and this time, she hung on, sensing his inner battle. The push-pull that had him holding her close, then going stiff, and relaxing all over again.

Yes, she wanted to say. *Like that. Relax. Trust. Whatever you do, just please don't shut down.*

159

She tilted her head, getting closer, ignoring the outside world. Her heart pounded and her blood rushed.

Love. This had to be love, didn't it? Not confusion. Not anger, nor fear. Just a feeling of rightness, of coming home.

When she opened her mouth, Tim did the same, and their lips did a slow, sultry dance. His chest rose and fell as hers did, until he finally pulled away. She kept her eyes closed, relishing the sweep of his thumb over her lips.

"Beautiful," he whispered.

When she peeked, his eyes were closed, and she smiled. She'd heard *beautiful* a thousand times in her life — photographers murmuring behind their lenses, ad execs gloating over designs, hairdressers leaning back to admire their handiwork. But Tim was talking about the moment, not her.

"Beautiful," she echoed, leaning her forehead against his. Then she smiled and tapped the cardboard beneath them. "Even this."

The air moved with Tim's chuckle. "Fancy, huh?"

She opened her eyes and took him in. "Perfect." *Like you.*

He took a deep breath and opened his eyes then motioned around with his smoothie cup. "To cardboard, parks, and sunsets."

"To smoothies," she added. "And kisses."

He looked at her, chagrined. "Those kind of snuck up on me. Sorry."

"I'm not," she said. She nearly said more, too, before the moment passed. Something like, *I meant that I'm not the least bit sorry. Can I kiss you some more?*

But Tim spoke before she could, standing and offering his hand. "Come on."

"What about the sunset?"

He grinned. "It will be even better where we're going."

Well, that certainly piqued her curiosity, and she stood. They left the cardboard beside the trash can and walked back the way they'd come, making one stop along the way.

"The Lucky Devil?" she asked as he slowed.

Chase was at the door, checking IDs, but when he saw Tim, he handed over a takeout bag and said, "Have fun."

"So we're not eating there, I guess?" Hailey asked as Tim tugged her on.

He held up the bag. "Nope. Got takeout. I hope that's okay."

Anything was okay with her — especially things that stretched out a lovely night. So she looked on while he wiggled the package into the saddlebags. When he was done, she hopped on behind him, and a minute later, they were cruising through town. They passed another few blocks of shops and eateries and a huge tree hung with party lights.

"Where exactly are we going?"

He pointed ahead. "Up there."

She stared over his shoulder and gaped. "All the way up there?"

He nodded. "Yep."

He spoke casually, but he was pointing to Haleakala, the ten-thousand-foot volcano that formed most of Maui. They had circled part of the base the first time they'd driven to Pu'u Pu'eo, but the peak had always been hidden in a crown of clouds. Now, she could see right to the top.

"Wow," she murmured, hugging him closer. Not just *wow* to the view but *wow* to Tim. He hadn't just been listening earlier that day, he'd been planning — and planning big.

To her right, the sea and sky were one wall of red-tinted blue as the sun slowly sank. To her left, the mountains of West Maui reared up into jagged, cloud-kissed peaks.

"Thank you," she whispered.

She hadn't expected him to hear, but he surprised her by responding. "You can thank me later if it works out. I might have cut it a little too close."

She smiled. Obviously, kissing in the park hadn't been part of his plan. But, hell. Even if they missed watching the sun set from the top of the volcano, the ride was worth it.

Tim revved the engine, stretching the speed limit. Not long after, he turned right on a road that began to climb in earnest, first in a long, straight shot, then in a series of tight bends.

"Silversword," Tim called over his shoulder as they passed a tall, spiky plant at the side of the road.

161

She'd read about them in one of the dusty books at Pu'u Pu'eo. A plant that bloomed once a century, or so she recalled. A little like true love — something a person got one fleeting chance at, once in a lifetime, and then it was gone.

She tightened her arms around Tim's waist and closed her eyes.

Sometime later, he pulled over at a bend in the road — and just in time, too. They both slipped off their helmets and gazed west.

"Wow," Hailey breathed, squeezing his hand.

The rocky outlook wasn't all the way up the mountain, but the view went on for miles — hundreds of miles, it seemed like — overlooking several other islands and what looked like half the Pacific. Three cars had stopped at the same lookout, and people snapped photos. But not even a wide-angle lens could do that view justice, so Hailey imprinted the moment on her mind. The rich, heavenly red. The warmth of Tim's hand. The jiggle in her legs after all that time on a humming motorcycle.

"Beautiful," she whispered.

Tim touched her cheek. "Your eyes are closed."

She shrugged. "It's so beautiful, seeing isn't enough to really take it in."

Tim went silent, and when she peeked, his eyes were closed too. Then he opened them, looked straight at her, and opened his mouth, suddenly serious. "Hailey, I really have to tell you—"

She leaned in, hoping for him to finally pour open his heart and soul. But one car beeped to another, and they both whipped their heads around. When she turned back, Tim was scratching his ear and looking at his feet. Then he looked up, lips tightly pursed, and finally spoke.

"You want a sweater?"

She shook her head. No, she didn't want a sweater. She wanted him to find the words he'd had on the tip of his tongue a few seconds earlier. But Tim kicked the ground, and the moment passed.

"I'm good," she whispered, climbing back onto the bike behind him.

The air grew colder as they climbed, but dusk stretched on and on. The sky seemed to go on forever, as did the last tones of sunset. Eventually, night won, spreading a dark blanket over the island, and Hailey listened to the motorcycle hum, clinging to Tim's warmth. When he pulled over and turned off the engine at the very peak, the silence was striking.

She pulled off her helmet and sat still for a moment, soaking it all in. Shivering a little. It was that cold, but incredible all the same. The wind whispered over the moonscape that unfolded around her, and crickets chirped.

"Wow," she breathed, looking over the crater, the views, and the sky.

"Hang on," Tim whispered, opening the saddlebags.

Hailey hugged herself, watching his every move. The man had promised her dinner and stars, and he meant it, all right. Within five minutes, they were huddled side by side at a picnic table with a blanket tucked over their shoulders. Tim struck a match, lighting a tiny candle lantern, and set it before them. The faint light flickered over the meal he unpacked and shone burgundy through a tiny bottle of wine.

"Screw top," he said, showing it to her with an apologetic shrug.

She laughed, and the sound carried through the night. Like anything could ruin her night now.

"Best dinner ever," she said as he poured wine into two paper cups.

"You haven't tried it yet."

"Doesn't matter. I just know."

Dinner was delicious, as it turned out — fish cakes that were still warm, together with potato salad and French bread that went down perfectly with the wine.

"I guess it's supposed to be white, huh?" Tim murmured, looking into his cup.

She nudged him in the ribs. "Special rules apply to picnic dinners on top of volcanoes. Didn't you know?" She took another bite. "It's perfect. Oh! Look!" She pointed as a shooting star streaked across the sky. "Make a wish."

But Tim, to her surprise, shook his head. "Mine already came true."

His words warmed her, but they scared her, too. Her wishes reached far into the future, but Tim sounded like he was content with what he already had.

He tipped his face up to the night sky and pointed. "The Milky Way..."

She leaned against his shoulder and followed his finger across that bright highway in the sky.

"Big Dipper," she murmured, finding it close to the horizon.

"Great Bear," he corrected.

"Same thing, right?"

He shook his head. "Looks more like a bear."

"How?"

He pointed. "See that star? That's the bear's back, and over there is the tail."

She tilted her head. "Are you sure?"

He nodded firmly, making her laugh.

"What makes you such an expert in bears?"

He scrubbed his chin with one hand for longer than she would have expected. "I guess I've seen enough to know."

She laughed. "The few bears I've seen, I ran from too fast to see much of."

Funny, Tim didn't laugh. He didn't even chuckle, and she wondered what was wrong.

"Maybe they're not so bad," he said after a thoughtful pause.

She laughed. "I don't ever want to get close enough to find out for myself." She huddled closer to him under the blanket. Why had he gone so stiff? "Are you warm enough?"

He gave a jerky nod.

She pointed left, trying to get the conversation started again. "My grandfather used to show me the stars. But it's been a while. I'm pretty sure that's Draco over there."

He nodded. "Draco. The dragon."

She chuckled. "I like that one."

"Why?"

"Fictional creature. Nothing to worry about," she joked. But then she frowned. "But I guess I thought werewolves were fiction, too."

"Wolf shifter," he said, quietly correcting her.

Obviously, the man was a stickler for terminology, but she decided to let that go. Lamar was gone, and she was determined to enjoy her first night of freedom in a long time.

They contemplated the stars in silence, and Hailey's mind drifted. So much had happened in the past days — enough to make it feel like more time had passed. She felt as though she'd known Tim — well, maybe not for years, but months, at least. Heck, enough had happened in the past twenty-four hours to make her mind reel.

She held out her cup for a refill, then pulled it back. "Oops. I'm hogging it."

Tim shook his head and poured her the rest. "I'm driving."

She looked at him. That was Tim in a nutshell. Putting her first. Keeping her safe as he'd done from day one. Would she ever be able to repay him?

She snuggled closer, closing her eyes. Being on top of the world had a way of making her think big thoughts. Confusing thoughts, like what a contradiction Tim was. The man was like the volcano under her feet — dormant, yet full of power. Mysterious. Utterly reliable yet unpredictable at the same time.

She sighed. Maybe she ought to try shrinking things down. Tim was a man. She was a woman. The future was one big mystery, and all she knew for certain was that they had this night. So why not use it well?

She inched closer, yearning for his touch. Inhaling, because he smelled that good. A minute later, she was nuzzling him and humming inside. Or maybe humming out loud, because a sound reached her ears.

Her eyes had slid shut, and when she opened them, she realized it was Tim humming in satisfaction while rubbing his cheek against hers. Marking her, almost, the way an animal marked its territory.

"Mmm," she murmured, shifting toward him. The blanket slipped off her shoulder, but she didn't feel the least bit cold.

"Hailey," he whispered before covering her mouth with his.

At first, his kiss was soft and gentle, but it soon grew faster and harder. Hard enough to make her pulse race. His hands wandered upward from her waist, and she moaned into the kiss. She wrapped her arms around his neck, mashing her breasts against his chest. Then she broke away with a gasp.

"Turn around," she said, surprised by her own urgency.

Tim looked up at her with eyes as bright as the stars.

There was only so much legroom at that picnic table, and she had to fix that, fast. She stood and stepped to the outer side of the bench. "Like this."

Tim slid around, still seated with his eyes locked on hers.

Quickly, before she lost her nerve, Hailey rearranged the blanket over his shoulders then straddled him, tucking herself good and close.

His eyes went wide, but his hands held her firmly in place. "Hailey..."

She kissed him hard, delving deep. A fireball rolled through her veins, and she moaned. Tim was a volcano, all right; she could sense the molten lava heaving on the inside. The simmering passion, waiting to explode.

She'd started out sitting closer to his knees than his groin, but Tim tugged her tighter, and even through two layers of jeans — his and hers — she could feel how hard he was. How hungry for her. Their tongues twisted and dueled, and their chests bumped.

"Hailey," he rasped, drawing back.

She shook her head. No way was she going to let him hit the emergency brake now.

"I want this. I want you," she said, locking eyes with him. "And you want it too."

He gulped and nodded.

"So, what's holding you back?" she demanded, then hurried on without letting him reply. "I'm not talking forever, Tim. So just for now. Just for tonight. Everything else can wait." She was panting by then, her chest heaving up and down. "Gonna be a long ride down, you know," she whispered

166

in his ear, grinding over his hips. "It will be torture if we don't get this out of our systems now."

He closed his eyes and rocked under her. "Up here?"

She giggled. This was freedom, and she liked it. "Why not? We have our blanket. A perfectly good picnic table. No one to see us but the stars."

He caught her hands before she could dip into the waistband of his jeans. "I can't tell you how much I want that."

"So, what's stopping us?"

His eyes clouded, and she could see that battle all over again. But when she rocked her hips, the fire in his eyes flared, and he spoke one word in a low, gritty voice before slamming his mouth over hers.

"Nothing."

She moaned, triumphant but still burning for more. Her life had been full of invisible walls before she met Tim. But there, under the stars, she felt totally wild and free. A little reckless but never so sure of anything in her life. Finally, she had her man, and nothing was stopping them.

Nothing.

Chapter Eighteen

Tim closed his eyes, relishing the sweet rush of heat. Fighting with his inner beast had been torture, but now, losing control felt good. Ridiculously good, like a dam breaking, and all he could do was go with the flow.

"Yes..." Hailey groaned, making his inner bear preen.

Show her, the beast growled. *Show her how good we can make her feel.*

Oh, he'd show her, all right. And he had a feeling she'd show him, too.

He wrapped the blanket tighter around both their shoulders and slid his hands down her rear, tugging her even closer. Hailey whimpered and swept her tongue over his teeth. He let her take the lead, chasing her with his tongue, holding her close. But the need in him grew until holding her wasn't enough. He had to touch her. Taste her. Possess her.

Moving slowly — agonizingly slowly — he gauged her reaction to his hands on her ribs... on her belly... on her breasts...

Hailey moaned, pulling her sweater free of her jeans. "Yes. Please..."

She went back to kissing him — hard — so he explored her like a blind man, inching his hands upward until he'd found the clasp to her bra. A second later, he released it, letting her soft flesh spill into his hands. He started circling his thumbs, nearly groaning at the sensation. Her breasts were small and delicate, and her nipples were already peaked and hard. He flicked the coarsest part of his thumbs over them, making her moan and thrust her shoulders back.

"So good..." Hailey mumbled.

Her hands tangled with his, and a moment later, she helped him pull up her shirt. Not all the way over her head — the mountain air was crisp despite the inferno building between them — but far enough to reveal the lower edge of one pert breast. He popped her pink nipple into his mouth, and she cried out, hitting a high note.

"Yes. . ."

He couldn't hold back a happy huffing sound as he rolled his lips. Hailey stretched higher and arched back.

He consumed her. Gorged himself on her. Lapped away until he was sure she would say no. But Hailey whimpered in pleasure, begging for more.

Give the lady what she wants, his bear ordered.

He nipped and suckled until his inner bear was roaring, and then he did it some more, because Hailey was going wild, and so was he. Dangerously wild.

Switching from one side to the other, he scrubbed his chin across her sensitive flesh. His bear was close enough to the surface to have made his clean shave grow out to a stubble, but Hailey didn't seem to mind. On the contrary, she clutched his head closer and moaned.

"Do that again. Please, do that again."

Hell yeah. He'd do it as much as she wanted.

The starlight was just bright enough for him to sneak a peek. Her nipples glistened like jewels from all the suckling he'd done, and he just about thumped his chest like a caveman. But he wasn't there to look, and he sure as hell wasn't going to let Hailey get cold, so he opened his mouth wide and went back to work.

Ha. His bear chuffed. *Work.*

Again, his mind registered that something was missing. Her necklace. In fact, he couldn't remember seeing it all day. But he wasn't going to stop and ask about it now. Not with Hailey quivering under his touch and making little coos of pleasure. He circled her nipple, then tweaked it, and finally smoothed it over with his tongue.

"Again," she murmured desperately. "Again."

It shouldn't have been possible for a man ten thousand feet above sea level to feel even higher, but Hailey did that to him. His mind grew fuzzier and fuzzier until all he sensed was the driving need to satisfy her. His jeans grew painfully tight, his touches ever rougher.

Hailey's cries held a note of wonder, and her breath hitched in surprise anytime he switched gears. He wasn't her first lover, but her cries were those of newfound pleasure.

So give her more, his bear rumbled inside.

Hailey must have been on the same wavelength, because she stood, fumbling with the clasp of her jeans.

"Damn it." She gave up on hers and went for his like a woman possessed.

Tim's eyes grew wide when he realized what she wanted, kneeling before him like that.

"Help me." She looked up at him with shining eyes. "Help me get these off."

He stared. "Are you sure?"

She laughed. "Do I look sure?"

She looked sure as sin, and he could practically hear the devil cackling when she licked her lips.

He stood just high enough to pop his jeans open — and nearly sighed in relief. When he shoved his boxers aside, his cock sprang free, hard and high.

Hailey's eyes bugged out and her mouth fell open, but a split second later, she was licking her lips.

"Oh, yes," she murmured, hunching over him.

Oh, yes did not begin to describe the flames that ripped through his body the second she kissed the tip, and it certainly didn't describe the wave of pleasure that rocked him — literally rocked him — the second she sucked him in. But Tim couldn't come up with any better descriptor, so he kept his mouth shut. Which was hard, because holy hell, did that slow, sliding action feel good. The squeeze of her lips, the extra pressure of her tongue...

Tim wove his fingers into her hair and threw his head back, groaning softly. His eyes were open, but the stars blurred and circled like little comets as he rocked in place. He gulped, telling himself not to clutch her hair or pull her closer, but it was hard. Really hard, especially when Hailey came up for air with a faint smacking sound. Then she went down on him again, gripping his thighs tightly.

Down she went, right down to the base, taking him deep. When she pulled back, she did so slowly, and her lips tugged his foreskin when she reached the very tip. Then she pushed forward with her whole body, swallowing him up again.

Tim's breath came in ragged pants, and every muscle in his body coiled. Any second, he'd explode.

"Hailey," he rasped, tugging gently on her hair.

She mumbled something but didn't slow down one bit.

With a supreme effort, he straightened and held his breath.

"You don't like that?" She looked up in surprise.

He'd made a mess of her hair, giving her a wild look that just about pushed his bear over the edge.

"I love it. But I want you in on this."

She grinned, ready to lean over him again. "Oh, I'm in on this, all right."

He shook his head and tugged her to her feet, hooking his fingers into the waistband of her jeans. "No, I mean all in. Both of us at the same time."

Her eyes sparkled. "All in. I like the sound of that. But I do want a rain check." She touched the tip of his cock, making it twitch.

It was amazing how his girl next door could not only turn on moments of *supermodel*, but *sex kitten* too.

"You got it," he growled.

She leaned in, capturing his mouth in a huge, sloppy kiss. Then she swiped her tongue over his a few times, spreading around an incredible taste that was part him, part her.

He groaned. "You are definitely getting a rain check."

She stood back, grinning, and let her hands fly over the zipper of her jeans. The second she shoved down her pants, goose bumps rose all over her legs. He threw the blanket over her shoulders, keeping her covered while she toed off her shoes and shucked her jeans. But when she got to her panties, she stopped and raised her hands.

172

"All yours."

His bear growled, and it took all his willpower not to extend his claws and rip those panties off her with one sharp click.

All mine, the beast rumbled.

His fingers trembled as he hooked the sides of her panties and slowly rolled them down. All the way down, because he didn't want to miss an inch of those long, perfect legs. After helping her kick off the panties, he drew his hands all the way back up again.

"Come closer." His voice was all scratchy and low.

Hailey stepped forward, straddling his legs. He slid his hands around her waist and down to her rear, reaching up for a kiss at the same time.

"Nice," Hailey whispered, closing her eyes.

Another one of those words that didn't capture what he truly felt. Her ass was round and tight, and her wide stance offered him an open invitation to explore.

"Yes," she panted, keeping her mouth near his while he touched her. She was wet and warm inside, and her hips gyrated slowly as his fingers slipped through her folds.

"Oh..." Her voice rose.

He found her entrance and circled a few times as another wave of heat ripped through his body. Hailey tipped her head back and circled in the opposite direction, moaning louder. Keeping one hand planted firmly on the left side of her glorious ass, he kept up the pressure with his right hand, slipping one finger in then another. Plunging deeper, circling harder.

Mine, his bear rumbled.

"Yes," Hailey cried, tempting him to keep that up just for the thrill of watching her come totally undone.

But he was coming undone too, his bear dangerously close to the surface. His cock ached, and his lips yearned to close around her nipple again.

"I don't have a condom," he managed to rasp, even though it would kill him if she said no. "Don't often need one," he admitted so she knew just how long he'd been waiting for someone like her.

Not someone like her, his bear growled. *Exactly her. Hailey. No one else comes close.*

"I'm on the shot," Hailey whispered. "And my sourpuss agent makes me get tested regularly. Like I sleep around or something." She chuckled. "Not with my mother standing guard all the time."

Finally, a reason to appreciate her mother. Then he shook his head. He didn't want to think about her mother. What he wanted was Hailey. All of her.

Hailey looked down at him through dazed eyes. Had she read his mind? Maybe she had, because a second later, she straddled his waist and lowered herself onto him.

"Oops," she purred, missing on the first try. Then she lifted and tried again, gasping when they connected.

Tim hung onto her hips, letting her take him in, one hot, straining inch at a time. Her mouth opened in a silent cry as she pushed harder, bottoming out.

"God, yes." Her head rolled back, and she gripped his shoulders, starting to rock.

Yes was the right word, because he'd never felt so connected or ready. So on the edge of a total meltdown. He rolled his hips and groaned at the tight squeeze she held him in.

"More," Hailey murmured.

He closed his eyes, settling into a rhythm Hailey matched, meeting each of his thrusts with a sharp flex of her inner muscles.

Bite her. Mark her. Take her, his bear growled.

"Touch me," Hailey moaned, making it even harder to resist.

No marking, he snapped at his bear. *No mating bite. Just touching, like she wants.*

She wants the bite. She wants us, the beast insisted, trying to seize power all over again.

With a supreme effort, he beat the beast down. *Not mating. Not tonight.*

Why he added that last part, he had no clue, but it did placate his rebellious bear.

Not tonight. But soon, his bear grumbled.

"Please," Hailey groaned, bucking over him. "Touch me."

He spread his hands wide across her stomach and slid upward. Her sweater had dropped down, and he rolled it out of the way. For a moment, he basked in the sight of her breasts, swaying seductively before his eyes. Then he leaned forward and captured the left side, squeezing it toward his mouth. The second his lips sealed around her nipple, Hailey shuddered and cried out.

"Yes. . ."

He flicked his tongue over her perfect, tight bead, working her into a frenzy. Licking, nipping, and thrusting harder all the time. Desire spiraled in him like a storm, and he could barely think. He thrust harder, making his cock burn. Making Hailey burn too, by the sound of it. Seeking out her clit with his free hand was pure instinct, and when he pinched, Hailey jerked.

"Yes," she cried.

She clamped down over him, and his vision flashed with blinding white light. Fire surged through his veins as he thrust harder. Then, with a sharp groan, he released deep, deep inside.

Mate, his bear cried. *Mine.*

Hailey mumbled and shuddered while he hung on, determined to fill her as long as he could. Even when his muscles relaxed one by one, he held her tight.

"Hailey. . ."

She jerked and cried out with an aftershock, then slumped. Her chin weighed heavily on his shoulder, and her cheek warmed his.

"So good," she whispered a long minute later, drawing lazy, uncoordinated circles on his back.

Slowly, his senses awoke from their blur of ecstasy, and he heard crickets chirp. Somewhere in the distance, a car started. Good thing he'd picked a table far from the rest. He wrapped both arms around Hailey, keeping her close, warm, and safe. Nuzzling her with his cheek, marking her as his.

Soon, we'll mark her for real, his bear murmured.

He clenched his jaw, concentrating on Hailey, who drew back far enough to look into his eyes and smile. "Can I just say I love your surprises? Especially this one."

That chased away the dark cloud in his mind, and he grinned. "That was kind of a surprise to me, too."

She tilted her head, studying him. "You mean you weren't planning to seduce me up here?" She waved a hand around.

The last of the wispy clouds were clearing out, opening a view to the lights of settlements far, far below. The sea and sky stretched indigo as far as he could see, and a universe of stars winked from above.

He laughed. "My plans only went as far as catching the sunset."

She chuckled. "You caught more than that, mister." Then she tightened the blanket around her shoulders and cupped his face in both hands. "Thank you. This is the best night ever. The most special."

Funny, he was about to say that. "For me too."

She looked around. "I guess doing it on top of a volcano is hard to beat, huh?"

He shook his head and spoke from the heart. "It's not the place, Hailey. It's not the stars. It's you."

Her mouth hung open a little as she stared at him.

You, Hailey, he wanted to say. *I love you. I need you.*

But he couldn't say that without explaining about his shifter side, and he just didn't have it in him to see her joy turn to fear of his bear. So he buried his face in her hair and sniffed, memorizing every aspect of his true love. Pretending he could keep her forever.

Forever, his bear growled, ignorant of the dark days he knew would come soon.

Chapter Nineteen

Hailey clung to Tim all the way down the volcano, kissing his shoulder from time to time. The motorcycle throbbed under her legs, and she blushed, thinking back to what they'd done. Had she really just screwed the world's most perfect man on a picnic bench?

The lingering heat between her legs assured her that, yes, she had. Not only that, but she'd gotten on her knees and tasted him too.

Her cheeks heated with a blush she was glad no one could see. Tim had given her a taste of freedom, for sure. And, wow. He might have created a monster, because she already craved more. More smoothie stops and walks in town. More stargazing, more talks. More night rides — and yes to more picnic table sex too. On her knees, in his lap, and maybe even spread out on the tabletop next time.

She hid her face in his jacket and leaned into the next curve of the mountain. Okay, maybe that was asking for a bit much. But it didn't stop her from fast-forwarding to new pleasures she wanted to explore when they reached his house.

Without realizing it, she let her hands drop lower into Tim's lap until they nudged his groin, and he swerved.

"Sorry," she called above the sound of the engine and forced her hands to the neutral territory of his waist. "But it is your fault."

"My fault?" he shot back, not sounding the least miffed.

"Yep." She pinched his biceps — as far around as her hands could reach, at least — then ran her hands over the washboard of his abs. "All your fault. Especially this part," she said, laying a hand over his heart.

He covered her hand with his, filling her with a deep sense of peace. Peace that stretched on even when he had to release her to negotiate the next turn.

Part of the drive back, she spent peeking over his shoulder, watching the scenery zip past. The quarter moon rose as they hit Maui's central valley, making the ocean glitter with silvery light. Then she closed her eyes and let her mind drift, and before she knew it, pavement gave way to gravel.

"Koakea," Tim murmured as they rolled onto the plantation grounds.

She looked up. Would anyone be up? Would it be obvious what she and Tim had done? She made a face. That wasn't anyone's business, so it shouldn't matter to her, right?

But Tim was close to his family and friends — incredibly close. So yes, it mattered. All the more so because they were good people who'd helped her again and again. It would hurt to have to face their disapproval, if that was what lay in store.

Luckily, the grounds were quiet, with everyone either asleep or out for the night, and she could stay as close as she wanted to Tim's side. Which was really close, because she just couldn't let go of him, already hungry for more.

So hungry, she pulled him over for a kiss outside his front door. A long, hungry kiss that she hoped was more of a beginning than an end.

"Any other wishes on your list?" he asked, stroking her cheek.

She smiled. There was that rain check, but...

"How about you get a wish?"

His lips twitched, and his eyes glowed. *Really* glowed, the way she'd imagined before. But it could have been her oversexed mind seeing things, too.

He smoothed her hair back. "I don't want to get all greedy..."

She grinned and pressed closer. "But?"

He leaned close, kissing her ear and nuzzling her cheek. "Wouldn't mind doing some more of this."

She laughed. The man was a champion nuzzler. Something she'd never come across before. But then again, before Tim,

178

her world had been filled with cool, standoffish types. The few men she'd slept with were the same — not following up sex with much cuddling or pillow talk. But Tim...

She pulled him toward the door. "Your wish is my command."

He laughed. "That's my line."

"Mine now," she murmured, leading him by the arm. It would have been so good to say that about him — *mine now* — but, heck. A girl could hope.

She paused inside the door, letting her eyes adjust. The condo she rented always felt empty and lonely when she first walked in. Tim's place might have been as dark and quiet, but it was homey and inviting at the same time.

"Lights?" she asked, letting her hand hover over the switch.

"Definitely," he murmured. "But not that one. Hang on."

He walked past her and switched on two reading lights that cast low, warm pools of light, leaving just enough shadow to maintain the mood while providing enough light to—

Hailey blushed, because her first thought was *Enough light to see each other's naked bodies by.* It was one thing to climb a man like a tree on a deserted mountaintop, because darkness had a way of masking one's inhibitions along with everything else. But to lie in plain view and let a man explore every inch of her naked flesh was different, somehow. No sheets to hide under and a glowing light to illuminate all her imperfections.

Her cheeks burned. Why did the thought of Tim looking at her turn her on so much? She'd never posed naked, and she never wanted to. But the urge to show Tim everything was overwhelming.

Tim reached for her, and she slid into his arms. Comfortably, naturally, like she'd been born to occupy that space. He combed back her hair with both hands and rubbed his cheek against hers. Softly at first, then harder, sniffing her the whole time.

"What?" he asked when she giggled.

"It's ticklish." The little puffs of his breath stirred her hair and warmed her skin. "But I like it," she hurried to add, pressing her cheek against his again.

"I like it too," he whispered in that rock-bottom bass she loved so much.

She tipped her head back, letting him work his way down her neck. He scrubbed every inch of her with his chin and cheeks. When he rubbed in one direction, the motion was soft in spite of his stubble. In the other direction, it was more of a rough scrape, and the contrast made her blood heat.

"Does that work all over?" she asked, mustering the courage to unfilter the thoughts darting around her mind.

"What do you mean?" he asked.

He was at her neck, and she took hold of his shoulders — on the second try, because they were so broad, her hands tended to slide off — and gently pushed him back. "I mean, if I did this..." She ducked, pulling her shirt and sweater off as one layer, and then dropped them to one side. Then she unclasped her bra and tossed that aside, followed by her jeans. "You know, to give you more space."

Tim made a low, hungry sound like a growl. "More space is good."

She stopped him just before he went back to nuzzling her collarbone and tugged at the hem of his shirt. "I think I need more space to try this out for myself, too."

His eyes sparkled in an echo of the starlight they'd absorbed, and he yanked off his shirt, then dropped his pants and boxers.

For an instant, they stood staring at each other like a couple of kids, naked for the first time. His hazel eyes swept over every inch of her body. Her gaze, on the other hand, moved in jerks, because his chest was a work of art. His abs looked like they'd been photoshopped, they were that defined. And below—

She gulped. Yeah, well-built was the term. Well-built and ready to engage.

Then her eyes flicked back up to his face and stayed there for just as long. Tim's eyes had won her over from the start — so honest and genuine. Lots of guys had good bodies, but how many had eyes like that?

Without saying a word, Tim went back to where he'd left off nuzzling. Up and along her jaw then down to her neck and onto her collarbone. While she fluttered her hands over his body, undecided where to start, he moved in long, purposeful strokes, like a painter intent on covering every inch of his canvas. With slow, barely perceptible steps, he backed her toward the bed, and when her calf bumped the lowest step to the loft, they broke apart.

"After you," he rumbled, kissing her hand.

Hailey was torn between staying close and lying back across the bed, but when she spotted another reading light, the decision was easy. She had to crawl halfway across the bed to turn it on, and when she did, she rolled and settled onto her back, totally open to his gaze. Tim came right to the edge of the bed, and she stared up at him. Up and up, given his height, her eyes locked on his.

She held out a hand. "Coming?"

She moved one knee, and his gaze jumped, following it.

"Coming," he rumbled, moving closer.

Hailey lay perfectly still, tingling in anticipation. Her nipples were already standing up, her body aching all over again.

Tim dropped slowly to all fours and inched over her, caging her in without actually making contact. For all she freely offered him — her wide-spread legs, her naked breasts — he didn't pause until they were face-to-face.

"Hailey," he whispered, so low and full of yearning, her heart swelled.

She waited, because there was more coming. Some great revelation or sweet words. Something he'd obviously wanted to say for a long time.

But a tree branch scratched over the roof, and Tim closed his eyes. His shoulder sagged the slightest bit, and a look of intense sorrow came over his face.

She touched his jaw and stroked it softly. "Whatever it is, it's okay."

He shook his head in a way that could have meant anything from *It will never be okay* to *Sure. Fine. Absolutely okay.*

"Tim?" she whispered.

He dropped down, buried his face in what seemed to be his favorite spot — the highest corner of her neck, over by one ear — and started nuzzling her again.

She held him for a moment. Was he truly okay? Should she let the moment pass, or should she try to drag whatever it was out of him?

By the time she got that far in her thoughts, though, Tim had charged ahead, nuzzling her harder than ever, and she couldn't help but arch into him. Maybe he was communicating whatever he'd wanted to say through body language instead of words. Maybe if she listened really carefully, she would discover the hidden message.

A moment later, she nearly giggled in guilty pleasure. Given the way her body was heating up, she could barely think straight, let alone unravel the secrets of her mystery man. But the more he kissed her, the less it seemed to matter.

She tilted her head back and curled a leg around his, pressing ever closer. Cooing and moaning, because it already felt that good. And when Tim skimmed one big hand over her chest, she arched in a silent cry for more.

A lucky thing Tim was fluent in reading her body language. Within the space of two heartbeats, he ducked and suckled her breasts just as she hoped he would.

"Yes..." she breathed, moving under him.

"Watch," he whispered, catching her eye.

Her breath caught. Had she heard him right? "Watch?"

He nodded and reached up, pushing a second pillow toward her.

"Please. Watch," he whispered.

Hailey plumped the pillow behind her head and managed a curt nod. And, whoa. Just watching Tim lick his lips half an inch away from her nipple nearly made her groan. When he caught it, she really did groan, feeling dirty-minded about watching, yet feeling incredibly turned on. He worked his lips, letting her nipple pop in and out of view, and the sight mixed with the sensation nearly made her come. Then he slid down her body, spread her legs, and—

"Watch," he said in a voice that said she wasn't the only one barely holding it together. Then he ducked between her legs and flicked his tongue.

She arched right off the mattress, crying out loud. So loud, she was glad no one else lived nearby. She'd never had a man do that before, and much as she loved watching, her eyes kept shutting from the sensory overload. The quick flick of his tongue. The soft push of his fingers. The rough scrape of his chin. Every move of his tongue, every slide of his fingers made her clutch the sheets tighter. Tim knew exactly what combination to use and when, pushing her to her limits, then letting her back down, only to make her cry with ecstasy again.

Unexpected sex on a starry mountaintop had been amazing, but this was something completely different. This was being absolutely, totally possessed. And if it had been anyone else, she would have gone running for the hills. But with Tim — it was scary, how right it felt. How much she wanted to be his.

He broke off abruptly, leaving her gasping. Before she could so much as open her eyes in surprise, he'd crawled back up her body and kissed her hard. With a quick, sweeping tongue, he spread the taste of sex around her mouth and finally broke away, staring down at her. His eyes glowed, and she swore she heard his voice in her head.

You are mine.

"Yes," she whispered, reaching for him.

A vein at the side of his brow pumped, and his chest heaved as he moved into place. She wrapped her legs around his waist, holding her breath.

Mine, she swore he whispered as he thrust in.

She howled, and when he withdrew and powered back in, she cried out again. The sweet burn, the achy stretch, the feeling of being filled made her head roll from side to side. Tim moved faster and faster, losing then regaining his rhythm as he fought to maintain self-control. She imagined two Tims, one more dirty-minded than the other, battling inside. One insisting he take his time, while the other howled to be set free. Which did she want?

Easy answer.

"Tim," she whispered, catching his gaze.

He paused, staying deep inside her, quivering with need.

"Anything you want, I want too," she said. "Please."

It was hard to find the words, because screaming *Fuck me as hard as your hottest fantasies* wasn't exactly her style. She did picture it, though, forming a wild scene in her mind. The details were fuzzy, but in the vision, Tim's movements were sharp and hard. His voice was low and gritty, like an animal's, and his eyes were wild.

That's what I want, she let her eyes say.

"Please," she whispered. "Anything you want."

For the next breathless seconds, she worried that he'd say something sweet and tame like, *I want whatever you want.* But then his eyes shifted color, going more green than brown, and his face went hard all over.

"Anything," she whispered.

It was one of those *Be careful what you wish for* moments, because a second later, he reared up to his knees, holding her hips high above the mattress. Then he started thrusting with an untamed expression that matched his flashing eyes. The angle intensified the pressure, pushing the limits of where pain ended and pleasure started. The blood rushed to her head, and she clutched the sheets.

"So good," she moaned again and again.

Tim's hands clamped over her hips, holding her up. Sweat gleamed over his face and chest. He pumped faster, filling her with indescribable emotions and a sense of her own power.

See what you do to me, woman? his wild eyes said. *See how good you make me feel?*

She clamped down with her inner muscles, making him groan. The gritty sound of his voice pushed her over the edge.

Now, she wanted to scream. *Now.*

Tim make a harsh, roaring sound as he exploded inside her, and a heat wave ripped through her body.

Hailey threw her head back and opened her mouth to shout, but no sound came out. Not even a pant, because she held her breath through the shudders that racked her body. Tim closed

184

his eyes, concentrating on the moment. Every vein near the surface of his body stood out, and every muscle clenched hard.

"Yes..." she whispered, finally taking a breath. Then an aftershock swept through her body, making her writhe all over again.

When Tim lowered her back to the mattress, it was like floating through a cloud. And when he lay down over her, spent, it felt like coming home.

"Hailey." He panted into the sheets next to her head.

She clutched at his shoulders, never wanting the sensation to end. The heat. The emotion. The passion. Surely there had to be some way of holding on to all that joy?

But it was closer to dawn than to midnight, and when Tim rolled and held her close, she peacefully, blissfully drifted off to sleep.

Chapter Twenty

Hailey woke at dawn, smiling at nothing in particular. Every limb felt loose and satisfied, like she'd squeezed a week of yoga into the previous day — and night.

She grinned. She was in Maui, so loose and satisfied was fitting, and the bear of a man slumbering beside her provided all the warmth and protection she could ask for.

They were spooned closely, her back to Tim's chest, and all she could see were his thick arms curled around her. For a long, quiet minute, she took in that view, replaying everything that had happened the previous night. Her cheeks heated, and she planted a tiny thank-you kiss on his arm.

Slowly, she slipped out of bed, trying not to disturb Tim. God knew the poor man needed his sleep. He'd been up at some point in the night, but she'd fallen right back to sleep. Now it was the other way around, and she couldn't lie still for another minute, not with so many thoughts bouncing around her head.

Standing quietly, she padded to the door. She needed some fresh air to clear her head and figure out what to say to Tim when he woke. If he didn't want another day of her, she'd catch the first plane out of Maui and never bother him again. But if he said yes...

Her chest swelled with hope she barely dared entertain.

She took a deep breath, trying to organize her mind. First, she'd take a little walk. Then, she'd return and wait until Tim woke. The second he did, she'd brew him a fresh cup of coffee. And once he was really awake...

What then?

She forced herself not to think of the outcome, only how to best express what she felt.

I love you, Tim. It's crazy, but I love you. And I'd really like to give us the chance to...

She paused. Would that scare him off? Maybe she should be a little more subtle.

Hey, Tim. Last night was great, and so were the past days—

She frowned, because having to face her mother, Jonathan, and a terrifying werewolf had been hell. Only the moments with Tim were good.

The more time I spend with you, the more I think we might have something special. Do you feel that too?

She pushed the front door open but stopped there and looked back. A ray of pink light stretched across the cabin floor, illuminating tiny particles in the air and making the cabinets glow. Beyond the point reached by the dawn light, Tim slept, looking more peaceful than ever.

Hailey nearly sighed, looking around. Maybe her stay on Maui didn't have to be temporary. Maybe she didn't have to pretend about having a quiet life with a good man.

She stepped outside, closing the door behind her. And, wow — the entire plantation glowed, taking on the colors of dawn. The dark green of the abandoned coffee grove had a golden tint, and the long, grassy slope that led to the ocean was a warm, yellowish-orange. Birds sang, and the quiet rush of surf carried from far below.

The beach was as good a place as any to start her walk, so she set off, breathing deeply. The air was as clean and fresh as the color of the sky — nothing like LA, which only got her thinking more. The long, low structure behind Tim's house appeared to be an abandoned coffee drying shed. That would be a fun project — getting a couple of acres of coffee up and thriving again. She could harvest her own beans... Make Tim the best coffee ever... Watch him breathe in the aroma...

She walked on, following a gurgling stream. Dreaming was one thing. Figuring out what to say to Tim was another, and steeling herself for rejection yet another. It was one of those days that could change her life, and she knew it, because it could end in several different ways.

Well, whatever happened, she'd never forget her time on Maui, that was for sure.

The slope folded more sharply as she approached the beach, creating a crease where the stream flowed faster. Something moved on the patch of sand ahead, and she stopped, watching.

Hi, Dell, she nearly called when she saw who it was. But he was doing yoga, and it felt wrong to disturb his peace. She nearly turned away to continue her walk, but he was just easing into a one-armed handstand, forming a diamond with his legs. It was amazing, that combination of sheer strength and delicate balance. He didn't wobble the slightest bit, and she tried to figure out how he did it. *Why* he did it, because Dell seemed more the type for a rough round of football than an introspective morning of yoga. Was there some trauma in his past he was trying to shake?

He eased out of the pose, going to two hands and then a plank. Resting on his knees, he tossed his shirt aside and went into a downward dog move that made Hailey think about finding her own quiet spot to do a little yoga, too. He held the pose for a long time, making her think *cat* more than *dog* for some reason. And finally—

Hailey frowned. The stretch went too far, as if he'd thrown out his back. But Dell kept right on pushing with his arms while his knees bent backward in a way that shouldn't have been possible. His fingers clawed the ground the way a cat might knead a blanket, and his shoulder blades stood out on his back.

Something was wrong. Something *had* to be wrong, because human bodies didn't bend like that. Was he having a seizure?

Hailey ran two steps forward then froze.

Hair broke out all over Dell's back in the reverse of what she'd witnessed Lamar do that awful evening on the beach. The blond scruff on Dell's chin extended all over his neck. His backbone stuck out, and every joint twisted the wrong way.

She opened her mouth to scream, but no sound came out. Dell the human was gone, and a lion stood in his place. An honest-to-God, full-grown lion with a long, tufted tail and a thick mane. The beast clawed the ground, digging deep furrows in the sand, then gave itself a mighty shake.

Hailey inched back, barely breathing.

Oh God. Dell was a shifter. A lion shifter that looked about to set off on a hunt. And since Maui wasn't exactly teeming with gazelles...

Hailey turned and ran, hoping he wouldn't hear her over the sound of the sea. The wind was at her back, which meant the beast couldn't catch her scent — hopefully. She sprinted for her life, straight for Tim's house, already planning to fling open the door and scream for help.

It wasn't possible. Not another shifter. Not here, where Tim said she'd be safe.

A myna bird — black with a yellow mask around the eyes — pecked at a dip in the ground beside the water pump by Tim's house. The bird fluttered away, and Hailey screeched to a stop, staring at the spot, wondering why that seemed important.

Then it hit her. That wasn't a dip in the ground. It was an animal track — one of several left in the soft earth around the pump. Big tracks — bigger than her foot — showing a triangular pad and five round toes.

Bear tracks.

Her knees shook. Lions and bears? She wanted to scream to alert Tim, but if she did, the beasts would hear and—

All the blood drained out of her face as it hit her. Tim had stepped out at some point in the wee hours of the night, and she'd been so sleepy, she'd barely registered it at the time. But now...

Be right back, he'd whispered, kissing her on the shoulder. *Just going to check on things.*

She stared at the tracks and then at the house.

Wolves. Lions. Bears...

A strangled cry escaped her throat.

Shifters.

Not all shifters are bad, Tim had once said. *But it's very hush-hush, and we have to keep it that way.*

Her knees shook, and she felt faint. Hush-hush enough for him not to tell her?

She whirled, looking from one part of the property to another, picturing Tim's friends. Connor, Jenna, and Chase. Cynthia and little Joey. Could it really be?

But they'd shown her every kindness. Had all that been some kind of ruse?

There are good shifters who wouldn't hurt anyone, Tim had said.

But, God. How could she be sure?

Still shaking, she tiptoed away from the house. She'd just spent the night in a bear shifter's arms?

Her skin crawled at the thought of those arms turning into bear legs and caging her in. Of his beautiful smile cracking into a grimace that showed off horrifyingly big teeth.

She broke into a run, heading toward the barn. The keys to Tim's pickup hung from a nail, and she grabbed for them, then abruptly stopped.

The flower. The pure white plumeria he'd given to her was right where she'd left it. She stared, clutching the keys hard enough for them to cut into her palm. What the hell was she doing?

Running, her mind screamed. *Getting away.*

But *running away* didn't go with *Tim.* Her body shook, rejecting the idea.

On the other hand. . . lions. Bears. Wolves. Her rattled mind had no idea what to make of it all. So she slipped into the driver's seat, appalled at herself. How could she steal Tim's car? But then again, how could she possibly stay?

When she turned the key, the engine sputtered to life, and she drove off quickly — too quickly — kicking up gravel as she went. Then she roared onto the main road and raced off, watching the rearview mirror as much as the road.

Okay, so. . . a plan. She desperately needed a plan. Which had to be heading to the airport and flying the hell away. There was no alternative. She could leave the keys in the car. Once she was safely on her way, she would find a way to get a message to Tim so he could retrieve the vehicle.

Her hands gripped the steering wheel harder. Could she really do that to him?

Then her jaw grew tight with resolve. How could he not have told her about himself? He'd seen Lamar shift, and yet he hadn't told her about himself. That made him a liar, right?

She forced her mind back to forming a plan. If there weren't a flight, she would go to the adjacent heliport, book a ride to Oahu, and take it from there. But, Jesus. Where could she go? It was bad enough to have Jonathan and the likes of Lamar tracking her down. What if Tim came after her, too?

Don't be ridiculous, a little voice insisted, speaking from her heart. *Tim would never hurt you.*

That's what she thought, but he'd lied to her all along. What other lies was he capable of?

She drove, clutching the wheel so hard, her knuckles hurt. Too shocked to cry, too frightened to do anything but stomp on the gas pedal.

"Damn it." She thumped the empty spot on her chest. Her great-grandmother's pearl. She couldn't leave Maui without it.

She stretched across the car, fiddling in the glove compartment for a map. Then she gave up on that and worked from memory. The house at Pu'u Pu'eo wasn't much farther than the airport, right? And traffic was light this early...

She leaned forward, egging the pickup on like an aging steed. Every few seconds, she'd peek back then jerk her eyes forward again. It took all her resolve not to exit for the airport instead of driving on the familiar road along Maui's North Shore. Long lines of surf pounded the cliffs, an echo of the emotions roiling around her mind. Twenty minutes later, she swerved onto the turnoff for the well-hidden property and revved up the rocky road. Then she ran up to the house at Pu'u Pu'eo—

She pulled up short, staring at the peaceful scene.

An owl hooted. The wind whispered through the trees. Somewhere in the distance, the crash of a waterfall could be heard.

She bit her lip. The six days she'd spent there with Tim had been the calmest and most peaceful of her life. How could it end like this?

It doesn't have to end like this, a little voice said.

Slowly, she ascended the stairs and pushed open the unlocked door. Then she walked through the empty house, touching the walls. Sniffing. Wondering whether the faint hint of coffee and flowers was really there or just in her mind.

All that was good, the little voice said. *Like Tim. Honest. Trustworthy.*

She stopped in the doorway to the room Tim had used, recalling how he'd rubbed his shoulder against the frame.

He protected you when you had nowhere to go.

A lump big enough to choke her formed in her throat, and no amount of gulping forced it down.

She moved to the bedroom in the back and reached under the mattress. The pearl immediately warmed her hand, and she found herself sinking down to sit on the mattress.

Please help me, she wanted to beg the pearl. *Please tell me what to do.*

A silent minute passed, and she snorted. What was a pearl going to say or do? She had to stop waiting for help and find the power within herself to decide her own fate.

The house was painfully quiet, but her memories were so vivid, it was almost surreal. Hailey rocked on the mattress, looking up at the hook where she'd always left her pink *Aloha* cap at night. The cap Tim had bought for her. Somehow, leaving that behind hurt as much as the thought of leaving her pearl. But the cap was back at Tim's house...

A stab of pain went through her. Was she really ready to leave Tim?

She slipped her necklace on, paced back through the house, and stood in the middle of the yard, listening as an owl hooted sadly from the trees.

Hoo. Hoo.

She looked up. The bird might as well have called, *Why?* Why was she running from Tim, who'd never done anything but protect her?

The hallway was unpainted. The gazebo just an image in her mind. The kitchen devoid of laughter and warmth. There was so much they hadn't gotten around to doing. So much she hadn't said.

She looked around, then swallowed hard. Her grandfather had always told her to listen to her heart, but damn. Did that apply when bears were involved?

She chewed that one over as she drove back down the road, much more slowly than the rush in which she'd arrived.

Let's say someone you know was a shifter, and you didn't even know it, Tim had once said. *A person you trusted. Worked with. Laughed with. Shared meals with. Everything.*

Her heart wept. Had he been trying to tell her?

Someone who was always there and you never thought twice about. Let's say you suddenly found out they were—

"A werebear," she whispered. Tim *had* been trying to explain. It was she who hadn't been listening.

It wouldn't matter, because you know who they really are and what they're like. That they're good inside.

A single tear trailed down her cheek. Tim wasn't good inside. He was golden. But she...

She looked in the mirror, finding too much that resembled her mother. The curve of her eyebrows. The suspicion coded into her pursed lips. The greedy, *I want more* sheen of her eyes.

Hailey blinked a few times. Was that really her?

She was about to pull over and think — really think — when a car passed her on the left, coming much too close. More than close, in fact. With an ear-splitting thump, the cars collided, side to side.

"Watch it!" she yelped, fighting the car back under control.

Instead of racing ahead or pulling over, the SUV remained in the oncoming lane. It jerked over again, smashing Tim's pickup a second time.

Hailey yelped, battling the wheel with stiff, outstretched arms. Was that driver crazy? The right tires of Tim's pickup rattled along the narrow shoulder, kicking up gravel.

"Stop!" she screamed, glancing left.

But the SUV didn't stop. It kept up the pressure until she had no choice but to swerve down a gravel road with a *Do Not Enter* sign. Bad choice, because the minute she flew out of sight of the main road, another SUV cut in beside her. One panicked glance showed Hailey the face at the driver's wheel — a face straight from her nightmares.

Lamar.

"No—"

Her scream turned into a gasp when the first vehicle banged Tim's pickup from behind, forcing her onward. The dirt road was barely meant for one vehicle, let alone three, and she wrenched the wheel from side to side, avoiding boulders and trees.

"Oh God..."

Straight ahead, the forest thickened, and there was no way through. She hit the brakes, jumped out of the car, and ran. Behind her, brakes squealed, doors slammed, and footsteps pounded. She raced through the trees and scrambled over a dune. Then she shot out onto an open beach pounded by surf so wild, there was no way to wade in and swim away. She whirled around just as a group of men crested the dune above her.

"Now what, sweetheart?" Lamar sneered. "Out of places to run?"

Hailey took two steps to the right, but another man appeared and cut her off.

"Miss me, honey?" he said with a self-satisfied grin.

She blanched. "Jonathan."

Chapter Twenty-One

Tim woke slowly, smiling before he even opened his eyes. His bear hummed lazily, still celebrating the experiences of the previous night. He tightened his arms and hugged Hailey closer, but she'd slipped out of his grasp. So he reached a little farther and opened his eyes.

Rays of golden morning light sliced through cracks in the weathered cabin walls, illuminating everything but Hailey. The kettle on the stove shone, begging to be put to use. Sunlight glinted off the copper plate of the old-fashioned coffee grinder, and the brown-and-purple colors of the braided rug on the floor were richer than ever.

But Hailey was nowhere in sight.

He closed his eyes and twitched his nose, engaging his keen bear sense of smell. Still no Hailey.

His eyes snapped open, and his heart revved. Where was she?

He stood quickly and pulled on the jeans he'd discarded the night before. It couldn't take long to find Hailey. Then he could sit her down with a mug of coffee and finally spill all. He had to, because there was no way he could let her go without trying to explain.

Outside, the air was still, the plantation quiet.

"Hailey?" he called softly.

Had she gone to the beach? He sniffed again. Hailey's honeysuckle scent hung in the air, but intertwined with it was. . . fear?

He froze, concentrating on his nose, teasing apart the thousand different scents in the air.

"Hailey," he whispered, looking around.

Panic was an unfamiliar emotion, and it rose in him like a wave, making it hard to think.

There were two scent trails that matched Hailey. One led toward to the beach and felt calm. The other was tinged with fear and headed uphill. He forced himself to walk slowly, looking at the ground.

"Crap."

He stared at his own footprint — a grizzly print, clear as day in the soft soil around the water pump. He hadn't thought of that the previous night when he'd gone out. His bear had been so excited about having Hailey close that he'd had to shift and amble around, satisfying the urge to rub up against every stump and fencepost, marking his turf and everything in it — including Hailey — as his.

Not far from the huge grizzly print were the marks of Hailey's flip-flops. The angle and impression showed that she'd gone from strolling to stopping to...

He looked up, feeling sick. She'd started running for her life.

"Hailey." He wanted to call for her, but it came out a choked whisper instead.

Seconds later, he raced up the hill and into the barn, where he screeched to a stop. The pickup was gone. Hailey was gone.

His first instinct was to race after her. The second was utter defeat. If she had figured out he was a shifter, there was no way she would ever trust him again.

I told you to explain to her before, his bear cried.

Before meant before sleeping with her, and his soul ached, knowing he'd never get to go to bed or wake up with her again. He stared out the open doors of the barn, ready to drop to his knees and yell. Or better yet, to drop and die. Why live if he couldn't have his mate?

He tried pulling a curtain over his mind to shutter away the emotions. Logic was better, and it didn't hurt. And for a short time, he even succeeded. But then his bear piped up.

Can't let her go.

All the pain rushed back in, and he really did drop to his knees.

But what was he going to do — chase after Hailey and force her to stay? That would make him no better than Jonathan.

Which was when it hit him that Jonathan was still out there. Lamar, too. Would they pressure Hailey when they discovered she was no longer under the protection of the Hoving clan?

Anger welled up in him, overriding the pain, and he sprinted for Connor's motorcycle. Even if he couldn't have Hailey, he had to keep her safe. Seconds later, he was racing down the road, doubling the speed limit, desperate to track her down before she left the safety of Maui.

He headed for the airport, because that seemed like the logical place for her to go. And that felt right, too, up until the last turnoff, where his inner compass pointed onward.

Focus, damn it, he told himself. The airport made more sense.

But his inner compass insisted, and at the last second, he swerved back onto the main road. Soon, he was on Highway 36, the road to Hana. A mile or two later, he pulled over, ready to roar in frustration. It made no sense. Why would Hailey go that way? All that lay in that direction was the house at Pu'u Pu'eo.

His insides twisted. Turning back to the airport was the logical thing, but instinct kept insisting he should follow the coastal road.

Logic, his mind insisted. *Less painful that way.*

But a little voice kept begging him to listen. *That way. Trust me.*

That inner battle, that push-pull, was something he'd never experienced before. Not even in the most desperate moments of his military career or the most lethal shifter fights he'd been dragged into. Why was it happening now?

Because she's our mate, you fool. Our destiny, his bear cried.

If he could have reached out and kicked destiny, he would have. What was the point of finding his mate only to lose her?

With a curse, he peeled off again, racing down the coastal highway instead of turning back to the airport. It would kill him to find out his hunch had been wrong, but hell. He leaned into every curve, driving at breakneck speed. Then the inner compass twitched again, and he eased off the throttle. Pu'u Pu'eo was another couple of miles down the road, but the compass pointed toward the coast.

An unmarked road with a *Do Not Enter* sign flashed by on the left, and he whipped his head around. The side road was fifty yards behind him before he recognized the scent carried by the wind.

Wolf shifter. And not Chase, nor their friend Boone.

"Lamar," he grunted.

Throwing his left foot down, he dragged the motorcycle through a skidding 180-degree turn and raced back the way he'd come. With every sense on high alert, he bumped down the side road. Beneath the *Do Not Enter* sign was a smaller sign marked with an ominous, *Dangerous surf. Beach closed.* Lamar was out there, and so was Hailey. He could tell by the scent. Jonathan, too.

Tim's heart leaped into his throat when he spotted his pickup standing with its door open, surrounded by three SUVs. The driver's side showed several huge dents, and his pulse soared. What had those bastards done to Hailey?

He jumped off the bike, letting it drop as he took off on foot through the trees. Fast at first and then slower, with his shoulders hunched to remain concealed. The onshore wind was in his favor, keeping his scent from the other shifters, but it also brought him the acrid scent of Hailey's fear.

He snuck over the last few yards and peered out from behind the last tree. Before him, the dunes dropped off to the beach. Lamar and Jonathan were there, boxing Hailey in.

Those two are about to die, his bear growled.

Tim fought off the urge to sprint in and let his grizzly rampage. Hailey would think him a monster, and there were at least four other shifters to consider — three wolves and a bear, if his nose was right. They must have flown in to Maui covertly that very morning, because they certainly hadn't been on the island last night.

Wait. Think. Plan this out, he ordered himself. Hailey was unharmed — for now. He had to turn off the emotions roiling around his gut and think.

To his surprise, his frantic bear — the beast who always rebelled when it came to matters of the heart — quieted and let him organize his mind.

Hailey. Four shifters plus one human. Basically, the kind of hostage situation he'd trained for, and he had the element of surprise.

Connor, he called through his mind.

His brother was miles away, across the island, but Connor's deep dragon growl sounded in his head.

What the hell is going on? Why did you rush off? And where the hell is my bike?

Tim didn't bother to answer. *Lamar and a couple of his cronies have Hailey cornered out here. I need backup. Fast.*

He couldn't name the location, but Connor would be able to track him as clearly as Tim had been able to track Hailey down.

Crap. Hold your position, Connor ordered. *We're on our way.*

Tim gnashed his teeth and crept closer. Normally, bears were among the most patient shifters, but that was Hailey out there, and his world was upside down.

"No, I did not miss you, you jerk," Hailey barked at Jonathan.

Her face was a patchy color, showing the white of fear and red of anger. Tim forced himself to take in other details of the scene — the position of each man, the angle of a long-abandoned lifeguard tower, and the distance to each end of the deserted beach that terminated in rocky outcrops. Lamar was clearly alpha among the four shifters, and the others were on edge, watching for some cue from their boss.

Jonathan tsked and touched Hailey's hair, but she smacked his hand away.

"I told you you'd regret leaving me," he said, oh so casually.

Every muscle in Tim's body coiled.

"And I told you my only regret is ever meeting you," she snapped. Then she looked around, worried. "Where's my mother? What have you done to her?"

Jonathan smirked. "So sweet of you to think of the old bitch. Don't worry. She's happily shopping in Waikiki. At least, for now." His voice dropped in a clear threat.

"For now?" Hailey stuck her hands on her hips.

Jonathan laughed — the ass — and smiled. "Last chance, baby."

Hailey shook her head. "What's so hard to understand about no? I don't love you, Jonathan. I never will."

Jonathan sighed. "I don't see why you're making such a big deal out of that."

Tim's bear growled. *Love is everything.*

Before he'd met Hailey, he hadn't understood that. But she'd opened the door to a hidden part of his soul and changed everything.

"I'll give you everything. I'll take good care of you," Jonathan went on. "Like a princess."

Hailey snorted. "What if I don't want to be a princess?"

Jonathan went on as if he hadn't heard. "All you have to do is follow my lead."

Tim scowled. Did Jonathan really think that was all a woman might desire?

"No." Hailey turned to stride away, but one of the others stepped forward, cutting her off. She spun back to Jonathan, furious. "You can't force me to go with you."

"Oh, but I can. You're the perfect wife, and I want you."

He might as well have said, *That's the perfect Mercedes-Benz* or *I want that Armani suit.* As if Hailey were just another accessory he needed to achieve his ambitions.

"You have a choice, Hailey. Two easy options." Jonathan grinned. "Option one, you marry me and live happily ever after. I'm going places, baby, and I'll make you the most glamorous First Lady since Jackie O."

Hailey scowled. "Why not the most glamorous First Lady ever, while you're at it?"

Tim hid a snort. Hailey could certainly do glamorous — he'd seen the magazine spreads. But that wasn't who she really was. Why couldn't Jonathan understand?

"Option two," Jonathan went on. "And let me warn you — you really need to consider this from my perspective. The next best thing to a Senate candidate with perfect credentials and a beautiful wife is a Senate candidate whose true love died tragically, leaving him mourning and alone, ready to serve the public in loving memory of his fiancée."

Hailey stared, and Tim's pulse went through the roof.

Connor, he growled.

We're on our way, man, his brother replied.

On the way was good, but the distance was such that his backup wouldn't arrive anytime soon. Tim wouldn't mind taking on Lamar and the other shifters, but that increased the risk to Hailey. His feet twitched, but he forced himself to watch and wait.

Hailey glared at Jonathan. "Your true love dying tragically?"

He made a face. "Yes, I like the first option better, too. The choice is yours."

"You're crazy."

Jonathan sighed. "Option two. Such a pity." He reached into his coat pocket, drew out a sheaf of papers, and clicked a ballpoint pen. "I'll need you to sign this, of course."

Hailey's jaw dropped, and Tim's did too. Jonathan expected Hailey to sign some kind of agreement before he murdered her?

Hailey smacked the papers away. "What the hell is that?"

"The instructions to your lawyer to turn your property over to your beloved fiancé without further delay."

Hailey's face went blank. "What property? I rent my condo and—" Her expression changed, and she whispered, "You want my grandparents' place?

Jonathan tut-tutted. "You really should have signed this over before."

Lamar scowled. "That stubborn old man should have signed it over while he had a chance. See if you're any smarter, Ms. Crusak," he said, drawing out her legal name.

Tim's mind spun. What did that mean? Why had Hailey suddenly gone so pale?

Then he remembered what she'd said that day they'd rushed over to Koakea after running into Lamar.

My grandfather was mauled to death by wolves.

Wolves — or shifters?

Lamar's evil grin stretched.

Hailey covered her mouth and whispered, "You killed my grandfather."

She whirled, ready to bolt, but Jonathan caught her arm. She twisted away, glaring at him. "You want to kill me, but you want me to sign over the deed first?"

Jonathan nodded, all matter-of-fact. "Easier that way."

"And if I don't?"

He grinned — really grinned, like that was the best part of his diabolical plan.

Hailey read his expression before Tim could, and she blanched. "You'll kill my mother if I don't."

Jonathan shook his head. "Oh, I won't kill her. Lamar will."

Lamar nodded and showed the points of his teeth. "With pleasure."

The last of the blood drained from Hailey's face, and she swayed on her feet.

"Either way, that property will be mine," Jonathan crowed.

One of the security guards shot a knowing smirk to another, making Tim do a double take. What exactly did they have planned?

"Sign the land over to me, and nothing will happen to your mother," Jonathan said. "If you don't, you still die, and the land goes to her. She will sign it over to me, and then she will die." Jonathan waved to the pounding surf. "It's easy to stage a drowning, especially in a place like this. Another wouldn't be hard. Or maybe a tragic fall..."

Lamar shook his head. "Something slow and painful."

Hailey stared. "You're ready to kill for a godforsaken piece of land?"

Jonathan snorted. "That godforsaken piece of land is sitting on one of the biggest virgin oil fields in the lower forty-eight." Then his lips curled into a wolfish grin. "I wouldn't have minded screwing your sweet ass either. Oh, wait. Maybe I still will. Second thoughts, baby? Option one is still open, you know."

"Just get moving," Lamar growled.

"Now, Lamar, don't get greedy," Jonathan chided.

Lamar's face flushed. Like any alpha wolf, he hated to take orders. When Jonathan turned to Hailey, Lamar gave his men a curt nod. They fanned out to new positions, surrounding Jonathan.

Tim's heart pounded faster. The shit was about to hit the fan, and Hailey was standing at ground zero. He calculated which of the men he'd have to kill and which he'd have to settle for merely knocking aside when he ran in for Hailey.

"Just sign it already," Lamar barked at Hailey.

Jonathan's face clouded. "You stick to your job, Lamar, and I'll stick to mine."

Hailey looked from one to the other and slowly backed away.

Yes. That way, Tim wanted to whisper to her. *Get over toward the guy on your left. He looks like the slowest of the bunch.*

But Hailey edged closer to another man instead. Tim wiped a bead of sweat from his brow. If only he could speak into Hailey's mind the way he could talk to Connor or Chase.

Still, Hailey was his mate, so it had to be possible. Tim mustered all his concentration and pushed an image toward Hailey's mind. *The other way. Go toward that other guy.*

She halted, looking around in confusion. Then she spotted the tiny opening to her left and edged toward it.

Yes! That way. Slowly. Keep going, he wanted to yell.

"I'm the one who put all this together for you," Lamar barked.

Jonathan snorted. "You told me about the land, yes. But you wanted to kill Hailey outright. My plan was much better."

205

Tim felt sick. Was Jonathan talking about his plan to woo Hailey and make her the last accessory he needed for a perfect political career?

Jonathan laughed, apparently unaware of Lamar's growing anger. Did he even know the man was a shifter? Tim doubted it.

"Besides," Jonathan scoffed. "You have no capital, no connections. You knew about the oil under that land, but you couldn't do anything about it. Which is why you need me. Don't forget that, Lamar."

"You need me," Lamar growled.

Jonathan made a face. "Yes, I do need you. I also pay you, Lamar. Like I said, don't get greedy. This is just one step on a long road. I'll make you even richer someday, you know."

Lamar didn't look like he wanted to wait for someday, and Tim crouched, ready to run in.

"You're the one who can't control one stupid woman," Lamar snapped.

Tim nearly growled out loud. Hailey wasn't stupid, and she hadn't been put on earth to be controlled.

Jonathan ignored Lamar and turned back to Hailey. "Like I said, baby. Last chance."

"How long do you really think she'll play along for?" Lamar cut in. "Only one way to keep a woman quiet."

"Oh, I'm sure she'll come to see the light." Jonathan grinned, looking Hailey up and down. "And you," he said, turning to Lamar. "Don't lose your head. I've got this under control."

It sure didn't look like it, not from Tim's vantage point. The security guards had all taken a step closer, and like any good betas, their allegiance would lie with Lamar, not their human boss.

"Lose my head?" Lamar turned bright red. "Lose my head?"

The air shimmered around Lamar's shoulders, signaling an imminent shift. Tim took a deep breath, ready to barrel forward.

"Maybe you're the one who needs to know about losing for a change," Lamar snapped.

"Uh, boss..." one of his men murmured, trying to calm him down.

The others looked on nervously. Whatever their plan had been, Lamar was about to blow it to bits. Even Hailey patted the air with her hand, signaling for Jonathan to back down.

But Jonathan just laughed. "Lose? I never lose."

Lamar clenched one fist, and Tim watched as wolf claws extended from Lamar's hand.

"You will this time," Lamar growled.

Jonathan snorted and turned to Hailey, putting his back to Lamar. A fatal mistake Tim could see coming from a mile away. He shot forward, racing toward the huddled group. Not to save Jonathan's sorry ass — too late for that anyway — but to save Hailey.

"No!" Hailey shrieked as Lamar raised his arm.

Jonathan didn't even look over his shoulder. "Don't mind him, Hailey. All bark and no bi—"

The word *bite* turned into a shocked gasp as Lamar lay his claws across Jonathan's neck and ripped savagely to the side. Jonathan dropped, clutching his throat, making horrific gurgling sounds.

"Jonathan!" Hailey cried.

Lamar pushed away the nearest of his men. "Either way, she has to die. And either way, the profit is all ours. We'll get that bounty Moira offered — and the oil field, too."

Moira? Tim narrowed his eyes as he ran. What did that scheming she-dragon have to do with all this?

"You beast!" Hailey screamed at Lamar.

The words filled Tim's mind as he ran down the dune. He shifted in mid-sprint, wincing at the thought of what Hailey would see. She'd cringe at the sight of a huge grizzly with its jaws held wide, ready to rip Lamar and his men limb from limb. To her, he'd be another murdering shifter she would never be able to face. A beast.

I love you, Hailey, he whispered, wishing she could understand.

Then he steeled his nerves and bared his teeth, ready to take out the shifters who dared threaten his mate.

Chapter Twenty-Two

Hailey stumbled back as all hell broke loose. Everything happened at once, and her mind could only process it in slow motion.

Jonathan fell in a pool of his own blood. Lamar stepped forward with a murderous scowl, holding out fingers that ended in claws. His teeth extended to inch-long fangs, and his ears peaked into canine triangles. Behind him, something huge, brown, and furious came hurtling down the dunes.

Hailey opened her mouth to scream, but no sound came out.

A grizzly. A wild grizzly...

Her thoughts caught, looping around and around.

A grizzly with hazel eyes that begged for forgiveness. The tracks she'd seen that morning outside the house. The familiar, knight-in-shining-armor determination in every rushed step the bear took toward the men threatening her.

She struggled to connect the dots until all those threads came together in one tight knot.

"Tim," she whispered, buckling at the knees.

Lamar and his men whipped around, half a step too late. The grizzly flung the nearest man aside. It bulldozed straight over the second man, intent on getting to Lamar. The others scattered, shouting, and Lamar snarled.

Run, Hailey! Run! she swore Tim shouted into her mind. The words were faint but urgent, and spoken in the lowest bass she'd ever heard him hit.

Years ago, her grandfather had screamed those very words, and she'd had no choice but to run. She didn't really have a choice now, but her grandfather's murderer — Lamar — stood before her, and running felt wrong. A spot in the center of her chest burned, but she swatted at it, only to feel her necklace jerk. Then she jumped sideways, dragging Jonathan with her just in time to avoid the collision of the grizzly and Lamar, who was fully in wolf form. They fell to one side in a flurry of vicious snarls and bites.

The sounds Jonathan was making terrified her in a different way, and she crouched over him, not knowing what to do.

The pearl around her neck warmed, comforting her the way her grandfather would have been able to with one *You can do this* look.

"Hang on," she said, stripping off her shirt to cover the gashes on Jonathan's neck. It was too late, and she knew it, but she had to do something.

Jonathan's panicked eyes landed on her with a surprised look, and she nearly huffed. Yes, she despised him. But, no, she wasn't about to watch while he bled to death.

"Hang in there," she said, dragging him another yard.

The pool of blood spreading around Jonathan was horrifying enough to behold, but when her eyes strayed to the side...

Tim had only ever been kind and gentle around her. Now, he was all warrior. Fast, furious, and ruthless. All wild animal.

Of course, wild animals weren't supposed to act selflessly. Not in defending humans, at least. But there he was, putting his life on the line for her.

Blood splashed, and Hailey looked away, trying to think. She could scramble over the dunes, get into the car, and lock herself in. She could drive off for help. She could—

"Run," Jonathan whispered with the wide-eyed look of a man who'd realized too late how dirty his own dealings had been. Then his eyes hardened on some point over her shoulder, and his body went stiff.

"Jonathan," she cried, shaking him.

His lifeless eyes stayed on the sky, unblinking.

Go, Hailey. Run! Tim yelled in her mind.

She forced herself to look up and around. Jonathan was dead. Lamar's men were slow to regroup, and if she hurried...

She forced her legs into gear, grabbing a bat-sized length of driftwood as she ran for a gap between two of Lamar's men.

"No, you don't," one barked, reaching out.

She swung the wood, smacking his arm away, and darted left. By then, the second man had noticed her. Make that, a *wolf* had noticed her, because there was a mangy gray canine where the man had been. It clacked its jaws, driving her toward the first man. Hailey sprinted onward, no longer intent on getting through them, just on reaching the lifeguard tower. The ladder was steep and narrow, with just enough space for one. A position she had half a chance of defending if she held her shit together long enough.

She sprinted like never before and leaped for a rung halfway up. Her foot slipped, making her shin bash against a steel rung, but she caught hold and hauled herself up just in time to avoid the wolf's outstretched jaws. The second she reached the top, she spun and swung the stick.

"You bitch!" the man exclaimed, falling back along with the wolf. Both had reached for her, and both dropped to the ground. The wolf snarled, licking the red welt across his snout. The man ripped off his jacket and arched his back.

Hailey gasped as the man turned into a beast. A bear like Tim, yet nothing like Tim, as it turned out. Tim's pelt was the same rich brown color as his hair, and the tips shone in the sun. Every move he made was swift and calculated. The man, on the other hand, turned into a bear that looked as if the winter had stretched on far too long. His fur was scraggly and unkempt, his eyes wild. He took two steps toward Hailey, and her knees shook. If he stood on his hind legs, he could easily reach the tower, and she doubted her stick would do much against that beast.

But the last of Lamar's men — the last in human form, at least — stepped over and yelled, "I'll get her. You help Lamar finish that bastard off."

Finish Tim off? Hailey nearly cried out.

Lamar had been joined by a second wolf, and the pair fought Tim, showing speed and agility a bear could never match. Worse, the dark-colored bear was lumbering over to join them, making it three to one.

Within seconds, the fourth man had turned into a wolf too, and kept Hailey cornered in the lifeguard station. It paced back and forth, showing its teeth. Staying out of reach, the bastard. All she could do was stare at the fight. Tim stood firm, taking powerful swipes at each foe, but how could he possibly beat those odds?

The dark grizzly charged Tim, and the wolves scattered, letting the two giants duke it out. Hailey cringed as roars split the air. She had no idea bears could pull their lips that far back and expose so many teeth, but Christ, they sure could. Their six-inch claws slashed at each other's flanks.

"No," she croaked. She'd never seen anything so brutal in her life.

That spot on her chest warmed, and she caught the pearl without looking down. Her fingers played over the familiar, uneven surface. The pearl had warmed in the past — just enough to make her wonder before shaking the feeling away as the work of her imagination. But her pearl had never heated like this, almost burning her skin.

When she looked down, the pink was radiant with a faint inner light. She gripped the tower's handrail tightly. The pearl had glowed at her on that first uncertain night at Pu'u Pu'eo, as it had at different points of her life — but it had never glowed this brightly before.

Out of nowhere, images rushed through her mind like a slideshow that started in the present and went way, way back. The images grew blurry, then paused, and Hailey envisioned a woman very much like herself, fingering the pearl as she gazed across the golden prairies of eastern Montana.

"Great-grandma?" she whispered.

A man came up to the woman and spun her around in a slow circle that ended with a long kiss and a whispered *I love you* that echoed in Hailey's mind. A baby cried in the distance, and both the man and woman turned, hurrying to shower it with love.

There were tropical images, too, of lush coasts and water-falls and crashing surf very much like the scene before her. Hailey blinked and looked around. Maui? Oahu? Wherever that was, the images came from a long time ago, she was sure. As in, centuries back. A woman giggled in a mountain stream, beckoning a man closer. A man in some kind of native island garb with a bare, bronzed chest and a crown of leaves. That image blurred into the next, of the same pair in a scene so sensual, Hailey blushed. Palms swayed over the intertwined lovers, and the nearby surf crashed in time to the man's thrusts, drowning out the woman's sounds of delight.

The ocean delivered up another crashing wave, and Hailey blinked, yanking her attention back to the present. The bears were fighting, the wolves nipping, and the lone sentinel still guarding her tower. But the sounds were muted except for that of the sea.

Hailey frowned. What? What did it all mean?

She went over the images all over again, then stared at the pearl. Love. All the images it carried had to do with love. Beauty. Contentment.

Love, a faint, woman's voice whispered sadly in her mind. *Look what it makes us do.*

Hailey thought of her great-grandmother leaving her island home. She thought of her grandfather, smiling at the memories of his parents and his own dear wife long after they were gone. Then she trained her eyes on Tim and gulped.

Look at what love makes us do.

She looked long and hard. Love made a good man help a stranger when she needed it most. Love made him hide his deepest secret for fear of losing her. Love made him rush headlong into a battle he couldn't possibly win.

"Tim," she whispered, holding the pearl tight.

He fought on, parrying the grizzly's swipes, then twisting to chase off the wolf sneaking up from behind. The others hadn't gained an inch, but she could see Tim flagging. Blood matted the fur of one shoulder, and he limped on his right side. One ear was tattered, and—

The dark grizzly barreled forward, driving Tim toward the surf while the two wolves harried him from both sides.

"Tim!" she cried.

The wolf guarding the lifeguard tower made a cackling sound that said, *Watch and weep, honey. It won't be long now.*

Hailey had never witnessed a bear fight before, but it was clear the other grizzly couldn't beat Tim on its own. It could, however, drive him into the waves with the help of the wolves and wear him down. Sooner or later, Tim would miss a critical feint, and they'd smother him like so many lions taking down a gazelle.

"Dell..." Hailey fumbled through her pockets, but her phone was gone. Had Tim been able to alert the others before he came charging in?

She nearly sank to her knees in shame and desperation. All this was her fault.

So, do something, the voice in her mind said. *Help him.*

She looked around. How could she possibly intervene in a fight of wild beasts? Every one of them was stronger than her, and each was armed with sharp teeth and claws.

Don't underestimate yourself. Tim had said that once, and the words echoed through her head.

But, Jesus. All she had was a stick.

You have love, a voice whispered in her mind.

Tears streamed down her cheeks as Tim stumbled back toward the water. The wet sand made his paws sink deep, slowing every step. A wolf leaped onto his back, chomping down, and he bellowed in pain. With a sharp twist, the wolf went flying and landed with a thump.

Serves you right, Hailey wanted to shout.

Even with that wolf limping, however, it was still three-to-one. And she was as useless as a princess in a tower, waiting for her knight to rescue her.

She froze at the realization. Was that really her?

Sure looks like it, a little voice taunted her — not the voice that came with the pearl, but one from inside her own soul.

Anger welled up inside her. No, she wasn't a princess.

So, show it. Get out there.

She wanted to protest that she'd get clawed and torn to bits, but she bit the words back. Tim was the one getting clawed and torn to bits. She was still hiding in her tower.

Her lips pulled back in an unconscious snarl. Her knight had his hands full, and she sure as hell wasn't the type to wait around.

So why don't you get moving? the little voice taunted her. *Afraid of breaking a nail?*

She clenched her teeth, ready to shout back, but there was no one there. Just her own pride and the stark reality that even a determined hero might not be able to win without help.

So she tested the strength of her stick with both hands and took a deep breath. The pearl warmed against her skin, glowing pink.

Love, the faraway voice said.

Get 'em, that other voice said.

It was like having a fairy godmother and a warrior inside her, each of them egging her on. One was the pearl — a crazy notion she didn't have time to question now — and the other a deeply buried part of herself that was fed up with being a nice girl. She took a deep breath. All that kickboxing she'd done had to be good for something, right?

"Okay, then," she murmured. "Princess to the rescue."

Chapter Twenty-Three

The wolf guarding Hailey was paying more attention to the fight than to her, which gave her a little boost. Being underestimated had its pluses. She eyed the distance to the ground while waiting for the wolf to pace in front of the ladder. Six feet had never seemed like such a long way to jump, but then again, she'd never been in a life-and-death battle before.

That scared her, but it made her more resolute too. Jonathan's lifeless body had been trampled several times in the fight, and his blood was everywhere. Tim was bleeding too, and Lamar had made no secret of his plan to kill her.

So, yeah. Life-and-death was right.

The thought should have terrified her, but mainly, it helped her focus. She stared at the wolf below her and clutched her stick, planning her move.

Now! her inner Amazon cried.

Without thinking, she jumped. Not just a sissy jump either. No — she tackled the beast, slamming it to the ground. The second they collided, she jabbed with her stick and yelled like a barbarian. A moment later, the impact of her tackle caught up with her, and she gasped for air. The wolf scrambled away and stared with shocked eyes that said, *Holy shit.*

Hailey jumped to her feet and swung the stick at its head. The wolf jumped clear — barely — and snarled.

She swung again, and this time, the stick struck the beast across the muzzle. It yelped, but Hailey didn't relent, batting it again and again, driving it back. Power beyond anything she'd ever felt coursed through her arms, making each blow land with a solid thump that made her murmur, "Holy shit."

Maybe Tim was right about underestimating herself.

She swung the stick with both hands until the wolf scuttled back with an expression that said, *You are some batshit crazy woman, you know that?*

Hailey waved the stick. Batshit crazy was fine if that was what it took to win this fight.

"Go!" she yelled, waving her stick. "Get out of here."

The wolf took one long, panting look at the bloody fight then cantered out of sight.

Right, then. Hailey checked her mental scorecard. *One down, three to go.*

She turned to the others, who were all so intent on gaining some advantage they hadn't noticed her come down from the tower. Which meant she had the chance to run, but the second the thought entered her mind, she chased it away again. Lamar and his cronies would be the ones running soon, not her.

She gripped her stick tightly and stepped closer. With one hand, she reached up to touch the pearl, thinking of her grandfather. Even with all the bloodshed around her, she didn't feel a burning need for revenge. All she wanted was for this to end.

So, end it, the little voice whispered.

She knew perfectly well only Tim could do that, because she was just the dwarf at the edge of a battle of giants. But if the dwarf could sneak in...

She crouched a little, picking a target, feeling strangely military, like she'd applied camo face paint and strapped a bazooka to her side. At the same time, she felt like an utter impostor. Was she even doing this right?

The wolf on the right was Lamar. The one on the left was lighter in color and slightly smaller, so she crept toward that side. Tim and the bear battled on, locked as close as a couple of weary boxers leaning on each other. The second Tim's eyes drifted over her, they went wide.

She couldn't read his mind, but his thoughts were perfectly clear. *Are you nuts? Get out of here!*

She shook her head and focused on the wolf. The moment she moved, the others would know she was there, and anything could happen. If they all came for her, she'd be mauled on the spot.

So, don't let them get you, the inner voice said.

She stepped wider and nodded in a signal. Whether Tim had seen it or not, she was going in.

She swung the stick wide and bashed the wolf's rear legs, wincing at the blow. The wolf howled and fell, and she rushed in with three more sharp hits to the same area before she retreated.

The pitch of the animal fight changed — just as loud, but more alarmed than before, with Lamar giving a *What the hell?* bark and the dark bear swinging its head around, chuffing in confusion. Tim grabbed the momentary advantage, slashing the bear's shoulder with his claws and following up with a bite.

For a moment, the battle lulled. But then Lamar growled, rallying his men.

Get her. Get him, his bark said.

From that point on, it was all Hailey could do to jerk the stick left or right to deflect the beasts that attacked. Whenever that failed, she unleashed her best kicks and screams. It was all a blur of fur and fangs, and she couldn't tell whether Lamar or the other wolf was coming at her. All she knew was that strength unlike anything she'd ever felt flowed through her body, letting her strike and kick again and again. Hard and fiercely enough to make her think she might have an inner beast of her own.

"Take that," she bellowed after landing one blow.

In any other circumstance, she'd be shocked at the idea of hurting an animal, but Lamar and the others were more than animals. They were the worst kind of men who didn't shy from applying their brute animal power for immoral goals. She learned to aim for their most sensitive spots — legs, eyes, noses — and to anticipate their moves. But then one of the wolves barreled forward, and the blow she aimed at it ended with a sharp crack.

"No!" she yelped as her stick shattered.

She stumbled back, flat on her ass. Flat on her back, in fact, and before she could so much as scramble up—

She froze, staring up into a pair of murderous jaws. The wolf snarled, looming over her. A long line of saliva extended from its lower lip. Its eyes shone red with an unmistakable message.

Gotcha, bitch.

Lamar.

She kicked wildly, catching him on the chin, and scuttled backward. But that had just angered him, and he stalked back up to her, shaking with rage.

Now you die, those jaws said. *Slowly.*

Hailey stared, unable to move except to reach for her pearl.

Love, she told herself, squeezing it tightly, knowing this was the end.

But then another bellow of pain broke the air, and both she and Lamar looked up. One bear was hunched over the other, savaging its neck before looking up, panting through bloody jaws. Then its eyes narrowed, and it stepped over its lifeless foe, advancing on its new target. The other wolf had retreated to a safe distance, holding up an injured paw.

Hailey's eyes went wide. Which bear was that? Was she its new target or was Lamar?

Its fur was stained with blood, making it impossible to identify the bear, but its snarling jaws made no secret that it was out for blood. Lamar turned to face it, and Hailey dragged herself back. Her heart thumped wildly. Was that Tim or the other bear?

Finally, she spotted the eyes and whispered in relief, "Tim."

Lamar crouched, recognizing him at the same time. He stuck his chin up, growling murderously, but his tail curled between his legs. Tim reared up over both of them, and his eyes jumped to Hailey, begging her to look away.

She turned away as snarls and barks erupted. Then she clawed at the sand, escaping the terrifying sounds of the final, frenzied fight. Then there was a sharp yelp, a crunch, and a dull thud.

"Oh God..."

The remaining wolf fled. Once his footsteps faded, the only sound was that of the never-ending surf and the pounding of her own heart. Hailey gulped. Then she forced herself to turn slowly and look.

Lamar was dead. Tim was covered in blood. His blood? Lamar's? She'd never seen anything so ghastly.

Tim took two steps away from the dead wolf then stopped and sank down, chuffing mournfully. He didn't look up; he just stared at the sand, utterly defeated even in his moment of victory.

Hailey's mouth fell open in a silent cry. Was he all right? Why didn't he look her way?

Then her own words echoed in her mind, and she understood. *What kind of monster is he?*

She'd meant Lamar, and that was back when the wolf shifter had first surprised her on the beach. But *monster* could just as well have applied to Tim, the way she'd said it.

She rose on shaky feet and walked slowly toward him. Monster? Shifters were terrifying, for sure — grizzlies and wolves alike. Lions too. But Tim was no monster. Neither was Dell or any of the others who'd helped her over the past week.

The pearl burned on her chest. *Show him. Tell him.*

She inched forward, telling herself not to add to Tim's injuries by showing her fear. Okay, he was a bear shifter. So what?

She nearly snorted out loud. There was a lot she could reply to *so what*, but now was hardly the time.

"Tim," she whispered, holding out her hand.

His head was on the ground, his eyes closed, and the big bear body didn't move except for the heave of his chest. An entirely different type of fear sliced through her, and she rushed forward. Was he dying?

"Tim," she cried, patting him all over, so desperate for a sign of life that she forgot about the grizzly part. "Please tell me you're all right." She fell over him, hugging that giant mass. "Please..."

He didn't respond, and she squeezed her eyes shut.

"No," she whispered as his breaths grew fainter. "Don't die. You can't die."

But the sharp heaves of his chest were flattening out by the second, and there was nothing she could do but cry.

"I love you," she whispered, desperate to get that much out while she could. Did shifters understand human words when they were in animal form? She stroked him gently, determined to make him understand. "I don't want to lose you. I owe you so much."

Tim didn't utter so much as a groan, and slowly, she opened her eyes, expecting the worst, like those beautiful hazel eyes glossed over and staring at death.

Then she blinked. The hazel eyes were bright and focused on her. Shiny — with tears? — and love.

"I owe *you* so much," he croaked.

Hailey scrambled to get to her hands and knees, wide-eyed. Tim was human again. Flat on his back and bleeding from a dozen wounds, but alive.

"Tim," she shrieked, grabbing him so hard, he winced. "Sorry!" She forced herself to let go, but a second later, she was lying over him again, mumbling between tears, "I'm so sorry I didn't understand. I'm so sorry I didn't listen."

"I'm sorry I didn't explain," Tim whispered. He touched her gingerly. "Really sorry. I should have—"

She shook her head. "You tried to. I didn't listen. I was too scared."

His Adam's apple bobbed. "Are you still scared?"

She held her breath then nodded. "Yes." She looked around. "Scared to death of all of this. Scared a little of this, too." She showed him the pearl. "Or maybe awed is a better word."

Tim glanced down with a *So? It's just your necklace* look, but a second later, his eyes went wide. "A pearl. A pearl of..." His hoarse whisper trailed off.

Pearl of what? She shook the question away, because that didn't matter now. "I'm scared of all this shifter stuff. But I'm not scared of you."

He held her arms, looking her over, and a smile slowly spread across his face. "Maybe I ought to be scared of you. You and that stick."

She helped him to a sitting position and looked around nervously. Jonathan's dead body was splayed across the sand, as were the bodies of Lamar and the other bear. The two injured wolves had fled, but who knew when they'd come back?

The sound of a truck's engine carried from beyond the woods, and Hailey cringed. "God, no."

Tim creaked to his feet and sniffed the air, alert for any sign of danger. But a moment later, a low hoot reached their ears, and he relaxed. Then he cupped his hands around his mouth, hooted back, and then turned to explain.

"That's Connor and the others."

Hailey exhaled then panicked when Tim sank back to the ground.

"Are you okay?"

He nodded wearily. "I just need to sit for a second."

A minute later, several men stepped into sight, and one of them whistled. "Holy crap."

That was Dell, and Tim held up two fingers in silent reply. The second he did, Dell, Chase, and one other man — Hunter — stalked off, tracking the missing wolves. Hailey's eyes drifted over the carnage on the beach, and her stomach turned. All that death and destruction... While it had been caused by Jonathan's wild ambitions and Lamar's unfettered greed, she still felt guilty. Wouldn't it have been better if none of this had occurred?

She shook her head, answering her own question, and went back to hugging Tim. Yes, but no. Without the greed of those evil men, she never would have found Tim.

"Destiny," he whispered, reading her mind.

She looked up and into his eyes, tilting her head. Was there really such a thing?

He nodded and cracked a tiny smile. "Destiny. I'll tell you all about it..."

"Later," she said immediately, hiding her face in his shoulder again. "Much later. Please. This is about all I can handle right now."

"Later," he whispered in her ear, holding her close.

Chapter Twenty-Four

Tim's wounds burned, and his joints had all locked up, but the moment Hailey relaxed in his arms, all that disappeared. The only thing that really hurt after that was his heart, and that was from sheer relief. Hailey wasn't disgusted or scared of his bear.

Of course, she's not scared, his bear snorted. *Did you see her fight?*

Yes, he had. And, wow. Who knew a nice girl like Hailey was capable of blows like that?

But, damn. She had been scared, and he had been too. The fight could have gone either way at any time.

His eyes fell to the pearl dangling from her necklace. It was an oblong, lumpy thing, not round and shiny like the couple of pearls he'd seen. But, hell. That had to be one of the legendary pearls of desire. He could feel its energy throbbing through the air.

"You okay?" Connor asked, stepping up to them.

Tim didn't look up. He just nodded over Hailey's shoulder. His eyes cracked open just enough to see the golden glow of Hailey's hair before shutting again.

Really okay? Connor muttered into his mind.

Tim hid a snort. Well, he was alive, and more importantly, Hailey was unhurt. But, damn. If he hadn't been holding her so tightly, his hands would be shaking, and he'd be a mess. Lamar had been inches from ripping out Hailey's throat, and everything had gone into slow motion for him. His feet had felt mired in mud, and the bear he'd fought seemed twice his weight when it came to shaking the bastard off to get to Hailey. Then there was how afraid he'd been — make that, how sure he'd been — that Hailey would reject him. And when she hadn't...

He tilted his head and inhaled her honeysuckle scent. Was she really hugging him back, or was all that a fantasy?

She patted his back and snuggled closer, making his weary soul soar.

Yeah, he told Connor. *All okay.*

Jenna came up next, and Tim could practically hear her unspoken cry of *Oh my God. Are you okay?* But she must have sensed that they needed each other more than anyone else, so she stepped back and surveyed the scene.

Tim didn't pay much attention to things after that, although when Dell, Hunter, and Chase came back, signaling to Connor with grim nods, Tim relaxed the last little bit. All Lamar's men had been eliminated. The threat was truly gone. But they couldn't stay out on the beach much longer — even a sheltered, off-limits stretch of beach like this. Sooner or later, a kitesurfer would sail by, and—

"We got this," Connor murmured, clearly thinking along the same lines. "You two can hit the road."

Neither one of them budged until Jenna crouched and gently touched Tim's back. "Come on. How about I drive you guys home?"

Hailey nodded before Tim did, and his heart swelled at how she'd perked up at the mention of *home.* Did that mean...?

"Home." Hailey nodded, pulling back far enough to cup his cheek. Her face was streaked with tears and her skin pale, but her eyes shone.

"Home?" he whispered. Was he a fool to hope she was picturing his place?

She nodded firmly and managed a thin smile. "That nice little place with a view of the sea..." But then her face fell again. "Your wounds..."

"We heal fast," he murmured.

Hailey didn't seem horrified by that either, and he pulled her into a tight hug, ready to pass out with relief. Eventually, Hailey helped him to his feet and kept an arm around him all the way back to the pickup. The vehicle was just as battered as he was, though it did have a beach towel in the back he could cover his naked body with. Hunter caught up and tossed Jenna the keys to the Land Rover, a much more comfortable ride. Hailey helped Tim into the back seat, and the second they hit the road, he drifted off into an uneasy sleep.

Back at Koakea, he couldn't manage more than a stiff, painful shower before falling into bed. He and Hailey spent the rest of the day and night in a strangely emotionless state, huddled like a couple of shell-shocked survivors of a shipwreck. But he woke the next morning more comfortable and cozy than ever before, probably because Hailey woke first and was touching him. Kissing him with light little touches meant to soothe and heal. He looked at her for a while before daring to speak.

"Hailey, I—"

She touched his lips and shook her head. "Coffee. I definitely need coffee first."

It was half joke, half procrastination, which was fine with him.

"Let me guess," she said as she poured two mugs a few minutes later. "Honey for you?"

He nodded wordlessly. What a fool he'd been not to have told her earlier. A fool who'd nearly paid the ultimate price.

The coffee — Hailey's best yet — chased away the bitter aftertaste of those thoughts, and they sat on the patio while he explained. *Really* explained, from the very beginning to the very end. It helped that the morning was a pleasant one, with sunshine, swaying palms, and calm, glittering seas. Connor was down at the beach with Joey, flying a kite, and other than the distant sound of a lawn mower, everything was still.

Tim told Hailey everything — maybe too much, but he wasn't going to keep anything from her ever again. He started way back from his first time shifting as a gangly teen and continued through the tight line he'd had to walk in the military, keeping his shifter side hidden away. He told her about his deadbeat dad, his bear shifter mom, and his brothers.

"So Chase is a wolf, and Connor is a dragon—"

Hailey had just about spat out a mouthful of coffee when he got to that part, but she composed herself with a gulp and wiped her lips.

"Dragon, huh?" she said slowly, staring at the two figures flying a kite in the distance. "Wait — even Joey?"

He nodded. "Well, he won't shift until he's a teenager, but yeah. He's a dragon like his mom, Cynthia."

He decided not to expand on that — especially the fact that Cynthia would flip out if she knew the kite was Connor's way of teaching Joey the basics of flying. Cynthia was highly overprotective of her son, having lost her mate in a dragon duel nobody knew much about. But those details, Hailey really didn't need to hear about right now.

He looked over. Hailey was staring out at the sea, as she did for the next long minute before speaking.

"I need to see. Please."

His heart rate tripled. "Uh — you sure you're ready for that?"

Her expression remained blank until realization dawned. "Not a dragon. God, no. I'm definitely not ready for that. I meant you. The bear. Please."

He took a deep breath before standing before her. His bear trembled inside, eager and terrified at the same time.

You think she'll like me? his bear asked, suddenly fretting.

Tim had no clue, but it took all his concentration to get his shaking hands to remove his shirt and pants. There was no use shredding another set of clothes, and he really didn't want to heighten the brutish effect of his shift. His body still ached, but with shifter healing setting in, he had no excuse to wait, and he didn't want to. Slowly, he kneeled a good six feet from Hailey and kept his eyes down while he shifted.

A slow shift could be agony, but Tim was so self-conscious, he barely noticed. His skin burned, the last of his wounds ached, and the usual tingle went through his body. But that was nothing compared to the anxious signals rattling his nerves. When he finished shifting, he clawed the hard-packed dirt of the patio area nervously.

Cut that out, he snapped at his bear.

The beast went perfectly still while he retracted his claws as far as he could.

Hailey didn't move. Not at first. Then she held out her hands wordlessly. He took one cautious step, then another, careful to keep his fangs out of sight.

Her hands closed around his muzzle in timid starts and stops, but eventually, she started stroking him all over. The bolder her moves became, the more he closed his eyes and hummed from sheer pleasure.

When Hailey chuckled, he looked up, startled.

"For a tough grizzly, you're pretty soft. Especially right here." She tickled his ears.

Told you she'd like me, his bear chuffed.

"And your tail..." She laughed outright. "You actually have a tail. It's kind of cute."

Soft? Cute? He expected his bear to growl, but the beast just cooed.

He cracked into a smile, then hid it before she could see his teeth. Then he shifted back into human form.

Already? his bear grumbled.

He nodded firmly. Better to quit while he was ahead.

"Good shifters and bad shifters, huh?" Hailey murmured, staring off into the distance while he dressed.

"Just like good and bad people," he said carefully.

Hailey frowned, and he thought of Jonathan, Lamar, and the others. But then someone cleared his throat, and they both looked up. It was Dell, though the usual swagger was gone from his step, and his normally boisterous voice was a whisper.

"Hey. Special delivery. Okay with you?"

He held up a paper bag, and Tim caught the scent of something sweet. A peace offering of some kind. He nearly growled Dell away, because it was all his fault for scaring Hailey the previous morning and setting off the events that led to the shifter fight. But Dell was Dell — as much of a brother to Tim as Connor or Chase, and it was hard to remain furious with him for long. Tim settled for grouchy and looked at Hailey first.

She had tensed, and Tim guessed why. Even with Dell in human form, the lion in him was impossible to overlook. The golden beard, the deep, yellow-brown eyes, the *I could pounce at any moment* demeanor. But a minute later, Hailey nodded, if a little nervously.

"Okay with me. Okay with you?" She looked at Tim.

He nodded slowly and kept his eyes firmly on Dell as the lion shifter approached.

"I just wanted to say sorry. For scaring you, I mean," Dell murmured, looking shier than Tim had ever seen him. "Really sorry."

"What do you have there?" Hailey asked, clearly trying to break the ice.

A shadow of a smile played over Dell's face. "Chocolate croissants. Tessa sent them over. They're perfect with coffee, you know."

Hailey laughed — really laughed, giving Tim hope everything might all work out after all — and beckoned Dell closer. "You guys are definitely corrupting me."

Dell flashed a smile and motioned toward Tim. "Nah. You deserve it. You know, for putting up with this dumb lug."

Hailey shook her head. "That dumb lug happened to have saved my life. And he's really sweet."

Tim glowed.

"Sweet?" Dell snorted. "Here, quick. Take these and let me go. I can't stand to see this."

"See what?" Tim protested as Hailey accepted the bag.

Dell motioned between them. "You. Her. The goo-goo eyes. God, you're worse than Connor and Jenna when they—" He cut himself off there and stepped back. "Anyway, I'm out of here. Enjoy the croissants." Then he stopped and looked at Hailey, all serious again. "And sorry. Again. Truly."

"All good," Hailey said.

Tim raised an eyebrow when Dell left. "All good?"

She smiled. "Well, mostly. I think." Then she leaned closer. "What did he mean about Connor and Jenna? When they what?"

Tim's mouth went dry. How was he ever going to explain about mating and mating bites?

"When they, uh...got together. Fell in love," he said. The words came out all awkward and choppy.

Hailey smiled faintly. "Goo-goo eyes, huh?"

Tim felt his cheeks heat. Okay, so maybe he did fall into a daze around Hailey. But that was hardly his fault.

"Maybe occasionally."

"Occasionally?" she teased.

He waved a hand. "It's kind of a shifter thing."

Hailey waited for him to explain.

At first, he couldn't form a single word, but then it all rushed out — everything about mating. How only the luckiest shifters found their destined mates. How instinct led them together, and how they bonded for eternity with a mating bite.

The plantation seemed quieter than ever when he finished, and he worried that Hailey might suddenly run.

Finally, she spoke, still looking stunned. "You want that with me?"

At first, his heart sank, because really, why would anyone want such a brutal-sounding thing? But then it dawned on him that maybe she meant something else.

"You want forever — with me?" she whispered.

"Of course I do. From the minute I met you, my bear wanted you." Then he winced, because that came out all wrong. "I mean, I knew you were the one. My destined mate. The one I'm meant for. Forever."

Her cheeks turned pink, making her freckles stand out the way he loved. "Mate, huh?"

He nodded slowly, breathlessly.

She fingered the pearl around her neck. "My great-grandparents were like that, I think. My grandparents too." Then she sighed. "My mom and dad — not so much."

"Most humans don't know about mates. They don't feel it as intensely as shifters do. But when a shifter finds his mate — when a bear finds his mate..." He trailed off there, because how exactly did he put all that into words?

Luckily, he didn't need to, because Hailey filled in the rest. "He'll do anything for her. Even a perfect stranger whose life is a mess. He'll shelter and protect her, and he'll forgive all her

231

stupidities." Tears welled up in her eyes, and before he knew it, he was on his knees, hugging her.

"No stupidities. No mess. And his mate does the same for him. She shelters him..." Just having her there made his house feel like a home. "Protects him..." He pictured her on the beach with the stick and an expression so determined, it could have knocked him back a few steps. "Forgives him all his stupidities."

He held her tightly with his eyes closed and his heart wide open, or so it felt. Gushing with all kinds of feelings that didn't seem half as scary as before. Then he dried her tears and kissed her. Light kisses full of hope, light, and wonder. Because, wow. That was his mate in his arms, and even the truth hadn't made her run. On the contrary, Hailey was hanging on like she never wanted to let go.

"Tim! Tim!"

A child's voice made them break apart and hurriedly brush away the last tears.

"Did you see my kite?" Joey called as he skipped past, flush with happiness. "Did you see me fly it?"

"Looks like you're getting really good with those, uh..." Tim searched for the right word, but between being a little dazed and not being a dragon, he stalled out for a second. "Updrafts."

Thermals, Connor grumbled as he shepherded Joey toward the main house. He didn't pause, and he barely turned his head, giving Tim and Hailey their space.

Tim held Hailey's hand and watched his brother go. When Connor had first met Jenna, it had been hard for Tim to understand why his brother had taken so many stupid risks for a woman he barely knew. But now, Tim knew. Boy, did he know.

Thanks, man, he called softly after his brother. *I owe you.*

Call us even, Connor replied in a casual tone.

Tim smiled. That was just like their army days. In their downtime, the guys picked on each other and complained about the tiniest, most insignificant things. But when it came to saving each other's asses with death-defying feats, they simply shrugged and carried on like it went without saying.

And, Tim supposed, it did. Just like his love for Hailey. Sometimes, words weren't the best way to express things. So he hugged her for a good, long time, assuring himself it wasn't all a dream.

"So what happens now?" Hailey asked, holding both his hands. "I mean, for anyone lucky enough to find their mate?"

Tim's chest rose and fell in a deep breath. There was so much he wanted to say and do. Where to start?

How about with a bite? his bear chipped in.

Much as he'd love to mark Hailey permanently as his — and better yet, let her mark him — he knew she'd need some time to be ready for that.

"We take it slow," he said. "One step at a time. As fast or as slow as you want."

"And after that?" she asked, holding his hand tight.

He took a deep breath. "If you're happy, then we make it permanent." He smiled, trying to lighten the moment. "I could get down on a knee and propose, if you want."

She swatted his shoulder, laughing. "God — please no. None of that."

He grinned wide. "Okay, well — we'll figure it out when the time comes. And in the meantime..."

Hailey arched one eyebrow, waiting.

He waved a hand over the sloping roof. "I happen to have a fixer-upper if you're looking for a project."

She beamed, letting her gaze wander. "Funny. I just happen to have some time to do exactly that." Then she frowned. "After I deal with my mother and my agent, that is."

He squeezed her hands. "This fixer-upper isn't going anywhere."

Really, *he* felt like more of a fixer-upper than the house, but as long as he could stick with Hailey, everything would be all right.

She shot him a wry smile. "It turns out I'm not bad at home repair, you know."

He slid a little closer, because the tease in her voice gave his bear all kinds of bad ideas.

"Oh, yes?" he teased back, sliding his hands around her waist.

She wound her arms around his neck and leaned to within a half inch of his lips. When she spoke, her voice was a sultry purr. "Mmm. Really good, when I'm motivated. And also good at a few other things."

He slid his hands lower to cup her perfect ass. "What kinds of things?"

Hailey nestled closer, winding a leg around his, and nosed her way to his ear. "Private things. Can't show you out where the neighbors might see."

His bear started calculating the distance to the front door and, more importantly, the bed.

"Better get you inside, then," he said in a low, husky voice.

She ran her fingers along the waistline of his jeans. *Inside* the waistline, making him forget the soreness he'd started the morning with.

"That would be good," she whispered. "Really good."

His bear just about groaned in need, and he nearly kissed her there and then. But once he got started with that, he'd never stop, so he *really* needed to get her inside. Pronto. Backing her up with a dozen fluttery kisses, he pushed open the door with his foot. Hailey's hands were wrapped in his hair by then, her body mashed against his, and the second he got her inside and backed against the wall, he covered her mouth with a crushing kiss. A kiss that made it damn clear she was his, even if he couldn't deliver the mating bite yet.

Yet, his bear chuckled, not rebelling for a change.

Hailey broke off the kiss long enough to flash her hungriest, naughtiest grin. "You know what you just said? 'Better get you inside'... ?"

He nodded, waiting.

She laughed and slid her hands to his groin. "My sentiment exactly. Better get you inside me, I mean." Then she tilted her head at him. "Wait a minute. Is this a bear thing?"

"Is what a bear thing?"

"This," she said, fanning the air between them. "This insatiable need. This cat-in-heat feeling that I'm going to die if I can't have you."

He chuckled, but it came out a low, hungry rumble that made Hailey's eyes spark even more. "Yep. I think it is."

"You think?"

"Never had a mate before." He shrugged, kissing her neck. Touching her sides, imagining the heat of her naked flesh against his.

"Me neither," she whispered, wrapping her leg around his. Her hands slid under his shirt, exploring. "You think we'll figure out what to do?"

He nipped her ear and slid a hand higher until it cupped the soft flesh of her breast. "I know we will, my mate. I know we will."

And that was the last thing he said for a good, long while, because it was one of those times when actions spoke louder than words. Much louder, in fact. Within minutes, they were wrapped around each other on the bed, groaning and panting. Howling, almost, because the contact felt so good.

"Yes," Hailey moaned when he thrust into her the first time.

Yes, he grunted with every one of his next hot, hard slides.

"Tim..." When she cried out a minute later, her voice shook with need.

Moments later, they both came, and he nearly roared. Hailey dug her nails into his back, crying out, and his mind just about blanked out.

Mate, his bear mumbled again and again, savoring her scent.

"Mate," he whispered, holding her tight.

Chapter Twenty-Five

Hailey sighed and snuggled closer to Tim. It was hours later, and her body hummed with satisfaction that dulled the layer of soreness and exhaustion deeper down. She let her fingers play over his bare chest, marveling at the fact that a bear lay hidden under all that smooth skin.

A bear, not a beast. She understood the difference now. It didn't matter what shape Tim took; he was still him. And those claws and fangs were more comforting than scary now that she knew they would only ever be bared in her defense.

She lifted her hand, flexing her fingers slowly. Tim had explained more about shifters in the lazy hours that had drifted by — and about mates. Apparently, mating would give her the ability to shift into bear form. That was pretty hard to imagine — not so much scary or repelling as plain old impossible to conceive. The mating part, on the other hand — the part about *destiny* and *forever* — she loved.

In some ways, the actual *biting* part sounded a little barbaric. And yet the idea made her tingle with anticipation and need.

"You okay?" Tim murmured from over her shoulder.

Oh, yes. She was more than okay.

She turned in his arms, coming face-to-face, and sucked a quick gulp of air. Just the thought of Tim being hers forever took her breath away.

"I'm great. Just having a hard time imagining something better than this."

Tim scrubbed his chin over her shoulder in that marking move she'd already come to love. "Well, everyone who's mated says the bite is amazing. Like the best sex of your life times ten."

She fanned herself a little. The sex she'd just had superseded all her previous experiences by a factor of ten. And a mating bite was supposed to make it even better?

"You sure that's not just a bunch of locker room talk from the other guys?"

Tim had laughed. "Are you kidding? The women are worse than the men. Just ask Jenna sometime."

"Maybe I will," she teased. Then she rolled to her back and sighed. "I think I'd feel guilty asking for more."

"No guilt," he whispered, kissing her forehead. "And no rush."

Hailey hugged him. Her whole life in recent years had been one big rush. She'd rushed from place to place, through every strictly regimented meal, and over contracts she'd never really had a chance to read. All of that was a rush toward "success" defined by someone else. But being with Tim was exactly the opposite. Peaceful. Serene. Sure.

She looked into his eyes, celebrating the fact that he was hers all over again.

Love. Look what it makes us do, a voice chuckled in the recesses of her mind.

Tim kissed her softly, and she closed her eyes, more than happy to spend another blissful hour making love with him. But Tim murmured and pulled away, checking the watch he'd left at the bedside.

"How much time do we have?" she asked.

He sighed. "Not enough."

Hailey bit her lip. She and Tim had to attend a meeting at the plantation house — a meeting with everyone who lived at Koakea and several of the neighbors from Koa Point. She'd met them already, but that was before she knew they were shifters — and before she'd spent a heated night in Tim's arms.

She fretted about that all the way over once she and Tim had showered and changed. "Won't everyone know we spent the whole morning having sex?"

He laughed and kissed her hand. "Believe me, they'll understand. Mostly, they'll be glad to see us alive — and to see us together. Finding your destined mate is a big deal for us. You'll see."

Still, it took everything Hailey had not to hang half a step behind as they approached the group gathered on the plantation house porch. She wasn't the least bit ashamed of being with Tim — but intimidated by the others? Hell yes.

But there was no teasing, no knowing looks. Only smiles and genuine joy from all around. The guys smacked Tim's back hard enough to make him wince, and the women hugged her like so many excited bridesmaids. Little Joey hopped up and down, though that had more to do with excitement over the shifter fight.

"How many were there? Were they big? Any dragons?"

Cynthia stuck her hands on her hips. "Joey, I've told you. Fighting is bad."

But the little guy's eyes remained wide, his face flush with excitement. "Did you really fight them all by yourself?"

Tim put an arm around Hailey's shoulders. "Nope. Not by myself." Then he shot an exaggerated look of annoyance around. "Of course, we might have had some help if my brothers had gotten their asses into gear faster."

Cynthia covered Joey's ears at asses, but the others just laughed.

"And let you miss your chance to play hero?" Dell grinned. "No way."

Connor nudged Dell, going serious again. He put a hand on Joey's shoulder, instantly calming the boy down. "We don't play, not when it comes to our territory and our lives. No heroes either, just brothers." He grinned and looked at the women. "And sisters. And we'll do anything to protect our own. Of course, we'd rather prevent trouble." Connor gave Cynthia a firm nod. "But if trouble comes to us — you know we'll drop everything on the spot and come running."

Hailey took a deep breath as Tim and Connor locked eyes, making all kinds of silent vows to each other. The others all went serious too, and an undercurrent of raw power filled the air. A grim, *we'll fight to the death* determination that befit a corps of elite soldiers. Which was exactly what Tim and his brothers had been — but Hailey sensed that extending to Cynthia, Jenna, and Joey, too. It was as if they were all members of the same unit — or the fiercest fighting family alive.

In a way, it was scary, because she'd experienced the dangers of the shifter world firsthand. At the same time, it was comforting to know she didn't have to face those threats alone.

"Anyway, all's well that ends well," Dell announced. "I'm starving. And you two must be absolutely famished after all that... fighting and all." He winked.

Hailey cleared her throat and gave Dell a *Watch it, buster* look before Tim did something like bare his teeth. She might be the new kid on the block — and yes, she really was starving after a morning of nearly nonstop sex — but a guy like Dell would keep right on joking if she didn't show him the limits early on.

"I could use a bite," she quipped with a wink at Tim.

His eyes went wide, and she might have blushed a little. She'd surprised herself with the innuendo, but the longer she spent with Tim and his family, the more comfortable she grew with the idea of shifters, destined mates, and even mating bites.

Dell's tiny nod of approval told her she'd passed the test. Jenna grinned and gave her a thumbs-up — plus a naughty wink that promised she'd share all kinds of raunchy details when they got the chance. Connor shot Tim a sly look, and Chase — well, the poor guy backed away, shy as ever.

Chase grew up in the wild, Tim had told her earlier. *All wolf, so he's still a bit... well, awkward around people.*

Hailey could have snorted at the time, because *awkward* didn't fit the tall, muscled soldier in the least. But he did spend more time looking at the floor than into people's eyes, and his restless pacing never ceased.

Maybe someday he'll find his mate, Tim had murmured absently.

Hailey looked around. Connor and Jenna both radiated the kind of bone-deep satisfaction she felt. Hunter and Dawn, too.

Cynthia looked a little pinched, but every time she turned to Joey, she beamed. Dell, on the other hand, was all *easygoing bachelor,* and Chase definitely had *loner* in his blood. But even Tim had admitted to never understanding about mates until he'd met her, so maybe someday...

Cynthia motioned to the table, and in no time, everyone was sitting, talking, and devouring the food laid out like a feast. It was like attending the Thanksgiving dinner of a big, welcoming family, and Hailey sat back, observing their gestures and words. She'd grown up an only child, and watching the others revealed so much about each person. Some were funny, others more serious, and everyone interacted with one another in a slightly different way.

"Told you shifters aren't much different from people," Tim whispered between bites.

She considered for a moment before answering. Not so different, yet different in little ways. They were certainly more intense than most people she knew, but she supposed that might apply to any group of tight-knit soldier types. Everyone held their emotions in check, yet the mutual love and devotion were perfectly clear. In short, a community of the very best kind.

Cynthia must have noticed Hailey fingering her pearl, because her intense, dark eyes dropped to Hailey's neck several times over the course of the meal. Cynthia had a whole string of pearls — big, perfect, round ones, all with a hint of blue. She toyed with them absently, staring off into the distance. When everyone had eaten their fill, Cynthia glanced at Connor. He nodded, and Cynthia tapped the table. The small talk died away, and the mood grew serious.

"So," Cynthia started with gravity. "An enemy defeated. But one mystery remains." Her eyes fell to Hailey's pearl, and she waited.

Hailey wasn't entirely sure what to do, but when Tim nudged her, she took off her necklace and held it out for everyone to see.

"You mean this?"

241

Cynthia nodded. "A pearl. But not just any pearl, from what I understand. What do you know about it?"

Hailey shook her head. "Not much. My grandfather gave it to me. It belonged to my great-grandmother..."

"And you felt it during the fight?" Cynthia asked.

Hailey nodded, but it was Dell who spoke first. "Hell, I could feel its power from twenty feet away. Just like we all felt Jenna's that day of the sea dragon fight."

Sea dragon? Hailey's eyes went wide. That story, she hadn't heard yet.

Everyone looked at her expectantly, so she did her best to explain. "My grandfather told me it was special, but I never thought he meant..." She struggled for a word. *Magical* sounded too unbelievable, but *unique* didn't begin to describe it.

"Powerful?" Tim filled in.

She tilted her head. "Sort of. But more like...like heat. Energy." She bit her lip. How to describe that feeling of being powered by a thousand-volt battery?

"Have you ever felt it do that before?" Cynthia asked.

She nodded slowly. "It's warmed up lots of times but never like at the fight. I've only ever felt it when I was alone." She gulped, trying to overcome the feeling that this was too personal to share. These people were her friends, and she could trust them. "When I was lonely...I could feel it then."

It had to sound crazy, but everyone hung on to her every word, dead serious.

"My grandfather used to make up all these stories about it — at least, that's what I thought at the time. He said the pearl held a reservoir of love. A whole river of it that it might someday unleash, and if I was really lucky..."

She looked at Tim then swallowed as emotions welled up inside her again. The first time she'd met Tim, the necklace had felt warm. Had that been the pearl, telling her she could trust him? And all those times around Jonathan — the pearl had seemed to cut into her, keeping her on edge. Warning her?

She stared as it warmed in her hand.

A river of love, she remembered her grandfather saying. *And someday, that river will find you too.*

Sunlight glinted off the pearl, and she swore she heard a faint chuckle in the depths of her mind.

Found you.

She looked at it more closely. Her mother had always said it was too lumpy to be valuable, but obviously, she was wrong.

"What?" Tim tilted his head at her bitter laugh.

"My mother said it was worthless."

Jenna snorted. "Worthless, my ass."

Cynthia winced and covered her string of pearls the way she'd covered Joey's ears.

Hailey sighed. "That might explain why my mother never had the love story my grandparents did." She looked at Tim, awestruck all over again. *The love story you and I have,* she nearly said.

His eyes glowed, and the corners of his mouth curled into a tiny smile.

"There they go again," Dell sighed. "Don't look, Joey."

Joey frowned. "You're not going to kiss, are you? Yuck."

Tim grinned. "Sorry, buddy. I'll try to control myself, but every once in a while..."

Dell rolled his eyes, looking to Joey. "You said it, man. Yuck."

Cynthia ignored all of them. "Where did your grandfather get that pearl?"

Hailey furrowed her brow. "My great-grandmother came from Hawaii. She met my great-grandfather when he was stationed at Pearl Harbor in World War II. It was a present from her family..."

She trailed off and stared at the sparkling sea.

"During the fight, I saw things. Places. People." She shook her head and started again. "It was like the pearl was remembering things, and I could see them too. Things from a long time ago — centuries ago, I think."

Cynthia leaned closer. "What exactly did you see?"

She waved at the craggy peaks of West Maui, rising behind them. "Mountains. Waterfalls. Pounding surf." Hailey blinked and looked around. "Just like here, or maybe Oahu. Wherever it was, it was a different era. I saw a woman and a man, both of them dressed like in olden times. Before Captain Cook came along. Grass skirts, that kind of thing."

"That's it," Jenna said, nearly bouncing in her chair. "Nanalani!"

Na-na-who? Hailey wanted to say.

Cynthia nodded slowly and whispered, "A pearl of desire..."

Then she shook her head and hurried into the house. A minute later, she came back with a thick, leather-bound book. The moment Cynthia opened the volume, the dry, dusty scent of time floated through the air. It looked as old as an ancient bible, and judging by the way Cynthia handled the volume, it wasn't far off in terms of significance.

"Here," Cynthia said, turning the book around.

Jenna leaned in. "Wow. It looks just like that one."

Hailey stood to look, following Jenna's outstretched finger. The bottom of the page was filled with an illustration of a tropical island with a waterfall, craggy mountains, and a golden strip of sand. A woman stood waist-deep in the ocean, not looking the least bit worried about the shark fin circling her. Instead, she focused on the pale spheres cupped in the seashells she held.

Hailey gasped. "Are those pearls?"

Cynthia nodded, and Joey crawled into her lap to look. "I can count them. Look. One, two, three, four, five. Five, Mommy."

Cynthia hugged him. "Good job, sweetie."

Dell gave the boy a high five, but Hailey's eyes stayed glued to the page. The pearls were all shapes and sizes, and the one nearest the woman's pinkie looked like hers — an uneven, oblong shape with a hint of pink.

"Pearls of desire?" she whispered, reading the swirly script.

Jenna took the book from Cynthia and put her finger on a spot in the text. Obviously, she'd read the book before. "This is the story of Nanalani, the daughter of the shark king."

Hailey's eyes grew wide. Shark shifters?

"It's a Hawaiian legend," Connor explained.

"Not just a legend," Jenna corrected him and started reading.

"Nanalani could only love from afar for fear of her shark side coming out. Terrified of wreaking death and destruction upon her friends the way her brother had done when he took human form, Nanalani kept herself sequestered in a cave for years. Finally, in her loneliness and sorrow, she called forth the spirit of the sea..." Jenna read faster, and everyone leaned in. *"Nanalani put a spell on her pearls — the pearls of desire. Her treasures allowed her to go safely forth as a woman and love a man she had admired from afar. Over the years, Nanalani had many lovers, though she never found her mate."* Jenna looked up at Hailey. "Here it comes. Wait till you hear this." She grinned and read on. *"As time went on and her lovers passed away, Nanalani threw her pearls back into the sea, one by one. 'Now I am alone again,' she sighed to the god of the sea. 'I give you my pearls, not to keep, but to safeguard for another worthy lover who needs their power someday.'"* Jenna looked up. "That's you."

Hailey blinked. "Me?"

"Yep." Jenna's eyes danced. "You. A worthy lover who needed the pearl's power."

Hailey looked at Tim. Her cheeks burned, but Jenna pulled out a necklace, making Hailey gape.

"This is mine."

Hailey stared.

Tim turned the book around. "That one does look like Hailey's..."

She lay a hand over the spot on her chest the pearl usually rested over. All those years, she'd been carrying a pearl with mysterious powers?

"But Jenna's and Hailey's pearls look different," Joey pointed out.

They did — totally different. But Cynthia just shrugged. "Pearls are formed inside oysters. Remember that book we read? They all come out different."

"Like babies?" Joey asked.

Cynthia broke into a huge smile and ran her fingers through her son's fine red hair. "All different, like babies."

"I thought pearls were round," Dell said.

Cynthia shook her head. "Not all. Some come out like that. It's called a baroque pearl."

Hailey smiled. "My grandfather always said it was perfect in its imperfections."

He'd said that about her, too, making her feel better about her freckles and everything else she'd obsessed about as a kid.

"And pink means...?" Jenna asked.

"Pink in a pearl symbolizes fame, success, and good fortune," Cynthia said.

Dell cackled. "That fits."

Hailey frowned. "Fame? I could do without, believe me. And as for success and good fortune — I only feel like I've found that now." She leaned against Tim.

"It doesn't have to be taken literally," Jenna pointed out. "Like mine — wealth and prosperity can mean a lot of things." She wrapped her arm around Connor's, and her eyes shone with love.

Hailey thought it over. Fame and success didn't apply to everyone in her family, but good fortune... She thought of all the times her grandfather had talked about her grandmother as if she were still there. The way he'd recalled the special connection his own parents had once shared.

Her eyes strayed to Tim's, and he smiled. "Good fortune. I like that part."

She did too.

"Are yours special too?" she asked Cynthia. Surely a string of pearls that perfect had to outdo hers.

Cynthia flashed a thin smile and touched her necklace. "Alas, no. Just a pretty piece of jewelry. My mother gave it to me." Her smile grew bittersweet until she looked around in alarm, like she'd revealed one detail too much.

Connor, Tim, and the other men exchanged looks, and Hailey made a mental note to ask Tim what that was all about. There certainly was an air of mystery around Cynthia.

But Cynthia didn't look happy about sharing anything else, so Hailey motioned back at the illustration. "What about the pearls having power?"

Jenna tilted her head toward the book. "It doesn't say so specifically in there, but it seems like the pearls — the genuine pearls of desire — lend the bearer their power. Sometimes, at least. Like mine did when I needed it most."

"You need to have it in you, though," Connor pointed out.

"Have what?" Hailey asked.

Tim tapped her hand firmly. "Courage. Determination. The ability to tell right from wrong."

She sucked in a slow breath. Did he really mean her?

Jenna nodded, all matter-of-fact. "The pearl amplifies what you already possess."

Hailey turned back to the book, hoping to learn more. *"'And so it was that the pearls of desire — one for every kind of desire known to mankind — were lost, though legend claims they remain slumbering under the surface, waiting to be reawakened to inspire great acts of love again.'"* She leaned back. "Every kind of desire?"

Dell shrugged. "You know. Love, lust, passion. All that."

"Greed," Connor scowled.

"Commitment," Jenna said, taking his hand.

"Yearning," Tim whispered. He tilted his head toward Chase, who stared off into the distance silently.

"Undying passion," Cynthia whispered in a voice laced with sorrow and regret.

Hailey looked from one to another, trying to puzzle each person out.

"So, we're all good," Dell said, smacking his hands in a single clap. "Can I bring out dessert?"

Hailey laughed, as did Tim, but Cynthia's expression was pinched, and the way her eyes darted around suggested encroaching danger of some kind.

"Not yet," Cynthia said in a carefully neutral voice. "That's not all."

Chapter Twenty-Six

Hailey's heart thumped as she waited for more. Why was Cynthia so grim?

"You can desire lots of things," Jenna pointed out.

"Yeah, like dessert." Dell sighed.

Cynthia ignored him and looked at Hailey expectantly.

Her mind spun. What other kinds of desire were there? A frown dragged her lips downward as she pictured Jonathan and Lamar. "Wealth. Power. Like Connor said — greed."

"Exactly," Cynthia said. "Though it depends on the bearer. A pearl that awakens passion in one person can bring out the greed in another."

Hailey shifted in her seat with a growing sense of unease.

Cynthia took a deep breath then leaned over her son. "Joey, sweetheart. Do you think you can go upstairs and draw me a picture like this?" She pointed to the thick book on the table.

Joey nodded eagerly and scampered off. Cynthia waited for him to get out of earshot, then leaned forward and spoke in a hushed voice. "One pearl awakens." She pointed to Jenna's, then Hailey's. "Soon after, another appears, and destiny brings its bearer here..."

Tim bristled. "Nothing wrong with that."

Cynthia shook her head quickly. "Of course not. Not in and of itself. But there are three other pearls." She pointed to the book. "When will they awaken, and who else might they bring to our quiet corner of the world?"

Hailey shivered despite the warm afternoon breeze.

"Greed. Power. Wealth." Cynthia ticked each word off her fingers, then stopped and looked around.

"Moira," Connor filled in.

Hailey frowned. Her mind was so overwhelmed, she couldn't place the name for a moment, though she was sure she knew it. She closed her eyes, thinking, as Connor went on.

"We have no indication—"

"Shit," Tim cut in, slapping his forehead. "Lamar mentioned her. Something about a bounty."

Cynthia's face turned red, while her knuckles went white as she gripped the table. "What did he say exactly?"

Tim frowned. "He said, 'We'll get that bounty Moira offered, and the oil field too.'"

"What bounty?" Connor grunted.

Tim scowled. "I have no idea."

"Moira?" Hailey blurted as it finally dawned on her. "Moira LeGrange?"

Everyone stared, and even Chase, who'd been quietly pacing, went perfectly still.

"You know her?" Connor demanded.

Hailey made a face. "I know of her. She's the owner of the *Elements* fragrance line, right?"

Jenna nodded. "The one my sister posed for."

Hailey twisted her napkin in her lap, trying to tie the threads in her mind. "They wanted me to do one of their photo shoots, but I was already contracted to a competitor."

"*Boundless*," Jenna said immediately. "The campaign that did so well."

Connor frowned. "Maybe it did too well. If Moira put a bounty on Hailey's head..."

Hailey paled. It hadn't just been Jonathan and Lamar after her — Moira LeGrange had been involved as well? "But why? How?"

Connor chewed it over for a moment. "I don't know. Tell us more."

Hailey stared at a spot on her napkin while a tornado of thoughts rushed through her mind. "I know she wasn't happy about my turning down the offer." She tapped on the table, trying to remember what she'd heard. "Apparently, she was so mad *Boundless* did better, she bought the whole company."

"So why would she put a bounty on you? That campaign was over a while ago, right?" Jenna asked.

Dell had been following along incredulously, but he suddenly sat straight. "Holy shit."

"What?" Tim and Connor asked at the same time.

Dell made a sweeping gesture. "What better way to get more mileage out of an old campaign than to create a new round of publicity?"

"How?" Hailey asked.

"By bumping off the model," Dell finished.

Hailey shrank back, and Tim growled, but Dell went on.

"Just think about it. Killing Hailey does two things for Moira. First, she gets revenge on the woman who dared turn her down. And second, interest in *Boundless* soars thanks to the publicity."

"That's ridiculous," Jenna said. "Who would buy perfume because the model was murdered?"

"Not because — not directly," Dell said. "But *Boundless* would be in all the newspapers. That's free publicity. Believe me, negative publicity works. Not that I've ever heard of anyone resorting to murder..."

"Moira would," Cynthia said, choking out the name like a poison.

If Hailey hadn't had Tim's hand to hold, she would have been shaking like a leaf. "Is Moira a shifter?"

Cynthia nodded grimly, but it was Jenna who spoke. "Dragon."

Hailey covered her face with her hands. She'd managed to draw the wrath of a dragon?

"Look," Cynthia said quickly, trying to reassure her. "Moira has targeted a lot of people in the past."

Her voice shook, and Hailey had to wonder what person Cynthia loved had been hurt by Moira.

"But she's fickle, like the worst of dragons," Cynthia went on. "My worry is not that Moira will come after you again — not now that she's seen what you're made of. But it won't be long before Moira catches wind of the pearls and their power. That's what worries me."

"We took out every one of Lamar's men," Dell pointed out.

Connor and Cynthia exchanged dubious looks, and Cynthia replied. "That might well be, but it's hard to tell. I could feel the pearl's power from across the island, even though I couldn't pinpoint exactly what it was. Sooner or later, Moira is bound to hear about the pearls — or sense them."

Connor scowled at the book. "We've been lucky that the two pearls came to us first. But if another one awakens, and Moira gets to it first..."

Hailey felt sick, thinking of all the ways a powerful, corrupt dragon could misuse the incredible power she'd felt coursing through her veins. And if Moira had as twisted a definition of desire as Jonathan had...

"...the repercussions could be disastrous," Tim murmured, reading her mind.

"Wait," Hunter asked quietly. "Why now? The pearls have been lost for generations. Why would they surface now?"

Everyone scratched their heads, but Cynthia pointed at Jenna, who looked confused.

"What?" Jenna demanded.

"I think it could be you," Cynthia said carefully.

"Now wait a minute," Connor said, turning red.

Jenna put her hand on his arm, calming him down. "Hang on. What do you mean, Cynthia?"

Cynthia pursed her lips. "I'm not placing any blame. Not in the least. But it could be that your mermaid blood—"

Mermaid? Hailey stared.

"—triggered them. At least, it might have called to the first one. And now that one awoke from its slumber, it could be calling to the others."

A quiet minute ticked by, and no one said a word until Dell spoke up.

"So, what do we do? Hunt down the others? Go after Moira?"

Cynthia shook her head immediately. "There's no defeating Moira on her home turf."

She spoke as if out of bitter experience, making Hailey wonder what had happened.

Connor frowned. "Moira might not have caught wind of the pearls yet. We're better off watching. Waiting. Hoping we get to the next pearl first." Then he sighed, taking Jenna's hand. "If another one actually turns up. You never know."

Hailey closed her hand around her pearl and held it close to her chest.

"It's hard to say," Cynthia admitted. "But it's possible these two will further stir whatever power it is that fuels the pearls. And that might wake the others."

Jenna looked around, aghast. "I'm so sorry. I never thought..."

Cynthia shook her head immediately. "Nothing to be sorry about. It's destiny, not you. We just have to be cautious."

Connor took Jenna's hand and caressed it, then looked around to reassure everyone else. "Look, there's no reason for paranoia, just for caution. So we go on doing what we came here to do. Working. Living. Making a better life." He smiled at Jenna.

Hailey squeezed Tim's hand, thinking of the construction business he'd been busy launching when she'd interfered. The second she could, she would devote herself to helping him the way he'd helped her.

"I agree," Cynthia said. "We look forward, not back. But we keep our eyes open."

"Aye-aye, captain," Dell said.

"Damn," Hailey muttered just as everyone was brightening again. "Oops. Sorry. I just remembered my mother. My agent." She hung her head. All the obstacles she still faced before she could throw herself into the kind of life Connor had described.

Dell laughed. "You faced all those shifters armed with — what? A stick? She can't possibly be worse."

Hailey managed a thin smile. "You don't know my mother."

Tim laced his fingers tightly through hers and kissed her knuckles, promising her she'd have a big, bad bear at her side when the time came.

"At least you don't have to worry about Jonathan and Lamar," Connor pointed out.

Hailey gulped, but Tim touched her shoulder. "What they did is their own fault, not yours."

"I know, but it's sad anyway. And what if someone traces them to us?" she asked.

"No one can trace them to us," Dell said with a dry laugh. "Connor and I took care of that."

Cynthia raised an eyebrow. "Do I want to know the details?"

Connor shook his head firmly and reached for a newspaper. "Let's just say Jonathan and Lamar took their final private flight. All hands lost when their chopper crashed into the deepest part of the Kaiwi Channel, and no witnesses."

He held up a newspaper, and Hailey stared at the headline.

"*Helicopter Crash Claims Oil Magnate's Life?*" Cynthia frowned.

Hailey stared. How could Connor possibly make the carnage of the shifter fight look like a helicopter crash? Then it hit her. He was a dragon. It wouldn't have been hard to take Jonathan's helicopter, dispose of the grisly evidence offshore, and then fly home under his own power.

She ought to have been angry at Jonathan for causing so much unnecessary suffering, but all she felt was sorrow. For him, and for his family. If Jonathan hadn't come after her on Maui — or trusted Lamar — he might still be alive. Alive and free to make a move on some other woman he deemed suitable as the future Mrs. Jonathan Owen-Clarke.

Still, she groaned. "God, the press is going to be all over this. I'm so sorry I ever got you involved in this mess."

Tim shook his head firmly. "I'm not sorry."

"Neither am I," Connor added. "Let word get out that the shifters of Koa Point just hired the world's best security force. Us. Let anyone dare come anywhere near us again."

His words were full of force and conviction, and Hailey found herself sitting straighter.

"Besides, we're lucky with the timing," Dell said.

Tim raised one thick eyebrow. "Lucky? How?"

Dell grinned, pointing to the newspaper's back page. "You're talking about a plain old helicopter crash. What you've got here is a juicy celebrity cheating scandal. You know that loud chick from the reality TV show?"

"They're all loud," Chase muttered.

Dell went on without skipping a beat. "Remember how that NFL star proposed to her at halftime of the Super Bowl? Looks like he just got caught in a hot tub with..." Dell tapped a finger over the blurry picture. "One...two...three cheerleaders, none of them dressed. I'd say the press will be all over that instead of boring old you."

"Boring old who?" Tim glared.

Hailey laughed. "Boring old me. And you."

"Mommy, what's a hot tub?" Joey asked, coming out of nowhere to appear at his mother's side.

Cynthia turned pink. "Never mind that, sweetie. What do you have here?" She clapped and held up his drawing. "Wow. Look at that!"

"Wow," Hailey said, and not just to compliment Joey. For kid art, it was really good. "You've got the waterfall, the mountains, everything. Did you draw it all from memory?"

Joey beamed, nodding a thousand miles an hour.

"Let's see," Dell said, and Joey skipped over, sliding into his lap. "Whoa, Cynth!"

She sighed. "Cynthia."

"You got a hell of an artist here," Dell said, ignoring her.

"Language, please," Cynthia murmured.

Dell looked at Joey. "Does she want me to say it in Spanish?"

Joey giggled. "She already speaks Spanish. And French. And Latin. And Welch."

Cynthia hid a wince. "Welsh, sweetie."

Dell waved a hand. "Whatever. Check this out, guys." He held up the drawing again. "It's amazing. So amazing, I think the brilliant artist has just earned his next Star Wars ride."

"Star Wars?" Cynthia looked aghast.

Tim laughed and whispered to Hailey, "She's trying to keep Joey civilized, and Dell is hell-bent on letting him be a kid."

Dell stood and hunched, motioning to his back. "Get on your X-wing, young Jedi, and prepare for takeoff."

Joey whooped and jumped onto Dell's back while Cynthia clutched her pearls. "Takeoff?"

Dell started running for the stairs at full tilt, calling, "Don't worry. The force is with us. At least, most of the time."

The last word was nearly cut off as Dell launched off the top stair, and even Hailey grabbed the table at the sight of them hurtling through the air. But Dell landed as smoothly as a cat and sprinted on with Joey whooping in glee from his back. "The Force is with us."

Cynthia slumped back in her chair. "I'm not sure the Force is with me."

Hailey made a mental note never to ask Dell to babysit if she and Tim ever had kids. Then she caught herself and choked down a laugh. Maybe it wouldn't take her long to get used to the shifter world, after all.

"Aw, relax, Cynth," Connor joked, doing his best imitation of Dell's drawl. "Lions are cats, and cats always land on their feet."

"Cynthia," she sniffed, reaching for the drawing. Slowly, her smile reappeared. "It is good, isn't it?" she murmured.

"Deserves a spot on the fridge, for sure," Jenna agreed.

Cynthia stood, and slowly, Hailey sensed the official part of the meeting wind down. She slipped on her necklace, and Connor helped Jenna put hers on. Chase wandered off to the kitchen, and Dawn started clearing away the plates.

Hailey stood to help her, but Dawn shooed her away. "We got this."

"But—"

Jenna stood to help Dawn. "Yep. We got this."

Tim took Hailey's hand and tugged her toward the stairs. "See? They said they've got it. And I'm sure Connor is dying to help."

"I am?" Connor asked.

"Yep," Tim insisted, sliding his arm around Hailey as they walked.

The moment their sides touched, heat rushed through her veins, and a whole different kind of hunger washed over her. When Hailey touched the pearl, it was warm, and she swore she heard a naughty giggle in the depths of her mind. Was that the ghost of Nanalani, happy to see her pearls in action again?

"You two off so soon?" Connor asked as he stood to help Jenna.

"Yep," Tim said without turning back. "See you later." Then he whispered to Hailey, "I think we have some research to do."

She worked her hand into his back pocket, cupping his firm ass as they walked. "Research? What kind?"

"You know. All the different types of desire."

Hailey grinned and walked on, tucked comfortably at his side. So comfortably, she could tip her head back to soak in the sun. And with every step she took, she shed another layer of fear, worry, and sorrow that had settled over her during the course of the meeting. She inhaled deeply and concentrated on Tim's reassuring warmth.

Yes, the world had its problems, and God knew she'd had plenty lately. But Koakea was a world apart — a blissful corner of the world where evil was hard to picture. Joey whooped in the distance, and a myna bird flitted by, chattering. Tim's leather-and-pine scent filled her nose, and it was all too easy to picture what he'd treat her to next. How he'd lay her out on the bed and slowly strip her of clothing, one piece at a time. How he'd kneel down and worship her — thoroughly — before bringing her to their next shared high. She'd get her chance to play, too, and her mind already spun with options on what to try next.

"And what is it you desire, Mr. Hoving?" she whispered when they got to the front door of his place.

He picked her up and backed her slowly against the wall, giving her a taste of the ecstasy ahead. "You, Hailey. You."

Chapter Twenty-Seven

Six weeks later...

Hailey walked along, smiling up at the midnight moon, staying in a straight line by keeping one hand on Tim's furry back. Well, close to a straight line, because bears tended to ramble, sniffing the faintest trails and sweetest flowers with their sensitive noses.

She flexed her fingers in his thick pelt, marveling as she always did. The outer edges were coarse, but the inner part was soft — especially up by his ears. She rubbed them absently, and he responded with a low, happy chuff.

"You like that, huh?" She giggled.

The first few times she'd faced him in bear form, she'd been as tense as a spring. But that felt like a lifetime ago, and she'd grown to love their moonlit walks. Tim went in bear form, and she walked along beside him, exploring the huge property. Even the sight of Tim dragging his claws down huge tree trunks didn't faze her any more. Lately, she was even starting to wish she could do the same. It all looked so... so... satisfying. Shaking out a thick coat of fur. Stretching and then padding along with her nose to the breeze. Nuzzling her mate...

Tim circled around and rubbed his side along her legs then stopped to nuzzle her hip. *Really* nuzzling, nearly pushing her back with his weight.

She laughed and stuck a foot out to brace herself. "Watch it, mister. You're too big."

Tim looked up at her with shining hazel eyes that said, *And you're just right. You're perfect.*

It was amazing how quickly she'd learned to understand his bear expressions. But lately, she'd found herself wanting more. To be able to talk to Tim — and to the others — without speaking, as all shifters could. To be able to let go of the stresses of civilization and tune in to the natural world. Maybe even get in touch with her wild side and run her claws down the trunk of a tree from time to time.

Not that she had a lot to complain about. Other than a crazy week after the shifter fight, it had been incredibly smooth sailing. Yes, she'd had to meet the press, but Dell was right — the quarterback hot tub scandal was the big story, and hers quickly faded away. She'd had to face her mother too, and as hellish as that had been, she'd stood firm. Within a week, she'd let go of her agent, signed the lease on the condo over to her mother along with half the money in her accounts, and transferred the rest of her earnings to a new account — one in her name only. A few modeling offers still came in, and she referred them all to Joelle Parks, the model whose career her mother and Jonathan had sabotaged. Joelle was on the rise again, and Hailey was more than happy to leave the modeling world to her.

As expected, Hailey's mother and agent had both flipped out, but even that had a happy end. Hailey's "childish" and "regrettable" actions — their words, not hers — had pitted her mother and agent together against a common cause, and they'd ended up having a torrid affair. Within two weeks of Hailey's departure from the modeling scene, her mother kicked off her own career as a mature model, represented by her new lover. She was doing jewelry, fashion, and had just announced plans for a nude shoot. Which ought to have made Hailey sick, but considering how happy her mother was — and how off her back — it was great.

As for Jonathan — she grieved for his family, but that was all. It didn't take his father long to announce a foundation in Jonathan's name — one Hailey hoped would truly do the good deeds it claimed rather than being a tax shelter of some kind. Tim had looked doubtful, and Connor had offered to investigate, but she'd shaken her head. The Owen-Clarke family was out of her life for good.

Her land in Montana, meanwhile, was all hers — and safe from greedy oil interests. She was letting the property lie untouched for the time being, but someday, she and Tim planned to fix up the cabin as their own little getaway.

"Lots of space for a couple of bears to roam out there," Tim had murmured dreamily when they had talked about it.

Bears. As in, her and him. The more Hailey thought about it, the more she liked the idea.

When everything had gradually quieted down, she found a new bounce to her step, a readier smile — plus a few more pounds of padding around her ribs, which wasn't a bad thing. She and Tim had thrown themselves into renovating his house — when they weren't screwing like bunnies, that was. They'd finished off the patio with huge, earth-toned tiles and shored up the roof supports. She'd registered for an online course in architectural design and had started weeding out the nearest coffee grove. Her mind was already spinning with dreams of cultivating it on a bigger scale, though she hadn't told anyone yet.

Tim had nearly turned down his first contracting job to help her design an addition for the house, but they'd decided to put that off for a while. He was still busy with his security job, and she'd insisted that his business come first, so he'd taken the offer of installing skylights on a nearby estate.

"Practice for our place someday," he'd half joked.

It hadn't taken them long to settle into a new rhythm, and their nighttime walks became her favorite. At those times more than ever, she had the feeling of controlling her life. A life she loved every part of, though one little detail still niggled at the back of her mind.

Tim was hers, and she was his, but they hadn't actually mated yet. She'd needed time to get over the last vestiges of her fears, and Tim hadn't pushed her. But lately...

She slid her hand over his back and tilted her head in the direction of his house. "Ready to head home?"

His eyes sparkled at the way she said *home*, and she could relate. Tim's little cabin was the first place she'd truly felt at home for years. And tonight...

She hid a naughty smile. Tonight could well be the night they mated for good. She closed her eyes, imagining what it would be like. Would it truly be all the pleasure of sex times ten?

Times twenty, Jenna had assured her in a giggly, girls-only conversation they'd had not too long ago. *The bite hurts — hurts so good, if you know what I mean.*

Oh, Hailey knew all about that. Tim had been treating her to all kinds of good loving over the past few weeks, and the urge for more was starting to build in her.

So she put a little swing in her hips and led the way home, grinning at the appreciative bear rumble that sounded from behind. Within a few steps, the soft pad of his bear paws turned to the quicker rhythm of a man's feet, and Tim took her hand in his.

"Oh," she squeaked, not so much surprised as amazed at how smoothly he could shift.

She peeked back. His hair was spiky, as it always was after a shift, and a slightly musky scent still clung to his shoulders. But the leather-and-pine mix she loved so much was there too, along with every hard muscle she'd memorized over the past few weeks. Her eyes drifted down, and she couldn't hide a grin at the other — ahem — hard muscle lower down.

"Men." She faked exasperation. "Always thinking about sex."

He grinned and pulled her close — close enough for her to feel his hard length.

"I was wandering along, innocently thinking of honey and flowers, when *somebody* started putting bad ideas in my head," he teased.

"I can't imagine how you got that idea," she said, sliding her hands over his ass. She arched her shoulders back, letting her breasts push against his hard chest.

"So, I'm wrong?" He sniffed her ear. "You really just want to go back to bed?"

She laughed. "Oh, I want to go to bed, all right. But not to sleep."

"I think I can help you with that."

She crooked her fingers, coaxing him toward the house. "I bet you can. And I wasn't just thinking of sex, you know. I might be in need of a bite too," she whispered, watching for his reaction.

But Tim just looked perplexed. "You're hungry?"

She nearly doubled over laughing. He thought she meant a bite to eat? The poor man. He must have truly settled in for a long wait if he didn't catch on to her hint.

"Not that kind of hungry," she chuckled.

They were nearly at the front door before Tim figured it out. She could tell by the catch in his breath and the careful way he reeled her back into his arms.

"You mean. . . ?"

It was a whisper with a hint of a growl, which meant both sides of him were talking — the man and the bear.

She grinned and tilted her head, running her fingers along her neck. "I was thinking somewhere along here."

Tim's eyes brightened, and his nostrils flared. And, damn. His arousal jumped right over to her, and her skin prickled. It felt good just touching herself. How amazing would it feel to have him touch her there?

She didn't have to wait long for an answer, because Tim laid his big, callused hand on her neck and slid it slowly around as if searching for a particular spot.

His voice dropped an octave when he finally spoke. "More like around here."

She closed her eyes and leaned right, craving more of his touch. Her body swayed in a silent dance, and when Tim's lips touched down on her neck, she arched in need.

"Right. . . about. . . here," he whispered, homing in on the spot.

With his free hand, he cupped her breast, making her moan for more.

"No fair," she whispered.

"No fair?"

"You're already naked, and I'm still dressed."

263

He grinned; she could tell from the curl of his lips around her skin. "Easily fixed."

She caught his hands before he did something rash like scissoring her clothes off with one extended claw. "Wait! This is my favorite shirt."

He pulled back to look at it with one raised eyebrow. "This one?"

She touched the middle section. "Sure. Recognize it?"

It was the T-shirt he'd bought her that first day in Waikiki, before she had an inkling of destiny, shifters, or mates. A pitiful existence, in retrospect, because her life was so much richer now. Every morning brought a promising new dawn, and every sunset crowned another satisfying day.

He grinned. "Now I remember it. But it still needs to come off."

He helped her pull it off while pushing the front door open with his foot. A moment later, they were inside, where he tossed the shirt to a chair.

"These need to come off too," he breathed, tucking his fingers inside the hem of her shorts.

She shimmied out of them, not too fast, not too slow. Anticipation might not be as good as the real thing, but damn, was it close.

"Now about these. . . " He cupped her ass with his two huge hands, one covering each cheek. For a minute, he toyed with her, dragging her panties around just enough to work the fabric against her most sensitive spot. Then he tucked his fingers inside the waistband and slid them off, kneeling as he went. When she stepped out of the panties, he caught her foot and made sure it was placed good and wide. A beam of moonlight sliced through the open door behind him, and when he looked up at her, she felt like a statue on the altar of a goddess.

A low, rumbling sound rose from his throat, and he leaned forward to kiss her stomach. Then he dipped lower, keeping firm hold of her ass. The wall wasn't far behind, and she leaned against it, burning with anticipation.

"So beautiful," he murmured, coming closer.

His breath puffed against her core, and his tongue followed. Gently at first, then harder. His fingers were next, and it wasn't long before she was writhing and clutching blindly at the wall. Her hips moved in languid circles, heightening the pressure.

"Up here," he whispered, hooking her leg over his shoulder.

Her eyes went wide first, but the second his tongue touched down, her head rolled back. It was one of those times she was glad they had no immediate neighbors, because it was impossible not to make noise. A lot of noise, and the more she made, the harder Tim drove her. Higher and higher until it felt like she was floating off the floor. Floating and crying his name, then clutching at his shoulders when she came with a desperate shudder.

"Yes..." she panted, slowly melting against the wall.

Only part of her mind noticed Tim inch his way up her body, discarding her bra as he went. The rest of her mind spun in a whirlwind of blurry pleasure until his lips covered hers. Her eyes flew open, because that taste was hers and his, all mixed together.

"You sure you're ready for this?" he rumbled.

His chest heaved up and down like he was seconds from coming, and his iron-hard shaft jabbed at her side. She wrapped a hand around it and lifted her knee high.

"Does this answer your question?" she breathed.

He grinned and followed her unspoken command, lifting her clear off the ground. She wrapped her legs around his waist as he pressed forward, sliding smoothly into her.

She gasped at the stretch, burning for more. When he started thrusting inside her, she sang out in raw pleasure. And when he hitched her higher, pushing deeper at the same time, she tilted her head back helplessly and moaned.

"So good..."

He held her up effortlessly, one arm under her ass, the other massaging her breasts. His faint murmurs resembled the sounds his bear made when rooting around a particularly fragrant flower bed, and Hailey grinned. Well, she did inside. On the outside, her face must have been drawn in tight lines as she fought the urge to howl.

"My mate," she whispered, trying the words out on her tongue. Weeks ago, they had sounded crude and foreign. Now, they felt just right.

Tim eyed her neck, making her blood rush. He slid a thumb over her skin, following instinct to the very spot he'd found earlier.

At first, she didn't feel more than the usual arousal, but all of a sudden, a thousand little lights flared at the same time.

"Right there," she gasped.

He nodded, looking more serious than she'd ever seen him before. "Right there. But not right here."

He wrapped his arms around her and carried her away from the wall. Toward the bed, she supposed, but before they were halfway across the small room, she found her legs sliding down to the floor. Apparently, bears weren't the only ones with instincts. Hers were suddenly calling out to her, loud and clear.

"How about right here?" she asked, pulling him to the floor. When they were both on their knees, she turned her back to him and nestled against his chest.

She couldn't see his eyes glow from there, but the heat of his gaze warmed her neck, and when he slid his arms around her waist, she knew instinct had guided her well. Sex against the wall was a special kind of pleasure, but for mating — biting — she needed a more stable foundation, like on all fours.

"Perfect," he murmured, sliding his arms around her once more.

They remained on their knees, and Hailey tipped her head back while Tim touched her. One hand caressed her breasts while the other explored between her legs, making her dance in place.

"So good..." she whispered.

Almost too good, really, and she wondered how she'd ever hang on.

"Tim," she panted.

It was as if she were the one with an animal side, because she dropped to all fours first. She pushed back against Tim and practically yowled like a dog in heat.

"What you do to me..." she whispered, shaking her head. The man turned her to putty each time.

"What you do to *me*."

His voice was a deep rumble as he came into position behind her. A position that promised exactly the kind of raw power she craved. He flattened a hand on the small of her back, then took firm hold of her hips and tugged her back. Then, with a sharp pump of his hips, he thrust in.

"Yes," she cried, dropping her head low. Concentrating everything on the perfect pressure inside.

He murmured something unintelligible, pulling back slowly then hammering back in.

Hailey's mouth hung open in an endless cry of pleasure as he pumped harder and deeper. Her necklace was the only item adorning her naked body, and it swung beneath her, rocking hypnotically in time with his thrusts. Her breasts jiggled, loose and free like the rest of her. How was it possible that a string of terrifying circumstances had led her to something so good?

They led you to your mate, something whispered in her mind.

She closed her eyes and rocked harder, suddenly desperate to complete the mating ritual. Living with Tim didn't make him her mate. Only the bite did that, and she didn't want to wait a moment longer.

"Please," she groaned, turning her head to one side.

Her hair cascaded to her shoulder, and Tim combed the last strands aside, still moving inside her. A bead of his sweat fell between her shoulder blades, then another. He leaned over her, close enough for his breath to heat her neck.

"Yes," she moaned as he scraped his teeth across her skin.

Weeks ago, a bite seemed terrifying. Now, it was all she desired.

The pearl swung back and forth, whispering to her of *love* and *forever*, all within her grasp.

At first, Tim's teeth were a straight row, but the longer their bodies meshed, the more two points stood out. His bear fangs were extending. The rest of his body stayed all man, all muscle. All of it intent on pumping in and out of her. Driving her to wild abandon as she cried out again and again.

"Yes... yes... "

Mate, she swore she heard Tim whisper in her mind. Or maybe he shouted it. She couldn't tell, because a split second later, he bit down, and her body jolted as if on fire.

She shuddered in the mightiest orgasm of her life, clamping her inner muscles down hard. An explosion of heat signaled Tim's orgasm deep inside her. Her neck burned, and flames raced around her body, lighting every nerve.

Her mouth moved, but no sound came out as a dozen disjointed images crowded her mind. Deep, dark forests and rushing streams. Jumping salmon. Fragrant wildflowers that swayed in an alpine breeze. The taste of the earliest berries of spring, sweet and sour at the same time. A sky bluer than anything she'd ever seen. Primal, bear sensations, all underpinned by Tim's voice, sounding clearly in her mind.

I will love you forever, my mate. I will protect and honor you to the end of my days.

She wanted to echo the words, but an aftershock of pleasure shook her, and she rocked back, begging his body for more. His teeth pulled at her neck, giving her yet another rush, and Tim stiffened, giving her one last, hard thrust.

"Yes... "

Her sharp cry faded to a moan until she finally drooped to the ground. Tim curled up behind her, panting hard. Hailey gasped for air and covered his hands with hers, keeping him as close as possible.

"That... was... amazing," she whispered between breaths.

Tim let out a panting chuckle, keeping her tight against his chest. "Amazing is a good word. For you, at least."

She shook her head. He was the amazing one, but she couldn't think clearly enough to protest. She closed her eyes, watching the bear scenes continue to play out in her mind. Deep inside, she yawned and stretched.

Wait — that wasn't her stretching in there, was it?

Everyone — even humans — has a hidden, animal side, Tim had told her early on.

She blinked hard, feeling transported to a different time and place. A different body. She was on all fours and slowly crawling out of a den after a hibernation that had lasted far too long. She blinked, half blinded by the sun, soaking in its warmth.

Then she blinked some more, and she was back on the braided rug on the floor, wrapped in Tim's arms.

"Wow. Did you see that?" she asked in a whisper.

Tim nodded against her back.

"How long does it take?"

The question wasn't all that clearly formulated, but Tim knew just what she meant. "Until your first shift?" He waited a second, placing a hand over her heart. "As long as you want. As long as you need."

She reached for the pearl and pressed it against her chest, then pulled Tim's hand over hers so both of them held it in place. The pearl felt warm and content, just like the vague sights, smells, and sensations that wandered through her mind.

"Something tells me that won't be long," she said, turning in his arms.

At first, she thought Tim's eyes were glowing doubly bright, but then she realized they were reflecting her own glow. The glow of a happily mated shifter gazing at her mate. Then another surge of images washed through her mind, a little edgier than the rest. Images of teeth and skin along with a man's voice, telling her *Yes. Yes. Yes...*

Her eyes went wide, but Tim just nodded like he'd expected as much.

"You saw that too?" she asked, staring at him. "Wait. What was that?"

He broke into a cheeky grin. "Your bite. The one you give me."

She stared. "You mean we're not mated yet?"

He laughed and hugged her closer. "Oh, we are, all right. One bite is enough. But you can repeat it anytime you want, and female shifters can bite too. Kind of like renewing wedding vows, I guess. You don't need to..."

A low rumble sounded, and Hailey was shocked to hear it coming from her — or her inner bear.

"Oh, I need to," she murmured, shifting her weight until she was straddling him.

Looking down at him gave her a ridiculous sense of power, and it was easy to imagine returning the bite. She'd ride her mate for a while first, driving them both to the razor's edge of ecstasy and desire. Then she'd lean over his neck for her own bite, and...

"Wow," she murmured, blinking the vision away. "Not that I'm going to try that anytime soon. But someday..."

Tim grinned a cheeky, boy-next-door grin. "Whenever you're ready, my mate. I'll be here."

She leaned down for a kiss that ended up delving much deeper and lasting a lot longer than she intended. Mating woke all kinds of extra desires, it seemed. She dragged her hips over his and narrowed her eyes on Tim's. Was it too soon to want him all over again?

His eyes sparkled, and his cock twitched, giving her all the answer she needed.

"I might not be ready to bite you yet," she said, trying to play it cool despite the fact that she'd been a howling mess a minute earlier. "But I could practice."

Tim slid his hands over the rise of her ass, locking her into place. "Practice always makes sense."

She rose slightly then lowered herself, slowly taking him in. Then she leaned back and started rocking like a cowboy at a gentle lope. Outside, leaves whispered in the wind, and in the distance, waves rolled across the beach, reminding her where she was.

"Where are you?" Tim whispered, reading her mind.

She rocked a little harder, going deliciously hazy again. Soon, passion would take over, and she'd work herself and her lover to another blazing high, followed by another soul-warming cuddle in the shelter of her mate's arms. So she spoke while she could, just a few words.

"Home. I'm home, my mate."

Sneak Peek: Rebel Lion

Rebel Lion - Aloha Shifters: Pearls of Desire, Book 3

Lion shifter Dell O'Roarke has never been serious about life, but life is about to get serious with him. The beautiful stranger who's just arrived in Maui isn't just looking for anyone — she's looking for him. And that's not just any surprise in her luggage — it's a baby who looks a hell of a lot like Dell. Soon, he discovers there's more at stake than his lifestyle as a swinging bachelor. Vengeful shifters are hot on the stranger's heels, making Dell wonder — are they after the woman, the baby, or him?

Marketing executive Anjali Jain hasn't taken a vacation in years — and she sure isn't on vacation now. She's simply keeping a promise, and then she'll be back to climbing the corporate ladder. But there's nothing simple about taking care of a baby — or handing that baby off to a handsome, mysterious stranger who feels like a long-lost friend. Easygoing, relaxed Dell isn't her type, but the more he reluctantly reveals of his hidden, soulful side, the deeper she falls in love — and the more mysteries she discovers. How can one man possibly awaken so many lusts and desires at the same time? What evil forces lurk behind the brutal murder of her best friend? Any why does she have the feeling there's something not quite human about the murderers — or about Dell?

Don't miss *Rebel Lion*, available in ebook, paperback, and audio! Get your copy today!

Books by Anna Lowe

Aloha Shifters - Pearls of Desire

Rebel Dragon (Book 1)

Rebel Bear (Book 2)

Rebel Lion (Book 3)

Rebel Wolf (Book 4)

Rebel Alpha (Book 5)

Aloha Shifters - Jewels of the Heart

Lure of the Dragon (Book 1)

Lure of the Wolf (Book 2)

Lure of the Bear (Book 3)

Lure of the Tiger (Book 4)

Love of the Dragon (Book 5)

Lure of the Fox (Book 6)

The Wolves of Twin Moon Ranch

Desert Hunt (the Prequel)

Desert Moon (Book 1)

Desert Wolf: Complete Collection (Four short stories)

Desert Blood (Book 2)

Desert Fate (Book 3)

Desert Heart (Book 4)

Desert Yule (a short story)

Desert Rose (Book 5)

Desert Roots (Book 6)

Sasquatch Surprise (a Twin Moon spin-off story)

Blue Moon Saloon

Perfection (a short story prequel)

Damnation (Book 1)

Temptation (Book 2)

Redemption (Book 3)

Salvation (Book 4)

Deception (Book 5)

Celebration (a holiday treat)

Shifters in Vegas

Paranormal romance with a zany twist

Gambling on Trouble

Gambling on Her Dragon

Gambling on Her Bear

Serendipity Adventure Romance

Off the Charts

Uncharted

Entangled

Windswept

Adrift

Travel Romance

Veiled Fantasies

Island Fantasies

visit www.annalowebooks.com

About the Author

USA Today and Amazon bestselling author Anna Lowe loves putting the "hero" back into heroine and letting location ignite a passionate romance. She likes a heroine who is independent, intelligent, and imperfect – a woman who is doing just fine on her own. But give the heroine a good man – not to mention a chance to overcome her own inhibitions – and she'll never turn down the chance for adventure, nor shy away from danger.

Anna loves dogs, sports, and travel – and letting those inspire her fiction. On any given weekend, you might find her hiking in the mountains or hunched over her laptop, working on her latest story. Either way, the day will end with a chunk of dark chocolate and a good read.

Visit AnnaLoweBooks.com

Made in the USA
Middletown, DE
03 December 2021